MW00896413

Final Pursuit

Mystery in the Adirondacks
With Whidbey Island Detective Shane Lindstrom

DAN PEDERSEN

Final Pursuit

Mystery in the Adirondacks

With Whidbey Island Detective Shane Lindstrom

BY DAN PEDERSEN

Books in This Series
Available from Independent Booksellers and Amazon.com

1. Final Deception: *A Whidbey Island Mystery*
2. Final Passage: *Mystery on the Alaska Ferry*
3. Final Escape: *Mystery in the Idaho Sawtooths*
4. Final Justice: *Mystery on Whidbey Island*
5. Final Pursuit: *Mystery in the Adirondacks*

Also by the Author:
Louis and Fanny: *15 Years on the Alaska Frontier*
Outdoorsy Male: *Short Stories and Essays*
Wild Whidbey: *The Nature of Island Life*
Whidbey Island's Special Places

Front cover image: Blue canoe, by Suzanne Pedersen
Email inquiries to Dan Pedersen, **dogwood@whidbey.com**
Copyright 2019 Dan Pedersen
All rights reserved
ISBN 13: 978-1091955998

DAN PEDERSEN

Characters

Shane Lindstrom – Whidbey Island detective and B&B owner
Elizabeth Lindstrom – Shane's wife and B&B owner
Billy Lindstrom – age 13, Shane's son from earlier marriage
Robert Yuka – Their friend, an Idaho State Trooper
Marie Martin – Robert's wife, former Federal Wildlife Officer
Martin Yuka – Robert and Marie's two-year-old son
Aunt Bonnie – age 85, owner of a Pursuit Lake cabin
Brad Haraldsen, Shane's friend in Stanley, Idaho
Irene Haraldsen, artist and rancher, Stanley
Andrew Dixon – sheriff, Crossington, New York
Leland Hanson III – chief deputy sheriff
Sarah LeComte – Amish teen currently on rumspringa
Harry Roush – Amish boyfriend of Sarah LeComte
Tim Wade – Amish, 20-year-old, troublemaker
Barb Brown – age 52, alcoholic mother of Kat Brown
Kat Brown – age 18, Barb's estranged teenage daughter
Steve Kowalski –Barb's hard-drinking boyfriend
Peter Stoltzfus, sheriff's deputy
Frank Hale – pilot, Lake Air, serving Adirondack summer camps

DAN PEDERSEN

Preface

This is book five in what started in 2016 as The Brad Haraldsen Mystery Series. All five are thrillers and cozy mysteries, following a group of friends from Whidbey Island to Alaska, to the mountains of Central Idaho and now to the lake country of Upstate New York as they solve mysteries.

In book five, Whidbey Island detective Shane Lindstrom emerges as the central character, working with Idaho friends, Brad and Irene Haraldsen, Shane's wife Elizabeth, and former Alaskans Robert Yuka and Marie Martin.

I owe special thanks to Suzanne Pedersen for introducing me to the Adirondacks, to summer life on the lake, and for her encouragement with the story. I am especially grateful for our friendship in later life, and to her dad for several flights in his Grumman Widgeon in upstate New York.

Fellow writers, Candace Allen, JoAnn Kane, Greta d'Amico, Regina Hugo and Dave Anderson helped me refine the story. Members of my writers group, they were the first to protest whenever the story left the rails.

Special thanks also go to author and friend, Elizabeth Hall, whose assistance was invaluable as my developmental editor. Claire Creighton undertook the thankless chore of proofreading the manuscript and helped me find many well-hidden errors along the way.

Intruder

The body floated upright in the lake about thirty feet down, arms forward, head bowed, the posture oddly penitent. The open mouth suggested an unfinished thought.

A large man, his feet were anchored to the muddy bottom by a wrap of chain. Gasses in his gut had expanded for several days and tried to float his heavy torso to the surface. A few bass and perch mouthed his eyes and nose.

Two small wounds in his chest carved a channel to his lungs, which continued all the way to his back, where the bullets exited in an ugly mass of torn and pulverized flesh.

Overhead, sailboats from a nearby youth camp criss-crossed the lake under blue skies and puffy, white clouds. It was another beautiful morning on Pursuit Lake, the quiet broken only by the squeals and shouts of happy children.

*

Several days earlier. Something brushed Shane Lindstrom's shoulder as he slept. His wife, Elizabeth, lay beside him and he was pretty sure she'd touched him on purpose – lightly, as not to startle him. The bed was deliciously warm and he willed himself not to move; he didn't want to awaken. When she did it a second time, it was sharp.

"Somebody's in the house!" she whispered urgently.

"Huh?" he mumbled, turning to face her.

"Didn't you hear it? A window sliding open downstairs."

9

Shane cocked his head to concentrate. Elizabeth's mouth was inches from his ear and she was listening intently. He could feel her breathe, short and fast. Shane glanced at the blue digits of the clock – 2:07 a.m.

"Are you sure? Not just the breeze?"

"There's no breeze."

Shane glanced at the cafe curtains in the bedroom window, dimly backlit by a quarter moon. They hung straight and still on this humid night. Beyond them lay Pursuit Lake and a handful of cabins linked by shoreline trails. How could anyone be prowling downstairs?

The isolated lake was one of hundreds in the trackless forest of upstate New York, a short drive from the village of Crossington. No one lived here year-round. But in the summertime, a seasonal community came together – friends and family connected across the generations, sharing meals and stories, and watching one-another's children grow. Ivy League Schools and old money were the common threads.

The next sound was unmistakable – a metallic crash and muffled moan in the kitchen below them. The moan was human and Shane was wide-awake now, too. He pictured someone lowering himself through the pantry window from the screened deck, probing for the floor with his dangling feet and kicking the galvanized pail Shane had left by the window in preparation to mop the floor.

Billy? He wondered. Their thirteen-year-old son wouldn't wander the house at night; he was a sound sleeper.

"Check on Billy," Shane said. Billy slept in the adjoining room, reached directly from the master bedroom by a connecting door that didn't require using the hallway. "Bring him in here with you and lock the doors. I'll take a look downstairs."

Shane folded back the sheet, swung his legs out of bed and stood. At six-foot-two, he was lean and fit. He lifted his jeans from the nearest chair. Stepping into his pants in the darkness, he fastened his belt, then slid open the bedside drawer and felt for the reassuring bulk of his Glock. In the drawer beside it was a high-intensity tactical flashlight, which he slipped into his pocket. It could temporarily blind an intruder.

Barefoot and shirtless, with the gun in his right hand, he turned the old, brass doorknob with his left hand and entered the upstairs hall, pulling the door shut behind him. He heard Elizabeth snap the lock behind him.

The floor squeaked loudly as he crept down the hall – century old boards pinned to bone-dry joists by ancient iron nails. He hadn't been here long enough to know where the squeaky boards were to avoid them, but it didn't matter – everything squeaked. Elizabeth's great grandfather, an Adirondack lumber baron from the turn of the century, had built this house as a lakeside getaway for his family. The rough men who logged these hardwood trees and milled this lumber in the 1800s were gone, and their children and children's children as well.

These days, the house was a family retreat for Elizabeth's East Coast relatives, tucked for protection inside Adirondack Park along with a third of New York State's territory. This getaway was Elizabeth's idea, to introduce Shane to another piece of her family heritage. The black-haired, lanky detective jumped at the chance to glimpse this additional side of his wife, who combined bookish intellect and style in a person he liked to characterize as a young Meryl Streep. Their Whidbey Island bed-and-breakfast, once a brothel, wasn't the only grand house in the family, she pointed out, nor was it the oldest. But they'd been here less than 24 hours and already the vacation was taking an unforeseen turn.

Shane's eyes were adjusting now. Standing at the upstairs landing, he could make out the shape of sofas and chairs in the great room below. He wished he knew this house better as he scanned the shadows for someone crouching behind furniture or standing with their back to the wall. In the dim light, the floor-to-ceiling rock fireplace and chimney were the defining features of the room below. He could see no shadows that didn't belong, no movement.

It seemed unlikely that a burglar or teenage prowler would carry a gun, but Detective Shane Lindstrom wouldn't make a stupid mistake now just because he was on vacation. Police procedure was the same, whether at home on Whidbey Island or here, on the other side of the country.

Holding his gun with both hands, and with his back to the wall, he started down the stairs, one cautious step at a time. Built-in bookshelves lined the descent, a nice touch by Elizabeth's great-grandfather. He wondered if, on some deep level, these bookshelves were the origin of Elizabeth's love of reading. Some of the books on these shelves were musty volumes he knew her great grandparents had placed there long ago.

He passed framed pictures of the family arriving at their newly built summer home in a horse-drawn buggy. In those days that's how they got here, on a narrow buggy road from the old logging camp called Number Four, New York. Today, the road was little changed, Elizabeth said. Third-generation descendants of those ancestors worked in high-rise office towers and flew here – some of them – by personal aircraft.

Just then he heard another bang – close and sharp – from somewhere much nearer this time.

The pantry, from which Shane believed the disturbance had come, was at the back of the house, behind the old kitchen. If an intruder had entered there and made a clumsy misstep, he had probably turned around and left quickly the same way after he heard the ceiling boards squeak and creak in response.

The lakeside "lodge," with its half-dozen bedrooms, was not like anything in Shane's experience, growing up on the West Coast. Isolated by harsh winters, it had never been used as a year-round home. The family called it their Adirondack camp. It had stood on this spot through more than a century of subzero winters, deep snows, pounding thunderstorms and sweltering, humid summers. With its old, bat-filled cupola and rooster weather vane, its wrap-around porch, great room, massive fireplace and ancient kitchen, it was a throwback to New York State's early industrial era. The claw-foot tub was original. The toilet and sinks were antique and rust-stained by decades of hard water.

Today, the property was owned by a family trust and managed by a New York lawyer.

But that wasn't Shane's concern right now. He was struggling with the intentions of a prowler at all. It didn't make sense. Most prowlers don't enter houses when they know someone's home. Most don't expect to find anything worth taking in summer places that sit unoccupied most of the year, where people leave little but a few tins of beans, some kindling and a half-used can of stale Folgers.

The answer, Shane supposed, was that this particular prowler didn't know anyone was in the house tonight. He and Elizabeth, and Billy, had arrived only yesterday on Lake Air, a charter service piloted by a balding, sociable local named Frank Hale. He had met their flight from Seattle in Syracuse in his World War Two amphibian, a twin-engine Grumman Widgeon, and flown them here. Pursuit Lake was just large enough for Hale's vintage 1940s aircraft to land and take off on a hot day if the load weren't too heavy. He provided this pickup and delivery service for summer people throughout the lake country and knew many of the families personally. He'd land at any lake large enough for his plane. Pursuit Lake was just about at the lower limit for that.

Shane reached the foot of the stairs, and stopped and listened. The house was dead quiet. Elizabeth and Billy must be in bed together, perfectly still. Shane pulled the flashlight from his pocket but didn't turn it on. Facing the back of the house, he peeked into the kitchen before entering it. Nothing looked wrong. Beyond it, in back, was the pantry. He stepped into the doorway and hit the switch on the flashlight. Blinding light flooded the room. No one fired.

The pantry was empty. The window was open, just as Elizabeth had predicted. The aluminum pail lay on its side halfway across the floor. Rushing to the window, Shane swept the trees with his light.

In the distance, just at the edge of the woods, his beam of light caught something in the shadows. A tall, catlike figure glanced back at the house and then melted into the forest.

Aunt Bonnie

Shane puzzled over what he had seen – little, really, but a slim figure in body-hugging black clothing and a brief flash of the intruder's face when he turned toward the light for a fleeting instant. That was the intruder's only mistake – looking back at the light – but Shane couldn't make out any details. What stuck in his mind was the prowler's stealth and sure-footed confidence, like a panther. He turned into the woods in darkness as if he knew exactly where to step.

Shane tried to estimate the prowler's stature – close to his own height, six feet at least, maybe six-two. The prowler was only one hundred sixty pounds or so, which added to the impression of being tall. He was clean-shaven and wore a stocking cap pulled low, and kept both hands free – again, confidence. No glasses. No gun or flashlight.

In the forest, in the night, someone unencumbered like that could go anywhere and would be impossible to find even a few feet away. The Adirondack woods were not Shane's turf. He shivered, remembering stories his dad had told of G.I.'s hunting the invisible Viet Cong at night in the jungles of Indochina.

He was letting his imagination get ahead of him. This was probably just some local delinquent prowling summer cabins. Shane pulled the pantry window shut and locked it tight, switched on the yard lights, then headed upstairs to check on Elizabeth and Billy.

At the bedroom door, Shane knocked lightly. "It's me," he announced. "All clear."

"Just a sec," Elizabeth replied. The lock clicked and the door swung open. "Thank god," she remarked. "That was frightening. Did you get a look?"

14

"Just briefly, one person. In the distance. Running away."

Billy had fallen back to sleep in the bed, but Shane and Elizabeth were so wide awake now, neither could imagine sleeping any more. They went from room to room, turning on lights and checking window locks and deadbolts, assessing what they could do to make the house tighter and get some peace of mind.

"I need to check something in the pantry," Elizabeth said. Together they returned to the back of the house. Elizabeth got a kitchen ladder from the utility closet and placed it in front of a tall cabinet. Then she climbed up and reached for a dusty cookie tin on the top shelf. She brought it down with her, placed it on the counter and pried off the lid.

Shane gasped when he saw the stack of $100 bills.

"There must be, what, several thousand dollars here?"

"Five thousand."

"My god, what's it doing here?"

"It's been here ever since Dad put it here," Elizabeth said. "I don't know how he got it and don't know if he ever told Mom. He said he liked to keep some cash around for a rainy day. It was his secret but he did mention it to me one of the last times we were together here at the lake. I must have been about twelve. That was just before he and Mom became Jehovah's Witnesses and we moved from Albany out to Washington."

"Your dad sounds complex," Shane observed.

"That's a good way to put it. He was gentle and low key, a good husband and father, but always seemed to be looking for something spiritual he couldn't find. I think he was torn between the low-risk life he was leading and adventurous fantasies he had on the side. He was an archivist for the university, which maybe explains where I got my own nerdiness. Maybe he thought he'd find the answers to life's mysteries deep in some dusty old volume."

"What happened to your summers at the lake?" Shane asked. "Did the family just stop coming here for some reason?"

"Mom and Dad died in a car accident a couple of years after the move and I lost all interest in coming back here. They left the camp to me and I set up a trust to keep it open to the family, since it was especially important to the East Coast relatives. I wondered if the money was still here but never came back to check. I should do something to safeguard it, but what? It's been here all this time."

"Judging by the dust, no one has opened this tin in years," Shane remarked. "Who else knows about it?"

"No one, as far as I know."

"Not even the family?"

"Not to my knowledge."

"I'll call the sheriff in a few hours and give him a report on the break-in," Shane said.

"Don't mention the cookie tin. And later this morning let's go next door and talk with Aunt Bonnie," Elizabeth suggested. "We need to say hello anyway and check on her, and let her know we're here, though I'm sure she saw the plane land and take off."

Bonnie, an eighty-five-year-old widow, drove up from Ithaca every summer and stayed in her lake cabin, Elizabeth said. "She's not my aunt but that's what everyone calls her. She has her poker-playing friends and her place is the de facto social hub of Pursuit Lake. If anyone knows what's going on, it's Bonnie."

"My god, an eighty-five-year-old woman chooses to come to this remote place every summer, alone, and stay by herself?" Shane asked. "What if she has a fall, or a heart attack or a stroke and no one to help her?"

"Well, she's eighty-five. That's a good, long life. I think if you're Bonnie, you'd just say that's okay. There are worse ways to go than being on your own in a place that you love, right up till the end. And besides, she knows everyone here, all the changing faces of the summertime, and people look in on her."

"What is it about the lake that brings her back, summer after summer," Shane asked.

"I think it's the memories of her husband. They built their cabin together, every stick of it, back in the days when this was a pretty remote place."

"This was their dream place?" Shane asked.

"Very much so. Imagine two young people at the peak of health, adventurous and active, who loved the outdoors – loved swimming in the summer and snowshoeing in the winter. When you see the pictures in Bonnie's cabin, you'll see he was a very handsome, dashing young man. Bonnie had won swimming championships in college and went on to become a topnotch skier. They were perfect partners for each other. I think they were deeply in love."

"Is there a trail to Bonnie's place?" Shane asked.

"Yes, but it's more fun to take the boat."

The previous day when the threesome landed at the lake, they had rowed ashore from the Widgeon in a dory the family kept tied to a float out front. Shane hadn't paid much attention to the camp's boathouse. To his surprise today, when they looked inside they found two exquisite wooden boats – hand-made of Canadian cedar strips coated with epoxy resin.

Elizabeth pointed out that the smaller of the two was a classic rowboat with oarlocks. The larger one was an inboard electric – battery powered – and was connected to a trickle charger. "Let's take the rowboat now, but maybe tomorrow we'll look around the lake in the electric boat. It's silent and just glides across the water."

Shane and Billy climbed in as Elizabeth un-looped the mooring line from the cleat and took her place on the seat at the stern. Shane, in the center seat, snapped the oars into their locks; Billy sat in the bow. Elizabeth gave them a little shove to drift free of the boathouse and they were under way.

Shane soon found his rhythm – *thunk, slosh, thunk, slosh* – as he swung the oars. The boat surged forward toward Bonnie's cabin on a promontory a quarter of a mile away. Billy was staring straight down into the water. "It's so clear I can see the bottom," he said.

"Keep your eyes peeled," Elizabeth urged. "You might see a few fish."

"Like what?"

"Trout, and maybe bass or perch," she replied. "But the real prize is to see a beaver. There are some beaver lodges near the inlet. We'll go take a look in a couple of days."

Within minutes the little boat was in front of Bonnie's cabin, also known as her own Adirondack camp. Elizabeth signaled Shane to lift up the oars and let the boat glide. She cupped her hands over her mouth, faced the shore and shouted, "Ahoy, Bonnie. Permission to come ashore?"

"Granted," came an unseen voice in return, apparently from behind one of the screened windows.

Elizabeth waved toward the cabin and turned back to Shane: "Ok, take us in."

Seconds later, the boat scrunched onto the sandy beach. Shane stepped over the gunwale in his flip-flops into bathtub-warm water. He pulled the boat higher on the shore and held it steady so the others could get out without getting wet.

Above them, on the deck, a wiry old lady in white Capri pants and a broad-brimmed straw hat stood and watched them. The set of her jaw and the expression on her deeply lined face were resolute. She couldn't be more than five feet tall and had her long, gray hair tied up in a bun.

Elizabeth led the little group up the path to the cabin and called ahead to Bonnie as they approached. "Bonnie, I don't know if you remember me but I'm Elizabeth Harlowe – my maiden name – from Washington, and this is my husband, Shane, and son, Billy."

"You and your folks used to come up every summer. I remember it well. You were a teenager then. I didn't see any of you after you moved out West, but I did hear something about a car accident. Terrible. It must have been devastating for you."

"That's right," Elizabeth said.

"Then at least I'm not senile," Bonnie remarked. "It's been a long time." Bonnie gave Elizabeth and Billy each a big hug and shook hands with Shane, then waved her arm to shoo her guests inside.

"We need to do some catching up," she said.

Shane liked this straight-shooting woman – equal parts bluntness and warmth. He felt instantly at home in her cheerful cabin, with sunshine streaming through the windows and a stack of trashy romance novels on the end table. The aroma of fresh coffee filled the room.

On the wall, a pair of old snowshoes held the place of honor. Shane assumed their significance had something to do with a decades old, black-and-white portrait of Bonnie and a dark-haired young man standing in front of an ice-covered, snowbound lake, in snowshoes.

"Your husband?" Shane asked.

"Oh yes, indeed. That was a long time ago, when we built this place." He imagined Bonnie coming back here summer after summer to the scene of that happy time, surrounded and comforted by the memories of her adventurous husband decades ago.

"You've been a regular at the lake all these years?" Shane asked.

"I haven't missed a summer since we built this place. My husband died in a skiing accident early in our marriage, and I wondered if it would change how I felt about this cabin, but it only made me feel closer to him here. Maybe I'm dotty but we still talk to each other."

Over fresh scones and strawberry preserves at Bonnie's kitchen table, Elizabeth told the story of last night's intruder. Bonnie nodded knowingly. "There's been a rash of break-ins around the lake, especially over the winter," she said. "I've never seen it like this."

"What was taken?" Shane asked.

Elizabeth glanced at Bonnie. "I should point out he's a detective," she interjected, nodding at Shane. Bonnie's eyebrows arched, so Elizabeth filled in the story of how she and Shane met at an Idaho ranch two summers ago. Once Bonnie was satisfied, she picked up her story.

"Nothing much – little stuff, food and clothing. But people here are frustrated with all the break-ins. The sheriff can't or won't do anything. In his defense, he has a tiny department and this is a big county with plenty of other lakes and summer cabins.

"It's like someone's been going from cabin-to-cabin for months mostly to sleep and find something to eat," she said. "People discover food left out, a jacket or sweatshirt missing, dirty dishes in the sink, beds unmade – that kind of thing."

"Have any electronics or guns been stolen?" Shane asked.

"Not that I've heard. Most people don't leave computers, guns and cell phones in these places over the winter. Nobody keeps valuables at a lake cabin."

Shane stole a glance at Elizabeth.

"So it doesn't seem to be kids stealing valuables to sell for drugs," Shane noted.

"No, there are enough drug problems in town," Bonnie replied. "There seems to be a little turf war with kids getting beaten up for not paying their debts – that kind of thing."

"Has anyone come face to face with the Pursuit Lake prowler?"

"No, he's been very successful at avoiding people and staying invisible. Seems to know who's home and who isn't. Doesn't take any unnecessary risks. And whatever's driving his break-ins, it really doesn't look like theft.

"Has anyone put up a webcam to try to get a picture of him?"

"Not that I've heard. The lake isn't exactly a hotspot of technology. Internet service is hit and miss, and besides, my generation are mostly Luddites anyway."

Shane laughed.

"The thing is, our problems with petty break-ins don't rate very high on the sheriff's priorities against more serious crimes," Bonnie said.

Shane's eye drifted to two gallon-size cans of paint and some brushes and stir sticks next to the patio door. Bonnie's eyes followed him.

"I'm getting ready to paint the deck," she said. "Hate that job with my rickety knees.

"You know," she continued, glancing back and forth between Shane and Elizabeth. "I wonder if your boy might like to make a few dollars this afternoon. I've got the paint and brushes right here and he might be just the one to save me some kneeling on these creaky joints. I could make some cookies to sweeten the deal."

Shane smiled. "Why don't you ask him?"

Billy was already grinning.

That afternoon, while Billy was busy painting at Aunt Bonnie's, Shane and Elizabeth went for a walk to see if they could trace where the intruder had gone after running from the house. Shane's crucial sighting gave them a starting point, and after a few minutes Shane picked up traces of a trail – just a game trail for rabbits and deer – leading from the spot where the guy had entered the woods. About two hundred feet further the trail became wider and better defined, more than just a game trail after all. From the hard-packed earth, it appeared that humans had come this way as well.

"I never knew this trail was even here," Elizabeth said as they climbed a gentle slope through sparse timber. "You can see a lot from up this way." They followed the trail for about twenty minutes, passing occasional signs that they weren't the first to walk this way. Shane pointed to a Snickers wrapper, and right after that Elizabeth signaled him with a hand sign to stop.

"Is that a handkerchief?" she whispered, pointing some distance off trail. Shane stepped over that way for a closer look. The red handkerchief was attached to a low branch of honeysuckle – tied there deliberately. Shane wondered what it meant. He looked around and noticed, further along, part of a shirt hanging from another branch. He waved to Elizabeth to follow him off the trail.

They were almost on top of the camp before they saw it. In a grove of maple and birch, on the brow of a slope, pieces of cord held the corners of a moss green tarp to nearby trees, about three feet off the ground. The tarp blended with the vegetation. Under the tarp, out of the weather, was a bedroll and a low-back plastic chair, a transistor radio, several books, a pair of binoculars and some open tins of spam and baked beans. A small fire pit was ringed neatly with rocks and held some ash. Shane took a stick and disturbed the ash, then felt with his hand for heat.

"Still warm," he said.

Shane straightened up and looked off in the distance. "Nice view of the lake. From this vantage he could watch the entire expanse of Pursuit Lake, and nearly all of its cabins and camps."

Something about the camp struck Shane as peculiar. He scanned the area for drugs and needles, cigarette butts and beer cans, but found none. Trash was confined to a depression in the earth just outside the sleeping area. Shane pawed through discarded food tins and candy wrappers, mostly Snickers.

"He keeps a tidy camp," Shane remarked.

"We know he has a sweet tooth and likes to read," Elizabeth noted. "Did you notice the books?"

Next to the bedroll were a book on astronomy, a geology text and something on edible plants of Adirondack Park.

"He doesn't feel to me like a lowlife," he said. "He feels more like a runaway."

Shane was glancing around. "Is it just me or does it seem like we're being watched?"

As he turned to look behind him, he imagined a figure in a black stocking cap ducking behind a rock outcropping. It would be easy to watch someone here.

"Let's not disturb anything. We'll go back and give the sheriff a call. We have something to report now."

Crossington

In the shadows behind the Duck Inn Bar, a tall youth in a black hoodie waited with an unopened bottle of wine in his right hand, behind his back. Heavy metal music boomed into the alley from the other side of the stage door. The door opened and a younger boy stepped out into the evening air. As the door swung shut behind him and locked with a click, the tall youth moved directly in front of him, his feet planted wide.

"Ducking out the back way?" he asked. "I hope it's because you have my money and figured I'd be waiting here."

"I'll have it tomorrow for sure."

"Oh, gosh, Monte, that's great to hear, but I feel for you because tomorrow is one day later than we agreed," the youth in the hoodie replied, raising the bottle in a quick motion and crashing it down on the boy's head. Wine and glass gushed down the boy's face as he fell in a heap to the asphalt alley, unconscious.

The boy in the hoodie pulled his belt from his pants, gripped it with the buckle hanging loose, and started to beat his victim. He worked the belt buckle up one side of the boy's ribs and down the other, then kicked his head several times and walked away.

In the morning, Elizabeth suggested Shane and Billy join her and drive to town to meet the sheriff in person, rather than call. "You haven't seen the area yet; the drive will put some things into perspective. Besides, isn't it easier to form a relationship with the sheriff face-to-face than over the phone?"

Elizabeth's family kept an old GMC Suburban at the lake for land excursions. "It's ancient but always ran pretty well as I recall, but the transmission is glitchy. So we'll have to finesse it from gear to gear."

Shane could tell from Billy's big smile that he looked forward to the trip. He was first into the car, freshly bankrolled with twenty-five dollars Aunt Bonnie had paid him for painting. Elizabeth was already making a list of groceries they needed. After lunch, Shane disconnected the trickle charger from the Suburban's battery, slammed the hood and turned the key. The engine turned over slowly a couple of times and then took hold in a cloud of blue smoke.

"Now what?" Shane asked.

"Listen up. I'll be your GPS. Schmooze it into gear. In 1,000 feet, veer right."

Shane scowled.

"What's wrong?"

"I've never had a GPS tell me to do that," he said.

"Just do it."

Shane pressed his foot all the way down on the clutch pedal and shifted the transmission into first gear, then eased up on the clutch and waited till the car started to shake and shudder with a sickening, grinding whine. To his amazement, the transmission engaged and the big Suburban started to move. He soon wrangled it into second gear. The gravel drive turned to pavement – a narrow, two-lane road through the forest. He got the Suburban into third gear, determined never to downshift again except to avoid a head-on collision, and maybe not then.

After a few miles he started to notice small clearings in the trees, where people had built houses, and still farther they came to larger fields and farms. Shane noticed that some of the houses were just daylight basements with nothing on top of the slab, yet there were vehicles and children's bicycles in the yard.

"People live underground here?" he asked.

"It's the depressed economy. There's so much poverty in the outlying areas, many people build their houses one floor at a time, starting with the basement," she said. "They live in the basement while they save money to build some more. Besides, that's the warmest part of the house in the cold winters, so if you're going to live anywhere, the basement is the best place. At some point they add a main floor."

Closer to Foreston, Shane noticed the farms became tidier and more prosperous. They passed pedestrians walking in small groups on the road shoulders. Many of the men wore white shirts and black trousers, supported by suspenders. The women wore white bonnets, ankle-length dresses with aprons, and practical, high-button boots.

"What is this?" Billy asked. "Those people are like something out of an old movie. Why are they dressed that way, in such old-fashioned clothes?"

"Because this is Amish and Mennonite country – Foreston and Crossington – Elizabeth explained. "They believe in living a simpler life, with fewer possessions."

"I've heard they don't use electricity," Shane remarked. "Can that even be true?"

"The Amish, especially, are pretty strict about that," Elizabeth said. "They use electricity in limited ways for safety purposes, such as batteries to power the lights on their buggies, but keep their homes off the public power grid."

"Isn't that a contradiction?"

"Not the way they think of it. The power grid would bring the outside world into their homes and make them reliant on others. Keeping it out of their homes, they can more easily wall out temptations such as television, cell phones, the Internet and such."

Shane could see in the rear-view mirror that Billy was leaning forward. "How do they make a living if they don't believe in electricity and are not part of the modern world?" he asked.

Just at that moment, Shane noticed a farmer pulling a plow with a team of two big draft horses, and pointed to him.

Elizabeth turned toward Billy in the back seat and explained, "The men work as farmers or laborers in sawmills or factories. Along with the Amish, there are Mennonites and Hutterites in this area, too, who follow similar ways. Shane, you've heard of Amish furniture, all handcrafted from hardwood."

"So this is where it comes from," he mused. "I had no idea such a community was just a few miles from the lake. It's hard to believe our intruder might be someone from this culture."

"Or not. The population here isn't all Mennonite and Amish. These groups are dispersed over a large area and most people think of Pennsylvania when it comes to Amish. But there are Amish here, too, and plenty of English capable of getting on the wrong track."

"English?"

"That's the Amish and Mennonite term for outsiders, who are not part of their community," Elizabeth clarified. "So just to be clear, we are English."

Shane parked the Suburban on Main Street, in front of a red, brick building he estimated to be more than a century old. Two sheriff's cars were parked in the police zone spaces out front, next to an antenna tower. He sent Elizabeth and Billy in search of ice cream while he went inside to find the sheriff.

The stenciling on the frosted glass door on the ground floor stated: Andrew Dixon, Sheriff. Shane tapped lightly, and then turned the knob. Inside he found just two people, a dispatcher and a grandfatherly gentleman with white hair and an ample belly, with a six-pointed star clipped to his olive-green shirt.

The white-haired man extended his hand. "Andy Dixon," he greeted Shane warmly, smiling and shaking hands firmly. "What may I do for you?"

"Sheriff Dixon," Shane began . . .

"Call me Andy."

Shane explained he was visiting from Whidbey Island. "I'm with the sheriff's department out there."

"It's always a pleasure to meet a colleague."

Shane went on to explain he had some information to pass along about a prowler who may be responsible for multiple break-ins at Pursuit Lake.

"Back up a bit. What brings you all the way across country to the Adirondacks?" Dixon asked.

"Vacationing – we're on a break from managing our B&B. Actually, my wife does most of the B&B work, since my day job keeps me busy."

"And you're staying where?" the sheriff asked.

"The old Harlowe family camp or lodge, call it what you will, on Pursuit Lake. I'm here with my wife, Elizabeth."

"I remember it. Gosh, that place has been in the family for generations. Your wife's great-grandfather was one of the original industrial tycoons in the county with his logging and lumber business, from back around the time Adirondack Park was created."

"That's right," Shane said. He filled in the sheriff on the break-in at lodge and his brief pursuit of the prowler. "I didn't know if he might be armed so I grabbed my Glock on the way downstairs. But he was more interested in getting away than in confronting me."

Dixon listened sympathetically but said he could not offer much hope that the prowler would be identified and brought to justice anytime soon.

"I'm sorry you got such a rude awakening on your vacation. That's the last thing you need."

"It was a surprise, but we understand from talking with others around the lake that there have been quite a few break-ins."

"It's an epidemic," the sheriff said, scowling and shaking his head. "We have a tiny department and have had a rash of these incidents in the last several years. I can't assign a deputy full time to Pursuit Lake, much as I'd like to.

"We know many of the troubled kids behind these cabin-prowls, but it's harder than heck for us to pin specific break-ins on specific kids unless we find identifiable, stolen possessions and the owners come forward with a claim. The kids often cache the stolen loot in the woods so it can't be found in their possession. Then they sneak back from time to time to get one or two items to sell."

"I sympathize, because it's the same back home in Island County, too," Shane said. "Plenty of geography but way too few officers to patrol it. Break-ins are low on our priorities unless we can solve a whole string with one key arrest."

Dixon listened pensively, staring at his hands, then added, "Our big problem is drugs. We're getting more drug violence in the streets all the time now, but the victims won't file a complaint for fear something worse will happen to them next time."

Shane nodded.

"As far as prowling is concerned, your report is more helpful than most because you actually got a look at the guy," the sheriff continued, "if only from behind in the dark. That's more than we usually get. These prowlers often aren't bad people per se, just kids going through a phase to find themselves. I was brought up Mennonite, myself, so I have some understanding of what it's like for these kids."

He continued, "The bad ones steal to support their habits. They give us fits because they soon lose their sense of right and wrong. We try to turn them around while it's still possible — remind them of their heritage and all the positive things about it. At some point, a few get bold or careless enough to start coming into contact with homeowners. Things can escalate fast till somebody gets hurt."

He added, "But I don't need to tell you that."

Shane wondered if the sheriff was politely warning him not to get carried away in confronting or cornering the guy. Maybe Shane shouldn't have mentioned he was carrying his Glock when he searched the house.

Shane nodded and added, "My wife and I are pretty sure we tracked him to his campsite in the hills overlooking the lake. I'd like to take you up there to look at it. Might give you a better picture of who's behind some of these break-ins."

"I'd like that," the sheriff said. "I'll drive up your way tomorrow afternoon if you think you can find the spot again."

"Absolutely. I'd be happy to help with that."

Back at the car, Elizabeth said she'd like to show Shane something special before they left town. Together, they walked a block to Community Hardware.

"This is what you wanted to show me?" Shane asked. "A hardware store?"

"There are newer stores in the malls – Ace Hardware if that's what you're looking for – but this is the store the men all love. It caters to a certain clientele," she said, opening the door. The bell overhead jingled as they stepped inside. Shane noticed they had to open and close the door behind them by hand – it did not sense their approach, and open and close itself.

It struck Shane that the aisles between displays were so crowded that customers would have to squeeze past each other. The displays were piled high with merchandise, and Shane wondered how the store employees watched for shoplifters. Maybe that wasn't a problem in this kind of store, in light of what he was seeing.

His eye had landed on a large display of cast iron buggy springs, wheels, wooden spokes and metal fasteners. He'd never seen such merchandise anywhere in any store, but if you owned a buggy, he assumed these would be the hardest parts to fabricate at home without special tools. There were also anvils, handsaws and hammers and clamps for those who might try. He browsed with fascination, trying to imagine how each tool and piece of metal was used. Hanging from the wall were several wooden sleds and fishing poles, simple but sturdy equipment for summer and winter sports. In a corner he admired a large collection of distinctive, locally-made bird houses.

At some point he looked down and noticed the hardwood floor was gray and worn from decades of foot traffic. No fancy tile for easy maintenance. He imagined many of this store's customers had first walked this floor as children, come back as adults, grown old and died, to be replaced by a new generation looking for much the same merchandise as their parents and grandparents. The wear in that floor, in a way, reflected their passage on Earth.

What he didn't see were mountains of plastic products, gadgets and "As Seen on TV" specials. There were no displays of junk food by the cash register, no ear buds for cell phones, no automatic coffee makers, no fancy housewares or remote controls for TVs and garage doors. Instead, there was an entire aisle of home canning supplies – large cooking pots, glass jars, lids and pectin. People in this community must put up a lot of food.

"Mom, look at this," Billy announced from the next aisle. Shane and Elizabeth followed his voice to an entire aisle of shoes and boots. It was like going back in time to another century – high button, lace up, black shoes for both men and women. It was well-constructed, practical footwear for long hours of standing and working.

"I think we just found where the Amish and Mennonites buy their shoes," Elizabeth said.

Rumspringa

Four blocks away, in a tumbledown rental house with long grass and a weedy yard, Sarah LeComte weighed what she knew was the most important decision of her life. Should she make love to Harry Loush?

She was ready to, but there were risks. Whether it was a good or bad idea probably depended on whether she got pregnant. If she did, her future was sealed. Going back to the Amish community was not an option for an unwed teen mother with a baby.

Secretly, she almost hoped that would happen. At age sixteen, she had left her parents' farm outside Crossington for rumspringa, known among the Amish as "adolescence" or "running around." During this time, teenagers were free to live among the English while deciding whether to ever return to the Amish community and get baptized, and give up all outside ways and distractions.

That was the problem – Sarah liked English ways. She liked having electricity and TV. She was addicted to cell phones and texting, everything to do with technology, and music, and especially everything to do with social media and Facebook. It was part of the attraction to Harry, who shared those same interests and could explain how everything worked.

Sarah was pretty, she knew, pretty enough to attract a good Amish man and do well in the traditional life of her community. She wore her waist-length hair in a long ponytail, deliberately playing down the beginnings of a womanly body and the radiant good health of a teenager.

She hoped she was pretty enough to make it in the much larger and more exciting English world, as well. She and Harry needed to talk. But most of all they needed to get away from an older Amish boy named Tim Wade. He had been Harry's friend back home, but had changed so much since leaving the Amish life that he scared her now.

It had seemed like a good idea, at first, to share a house with Tim and split the rent three ways. By doing that, the three of them could live in town. Sarah paid her share by providing childcare for a local professional couple who both commuted to jobs.

Tim, two years older, was well into rumspringa by the time Sarah joined the household. He made his money selling drugs, and had made his decision already never to return to the Amish community. Sarah knew that his mother had died of influenza in her early thirties and Tim's dad had raised him alone, relying on severe discipline to bend the boy to his will and make him help with the farm chores.

"I hate the guy," Tim said of his father. "He's a goddam dirt farmer who doesn't know anything except how to take out his belt and beat me. We don't even have electric lights. For crying out loud, this is the modern world."

Tim's pain was obvious and Sarah felt bad for him. In the Amish community, his dad was well known as a bitter man who'd been denied the large family he wanted by the untimely death of his wife. Sarah wondered if Tim hadn't inherited some of his dad's temper. To make things worse, he was spending more and more time with a group of lowlifes in Crossington, spinning out of control.

Sarah emerged one morning from the bedroom of the dilapidated bungalow and surveyed a scene that was increasingly familiar. Empty beer bottles littered the floor and end tables. A half-finished bowl of chips sat on the sofa, along with the bag they came in. In the kitchen, the sink and counter were piled with pizza boxes and half-eaten crusts. It would take an hour to wash dishes, haul out the bottles and boxes, and straighten the living room enough to sit down. Pepperoni and cheese were stuck to the linoleum in the kitchen. She'd deal with the floor later.

Since Sarah's arrival in the house, Tim had started leaving messes everywhere for her to clean up – women's work, he said. But the real problem was his unpredictable moods. He couldn't contain his anger, seemed to enjoy fighting, carried a knife and frequented the bars in town.

He also watched her a little too much, especially just out of the shower. She wondered if Tim was waiting for a chance to be alone with her and force himself on her. Sarah told Harry she was frightened of Tim and he'd bring trouble to their door if they stayed under the same roof. Sarah was pretty sure Tim and his English friends were involved in a rash of cabin prowls and burglaries. The refrigerator was full of their beer.

But it was worse than that. One evening, when Tim and his English friends were drinking, Tim beckoned Sarah to a back bedroom. "I've got something to show you," he said, as he pulled a gun from the front pocket of his baggy pants.

Sarah felt a chill.

He's going to use it, she thought. "You've got to get us out of here," she told Harry.

Sarah had gotten to know Harry gradually – watching him at barn raisings and community potlucks. He was a handsome, somewhat shy boy from a neighboring farm. He seemed more quiet and sensitive than most, serious and hardworking, but not so inhibited as to turn away from her long glances from across the room.

He returned her interest at church socials and when they met running errands in town, his gaze lingering long enough that there was no question. In time they found moments to sit next to each other at meetings or bump into each other at dinners, but the brief encounters only left her unsatisfied. In time, Sarah told him about the old oak on her farm, where they could leave notes for each other in the crook of a large limb. They both watched for times when it was safe to meet after dark and talk for a few minutes alone.

After Harry left the community a year earlier, he kept in touch with her and urged her to follow. Several months after Harry left, Sarah found a note from him in the old oak. She snuck away several nights to meet secretly with him, and then told her parents she was leaving on rumspringa.

"Come back and be baptized when you have seen enough," her father told her. "The English life leads nowhere but to misery."

"Don't throw your life away over a boy," her mother admonished. "This will pass. Boys always do."

Sarah had found the boys living like animals in the communal house, sometimes eating what they foraged or pilfered from the garbage cans behind restaurants in town. Tim, a string bean of a youth, did most of the pilfering. The more cerebral Harry, by his wits and charm, had accumulated a roomful of computer equipment and electronics, and spent most of his time absorbed in what he could learn. He found a part-time job in a computer store, helping customers with their problems.

As the only female in the household, Sarah fell into the traditional role of cook and mother to the two, who didn't know much about laundry or dishwashing. With little proper food in the house, she fell back on what she'd learned from her own mother about soups and stews. She could not see a future for herself living this way. But Harry was smart. He could be her ticket to a whole new world of possibilities.

Inside the glass cage that was Sheriff Andy Dixon's private office, the sheriff and mayor leaned toward each other and spoke in subdued voices.

"I think we've got to do something, Andy," the mayor said. "It'll be an unholy mess, but we both know it's better to deal with it now than later. He's just getting bolder and more reckless. I want you to know I'll back you all the way."

Dixon knew the mayor was right. "I appreciate that," he said, standing and shaking hands. The mayor opened the door and walked out, smiling at chief deputy Leland Hanson as he crossed the room and opened the door to the hall.

The sheriff went back to his paperwork.

At 6 pm, Sheriff Dixon pushed back his chair, stood and crossed the quiet room to where Deputy Leland Hanson sat at his desk. Tension filled the room. The two men were finally alone. Dixon waited for Hanson to look up.

"Lee, I'd like you to resign."

Hanson set his jaw and looked up at Sheriff Andy Dixon. "You *what?*" He leaned back in his swivel chair, put both hands in the air and laughed so hard he coughed and gagged to regain control.

Dixon took a step closer to the deputy, sat down on the corner of Hanson's desk and looked down at the deputy's eyes. The sheriff's face was red. "I'm dead serious, Lee."

The sheriff had been waiting for this moment when they'd be alone. Confrontation did not come easily to him, but he'd been building up to this for months. *Praise in public; criticize in private,* he believed. He lived by this principle.

"Our styles of policing are entirely different. You know it and so do I," the sheriff expressed, pounding his finger on Hanson's desk for emphasis. "I don't believe there is any justification for the way you treat suspects. It's not professional, nor is it what this department stands for. I don't believe you can change, nor that you want to."

"You're out of your fucking mind," Hanson protested, raising his voice. "I get results. You get nothing. You're a joke in this job, the old grandfather who just wants to be liked."

"I've got kids in those cells with cuts on their heads, and with arms dislocated so badly they're in slings," the sheriff said, pointing toward the holding cells. "They weren't that way when you brought them in. I ask them what happened and they say they slipped and fell. I don't know what goes on here when I'm away. They're afraid to tell me about it. But I'm going to find out, and when I do, I think you're going to be in deep trouble legally."

"Those kids respect me," Hanson said. "If I ask them a question and they don't reply, I let them know who's boss. I use the persuasion necessary to gain their cooperation and get some straight answers."

"What? You hold them for a few hours, rough them up, and then release them because we've got no basis to charge them? Is that what you call results?"

"They think twice before they sass me again," Hanson replied.

"Either you resign and go quietly, before I document my case for dismissal, or I write you up and we have a big, ugly fight about it. You'll end up in jail yourself facing charges that will prevent you from ever working in law enforcement again. Not that I would wish you on any department, anywhere."

Hanson stood up and moved toward Dixon's face, and looked down at him as he sat on the desk.

"I'll tell you what's going to happen," Hanson said. "I'm going to run against you in the next election and take your job. I'll come at you for employment discrimination and you'll be history, and I'll be the sheriff. You'll be out on the street. That's exactly where this is going, and I think you know it."

He stood up, turned his back on the sheriff, and walked out the door and slammed it behind him without another word.

It was early the next afternoon when Dixon rolled up to the lodge in his SUV with "Sheriff" printed prominently on the sides, and a blue-and-red light bar on the roof. Shane met him out front and they shook hands warmly. They were just exchanging pleasantries as Elizabeth emerged from the house.

"My wife, Elizabeth," Shane said as he introduced her to Sheriff Dixon.

"You're one of the Harlowes," the sheriff declared. "I've met a lot of your cousins and nieces and nephews over the years, but not you."

"This is the first time I've been back since Mom and Dad died," she said. "I was just a teenager the last time I was here, twenty years ago. I thought Shane should see where I spent some of the happiest times of my childhood."

"I remember your parents," the sheriff said. "I spent several summers at the lake back then running the youth camp for a while. I was just going back through some dusty old files in my cabinet and found one from the 1970s mentioning your dad. Of course, I was much younger then, myself, and that was long before I had this job."

"Wow, how did Dad ever end up in your files?" Elizabeth asked. "This is something I never knew."

"It was after the D.B. Cooper incident, when someone hijacked a Northwest Airlines jet and bailed out over Southwest Washington with two hundred thousand dollars. The case was never solved – the only hijacking in U.S. history that's still open and unsolved. People came forward with hundreds of tips, and one of them was about your dad."

Elizabeth's mind was racing. It's true that her dad, as a younger man, bore some resemblance to sketches she'd seen of the hijacker. But so did lots of other men. It struck Elizabeth that the sheriff was sharing a lot of information, and she wondered if he was doing it to see how she reacted.

"Apparently your dad seemed to be flush with cash around that time," the sheriff said. "People noticed it around town and wondered, but nothing concrete ever pointed to him. The D.B. Cooper cash was all marked, and none of the bills your Dad spent matched the serial numbers of the Cooper cash, so the whole thing petered out. Still, it was curious that he didn't seem to have a bank account. They say he didn't trust banks."

"No, he didn't. I remember that well," Elizabeth said.

"Sometime after that I guess he and your mom became quite religious and affiliated themselves with – how should I say it? – non-mainstream beliefs."

"That's a good way of putting it," Elizabeth said.

"But that's enough gossip," the sheriff said, turning to Shane. "We should get started with our hike."

While Elizabeth and Billy stayed behind to finish chores, Shane led Sheriff Dixon up the trail to the overlook where he and Elizabeth had found the camp. He set a moderate pace, but still, the heavier Dixon was breathing hard when they finally stopped.

"This is what you brought me to see?" Dixon asked when Shane pointed to a tidy clearing in the grass overlooking the lake. "The view is nice, but didn't you say there was a camp here?"

"There was yesterday. Right here. It must be around here someplace." Shane hurried off thirty feet in one direction, then thirty feet back in the other. "This is the place. It's exactly the place. I don't know what to say. It seems to be gone."

"Let's go over everything you found here," the sheriff remarked, sitting down on a log and pulling out a small yellow pad. All traces of the camp were now gone except for some matted grass and a few cold ashes where the dismantled firepit had been. Gone were the tarp, the books, the bedroll, the binoculars, the handkerchief tied to a branch. Someone had taken pains to clean it all up.

"Do you have any suspects?" Shane asked.

"Too many, I'm afraid. But one I've got my eye on is an 18-year-old named Tim Wade who left the Amish community a couple of years ago," the sheriff said. "He has a mean streak and has been linked to some violent assaults and more serious burglaries in Crossington. One of the items stolen is a semi-auto handgun. We don't know if he has the gun but it makes me nervous – a gun, let alone a rapid-fire weapon, in the hands of a teenager with a known temper problem."

Shane understood now why the sheriff had given him the veiled warning earlier about things escalating if a homeowner cornered the intruder.

"Of course," the sheriff continued, "these break-ins at the lake may just be kids on rumspringa. We've always got some group-households of kids in the county. But unless I can catch someone in the act, it's all just speculation.

"It would have been helpful to see this camp earlier, before someone cleaned it up, but at least we have your description of it and of the intruder, which is more than we had before. Up till now no one had put eyes on the guy."

Shane couldn't take much comfort from that. It was clear the intruder had watched Elizabeth and him discover the camp and had quickly dismantled it so they couldn't show the authorities. But he liked a challenge, and he knew that if this camp was gone, there would be another somewhere, maybe more than one. Shane promised himself he was not going to be the chump in this contest of wits.

By the time Shane and Sheriff Dixon got back to the lodge, Elizabeth and Billy had finished putting fresh linens on one of the guest beds.

"How'd it go?" Elizabeth asked.

"Total bust. I'll fill you in later."

Elizabeth seemed puzzled. She told Billy that Frank Hale was coming back in the widgeon today to deliver a surprise to them. That was all Billy needed.

He was out on the deck, listening and watching the sky, and was the first to hear the lumbering amphibian approach from the southwest and circle the lake. It came in low over the trees to crease the water with its hull and then settle all the way down till the pontoons on its wings were helping support it. A big cloud of spray trailed behind the plane as Hale fed power to the engines to taxi toward the bay where the family camp was located.

"Take the electric boat to meet the plane," Elizabeth suggested to Shane. "It's large enough for all three of them and their luggage."

As Shane and Billy glided clear of the boathouse in the electric boat, the plane was taxiing loudly in their direction. Shane waved a greeting and the pilot cut the throttles and let the plane drift. Shane pulled up alongside it, and the door on the aircraft's hull popped open.

There, framed in the opening, were Shane's friends Robert Yuka and Marie Martin, and their two-year-old son. Robert had been an Alaska state trooper and Marie was a federal wildlife agent when they met Shane.

Robert reached out and shook hands with Shane in the boat. Robert and Marie stepped carefully into the boat, steadied by Shane's hand. Then Frank Hale opened the plane's cargo bay and began handing suitcases and backpacks to them.

Shane knew this visit would be extra special for Elizabeth and Billy, for all three of them. He was also looking forward to sharing a little mystery with his guests – filling in Robert and Marie on his encounter with the prowler. That could wait till later.

When the whole group was settled in the electric boat, Shane backed smoothly away from the plane. He watched Marie adjust Martin's floppy hat to keep the sun off his eyes and face. Then she cinched the straps on his child floatation device.

Once they were a hundred feet from the airplane, Hale hit the starter and engine number one coughed to life in a cloud of blue smoke, followed shortly by number two. He gave Shane a thumb's-up through the cockpit window and shouted, "See you in a week." Then he slid the panel shut, advanced the throttles and began a slow turn and a long taxi toward the distant end of the lake. The group in the boat began the short hop to shore.

They were already back at the boathouse ten minutes later when the plane roared toward the bay from the far end of the lake. Billy, standing alone at the water's edge, saw Hale salute him from the cockpit. Billy waved back and watched the plane lift free of the water and climb low into the sky with a goodbye dip of the wings for him. A moment later, the tiny dot disappeared into the clouds. Billy ran back upslope to the lodge, where it was hugs all around for the new arrivals.

"This place is like something out of a fairy tale," Robert declared as he took in the old building, with its screened deck and cupola. "Getting here in an amphibian adds a nice touch. Growing up in an Inuit Village did not prepare me for how the landed gentry lives."

"Technically, it's how they lived a century ago," Elizabeth corrected, "minus the airplane. In the summertime, the lifestyle here is hot and tropical. In the winter, the lake is covered with ice and snow, and nothing moves except for a few snowmobiles and intrepid locals on cross-country skis."

Marie looked at Robert. "We're not complaining. I'd say Robert has adjusted to our new life in Boise just fine, now that he's the governor's driver and bodyguard. We get invited to dinner at the mansion once in a while," she added with a wink toward Shane. "It's a pretty nice perk. Life is good for us in Boise."

Elizabeth gave the new arrivals a one-minute orientation session. "Adirondack Park is the largest protected natural area in the lower forty-eight states," she said. "It occupies a third of New York State's total area."

She clarified that it's not a national or state park, just a park. But it's larger than Yellowstone, Everglades, Glacier and Grand Canyon national parks combined.

She led them all inside. The expressions of awe started all over again when Robert saw the massive, stone fireplace in the great room, the book-lined staircase and all the old family portraits on the wall.

At five-foot-six, the stocky Robert still had the commanding presence that had impressed Shane the first time they met on the Alaska Ferry. He remembered how relieved he was when he saw who was going to help him on that case. No doubt Robert's boss, the governor, had felt the same way when he first set eyes on him. Robert's native features and black hair added to the effect.

Marie, for her part, had the lean figure of a serious runner, but her oversize sunglasses and big smile made her instantly approachable and fun. Shane had seen what she could do as a federal wildlife officer and would never underestimate her.

"Martin has grown," Shane remarked, making eyes at the two-year-old at his feet. Martin smiled and made a goofy face back at him.

"He still likes to do that," Marie said. "But along with the cute stuff, he's now a major handful all day and night."

Martin took a few steps and found himself on the floor again.

"Did he just walk?" Elizabeth asked.

"Absolutely. Things are getting interesting now."

"Your room is on the left just upstairs," she said, pointing to the book-lined staircase. "We have a child gate to keep him from exploring the stairs."

"This is way cool," Marie remarked, "this whole place. This is where you spent your childhood?" she asked Elizabeth.

"We came here every summer as a family. Those were some happy times for me – swimming and boating, sharing meals on the deck, getting to know my cousins."

"Is this where you developed your interest in nature?" Marie asked.

"Absolutely. This is where it started. I read a book and learned there were flying squirrels here. I stayed up night-after-night trying to see them, but it's almost impossible to see a dark animal falling from the sky on a dark night. Then I learned I could just listen for them, and hear them plopping onto the roof in the middle of the night."

"That's funny."

"Yes, but there's so much more – like that Boreal Chickadee on the spruce tree behind us."

"Do you have eyes in the back of your head?"

"I heard it call. It looks and sounds a lot like the Black-capped Chickadees we have at home, but its call is slower and has a buzzing quality. I could sit and listen to the birds all day – Gray Jays, Spruce Grouse, Black-sided Woodpeckers, Crossbills and of course the loons in the early morning on the lake. There is nothing more haunting than the lonely call of a loon on a glassy lake around dawn."

"That's something I want to hear before we go back. Has Billy been out investigating the woods since you got here?"

"He has already been down to the water looking for bullfrogs, salamanders and turtles. There is a lot to see in the lake and wetlands close to shore. I think that's really what he's zeroing in on – amphibians and reptiles."

"He's a typical boy," Marie said. "I hope Martin gets interested in something like that so he becomes a little less demanding on Robert and me. Right now he's a total handful."

"I hear you. For me as a pre-teen, there were always people around the camp and they were always changing – new people arriving and other people leaving. Girls are probably more social anyway. One thing that hasn't changed is Aunt Bonnie, next door. You'll meet her soon. She was living there when I was a kid and she's still there now, older but just as spirited as ever."

Hours later, in the heat of a sultry afternoon, Marie tried to feed Martin at the kitchen table. She was sweating and her shoulder-length hair was stringy and wet. Martin had plastered scrambled eggs all over his shirt and the floor around his chair. Marie had toasted some bread with jam, and he had eaten some, smeared some more on his face, and dumped the rest on the floor. Nothing seemed to make him happy except the mess he was making.

Just at that moment, Martin released an ear-splitting shriek that made Marie's flesh crawl.

Robert came walking into the room. "Let me spell you off," he suggested, taking one look at Marie. "I'll clean this up and get Martin into some fresh clothes. He must be getting tired and that's why he's being so difficult; it's been a big day so far."

Elizabeth was watching all this, speechless.

"Come with me," she finally suggested to Marie, "and bring your book."

Elizabeth led her to a deck chair on the screened porch to spend some time with trashy novels. The heat brought back memories, sapping one's desire to get up and move at all. Elizabeth had always liked the feeling. Afternoons were meant for daydreaming, not for doing battle with a fussy two-year-old.

"He's a terrorist," Marie said.

"Martin?"

"They say all two-year-olds are. They push you right to the limit of human endurance."

Elizabeth smiled. "I see what you mean. I don't know how you keep your sanity. She let a moment pass, then sniffed the air and declared, "It's going to rain, "Wait till you see what we call an afternoon thunderstorm here." The sky had grown dark and it was suddenly hard to read the words on the page.

"Bring it on," Marie replied. "We have a front-row seat, nice and dry."

Billy was playing with the old radio in the great room, which, Elizabeth recalled, received only one station. She recognized the theme music of the Foreston Swap n' Shop Show, a mainstay of local radio here for decades, but the static was growing bad, no doubt from electrical activity in the area.

Elizabeth had last heard the swap-and-shop theme when she was a teenager. She couldn't believe it was still on the air in the format she remembered from her childhood. To submit an item for broadcast, listeners stopped at broadcast house and filled out cards for the announcer to read over the air. She wondered if that primitive method were still how it worked. It wouldn't surprise her, because things changed slowly here. People here liked their routines.

Will trade four mostly bald Volkswagen tires for ten laying hens and a rooster. Call Ambrose at . . .

40

For sale, trailing tandem disc harrow in fair condition, ideal for someone with welding equipment . . .

Wanted, aquarium with air pump and under-gravel filtration system . . .

Seeking ride to Ithaca on Tuesday mornings starting August 10. Will trade sewing or light housework . . .

It struck Elizabeth that a web page, or email, would be a much more efficient way for the radio station to receive and publicize such items. But then she remembered that the Amish and Mennonite communities didn't believe in computers. She wasn't even sure they believed in radio, but perhaps radio was more accepted than computers. She had heard that Amish homes didn't have telephones, either, though the Mennonites had adopted this convenience.

Robert planted Martin on the sofa in the great room and soon he was breathing heavily through his mouth and falling into a deep sleep. With luck the nap would last an hour or two and he'd awaken in a happier mood.

Robert advised Marie that things should be quiet for a little while now, then left with Shane for the boathouse. He forgot that a thunderstorm was imminent, and that it would test Martin's ability to sleep like nothing he'd ever experienced.

Shane wanted to show Robert the camp's blue canoe and give him a closer look at the electric boat in which he had ferried them ashore. Robert marveled at the exquisite wood grain and classic lines of the boat.

"People here really take pride in their craftsmanship," Robert remarked.

Shane noted that black thunderheads were piling high in the sky overhead.

"Does it rain every afternoon?" Robert asked.

"Not always, but often. Elizabeth says it's common on these hot summer days. It usually doesn't last long – half an hour, maybe an hour or two, just till the cell passes over us. Actually, the rain isn't the worst of it. What everyone dreads is the electrical storm that comes with it."

From the shelter of the boathouse, Shane pointed to the first few drops dimpling the glassy surface of the lake. Moments later, a furious downpour of wind-driven rain erased the lake from view.

"This is a white out," Robert remarked.

41

A brilliant flash of lightning lit up the sky. The concussion followed immediately and shook them both.

"That was close," Robert said. "Jesus, I'm not used to weather with concussions so loud you jump out of your skin."

Shane pointed to the seats in the electric boat. "We might as well sit down right here and relax. We won't be going anywhere for a few minutes."

When they were settled, Shane looked up at Robert and began, "Long as I've got you here, we've uncovered a little mystery."

Robert grinned broadly and leaned forward. "I knew it! I knew we weren't going to sit around in Adirondack chairs for a week and look at the view. Marie and I were wondering how long it would be till you rolled out a mystery for us." He laughed.

Shane was mindful that every time they'd ever been together, they'd ended up solving a crime.

"What is it this time?" Robert asked.

"It's nothing big. Nobody's dead, as far as I know. It's just that there has been a whole series of break-ins around the lake this year. The first night we were here, we heard someone breaking into this house and I chased them off."

"Did you get a look at them?"

"A fleeting look – one guy, tall, lean, dressed in black. Moved confidently without light."

"Did you call the sheriff?"

"No, we actually went and met him in person! Nice guy. We drove into town and talked with him face-to-face yesterday. He has a long list of teenage suspects but no solid leads and very few officers to patrol the entire county. Elizabeth and I found what we think was the prowler's camp about 20 minutes away in the woods, but by the time we came back with the sheriff the next day the whole site had been cleared."

That the nature of the community added another variable to things, Shane said. Many of the teenagers involved in break-ins and other minor crimes were likely to be Amish or Mennonite kids experimenting with life outside their own culture. They'd been raised with a strict moral code, and many of them would probably go back to the values their parents had taught them, after a period of living wild.

He added that the sheriff cautioned him politely about confronting any prowlers with a gun, since one of the young suspects is believed to have stolen a semi-auto pistol in a burglary in Crossington.

"Well that takes it to the next level," Robert said, the smile now gone from his face.

"Yeah," Shane replied. "If we start pulling our weapons on prowlers, we need to be aware we might run into someone who is both armed and scared."

"A bad combination," Robert said.

"Bad," Shane agreed. For now, he decided not to bring up the D.B. Cooper story he'd just heard. That was just a rumor anyway, probably nothing.

Trailer Trash

In the woods outside Crossington, Steve Kowalski had been working on getting drunk since afternoon. Now, as the shadows deepened, flames flickered in the firepit. He stood facing the yard from the step of the mobile home and watched his old lady, Barb Brown, toss a chunk of wood onto the fire. She seemed in a trance, staring mesmerized as a cloud of sparks erupted like fireflies. Then she threw back her head and drained the last sips from a can of Pabst Blue Ribbon.

Steve watched her crumple the can in her fist and toss it on the ground next to three dozen others. "Bring me another, dipshit," she called over her shoulder. "We got any weenies in there?"

"Just the one in my pants, honey bun, and it's hot for you," Steve's gravelly voice replied. Even drunk as he was, he struggled with the mess of this woman and her disgusting trailer. Plastic tarps covered part of the slimy green roof. A cracked window was secured with duct tape, and the screen door hung from the lower hinge only.

"You're not wearing pants, Steve. And don't wave that thing at me 'les you want to lose it," Barb replied.

She turned and stared at Steve as if studying a grotesque insect. He could read the familiar insult she was about to deliver – that he was fat, hairy and stinky. A heavy equipment operator, he had simply stopped working since he moved in with Barb and took up serious drinking. He hadn't trimmed his foot-long beard in months, nor the haystack of black hair on his head. But he was pretty sure he knew what she was thinking. She calculated it was better to hook up with a wreck of a man than none at all, because it's tough out here in the woods for a woman alone.

And if Barb were honest, she'd admit she hadn't showered or cleaned up in days, either. She might do that when the beer ran out, but Steve knew she tried hard to avoid getting sober. The kitchen counter was piled high with unpaid bills; maybe that was part of it.

The trailer sat in an isolated clearing on three acres of woods outside Crossington, New York. Barb rented it from an absentee landlord in Tucson, Arizona. She was well aware she was several months late with the rent. She told Steve angry notes and threats had been flying back and forth between them, and she threw most of the guy's letters into the trash unopened.

The trailer was reached on a rutted, gravel drive Barb had marked with hand-painted signs: "Keep Out," "Trespassers Will Be Shot," and "Protected by Smith and Wesson." Barb's broken down Dodge truck sat at the clearing's edge, next to Steve's newer Toyota land cruiser.

Barb's husband had just packed up and left one day. That was the story Barb told Steve, though she knew he secretly wondered if there might be a grave on the property, and maybe a spot for his own.

Barb knew she was no prize. At 52, she walked with a stoop from back problems and overflowed her comfort waist jeans with a roll of flab. She assured Steve she had been pretty in her 30s, with a willowy figure and long, blond hair. She worked for a few years in an office in Crossington, but that was before it all went to hell – marriage, childbirth, abandonment, unemployment and drinking.

"You sit on your butt too much," Barb called to Steve. "My husband worked."

"Well, just say the word and I'll lay some pipe."

"I'm going to puke," Barb replied, giving him the finger.

He patted his gut through a stained T-shirt, then wobbled off balance as he turned back inside to open the refrigerator in the kitchen behind him. He made a show of bending to look deep inside, displaying the full glory of his ass crack, as he grabbed another beer and delivered it to Barb. Then he stepped out the door toward the fire pit, turned and peed before dropping heavily into the chair next to her with a "huaaaah." He stared at the fire for a moment.

He looked at Barb. "No weenies," he declared, half speaking and half burping.

"I'm gonna beat the fuckin' shi . . . shit . . . out of that girl," Barb slurred. "She ate all the weenies and didn't get any more."

"Hell, she don't hardly ever come around anyway."

"Only to raid my fridge."

Kat watched from the shadows at the edge of the clearing. No one was going to beat the shit out of her tonight. Steve and her mom would fall asleep soon, she knew, and then she could slip inside the trailer. She wished her mom weren't such an angry drunk – weren't drunk at all – because she remembered better times when she had a "real" mom who went to parent-teacher conferences and baked cookies for her after-school snack. But after Kat's dad left, her mom fell into drinking and tantrums of yelling and beating her. Kat started skipping school, and getting into fights when she did go. She hid her bruises from teachers and social workers for a while, and then moved out altogether to stop the pain and live in the woods. The outdoors was her safe place.

At some point her mom started bringing home men – drunks and losers. Kat pleaded with her mom to stop but it did no good. At least this Steve Kowalski hadn't raped or beaten her like the others. She realized early that it wasn't her mom the men had their eye on – it was her. Steve was different in that he didn't want Kat around at all. Kat had just two overriding goals in life – to be as different as possible from her mom and to stay as far away as possible from the men in her mom's life.

As Kat watched, she became aware that the bickering had stopped. Her mom's head lolled to the side and she snorted, the first sign she was down for the count. Steve lay back on an aluminum lounge chair and dropped his beer on the ground. They'd sleep until late-morning, she thought.

It was getting harder and harder to visit her mom. When Kat was able to telephone her, Barb told her that sheriff's deputies and Child Protective Services were visiting the trailer often, looking for Kat and asking to search the premises for stolen merchandise. They had no search warrants and Barb ordered them off the property with a shotgun.

Kat waited till her mom and Steve were both snoring. Then she picked up her backpack and crossed the clearing to the trailer. She pulled open the broken screen door and slipped inside. The place was a health hazard, counters piled with dirty dishes and beer cans. She pushed an area of the mess aside to create a small clearing and arranged several cans on the counter of beans, stew and vegetables from her pack.

She pulled a sticky note pad from her pocket, and drew a smiley face on the first sheet, which she attached to the display. Then she slipped out the door again and disappeared into the night.

Cookie Tin

Flashing red and blue lights woke Barb from a confused and headachy sleep the next morning. She was still slumped in the lawn chair by the now-dead campfire, surrounded by empties. Steve was snoring loudly in the next chair. A sheriff's vehicle was sitting in the clearing and she recognized Andy Dixon standing in front of her with a piece of paper.

"What the fuh?" she slurred. "Get off of my property! Can't you read the signs?"

"It's not your property," the sheriff replied. "This is an eviction notice issued by the court and you have seven days to vacate the trailer and this land or I'll come back and move your possessions out to the highway for the garbage truck. Do you understand?"

"Nobody's doing any such thing," Barb replied.

"You've ignored repeated warnings."

"I don't have the money right now but I'm going to get it."

"Then that's between you and the court, but my orders are to serve you and start the process of moving you out."

"You mess with me, you're going to be sorry. Nobody pushes me around."

"It's not personal, Ms. Brown. It's the law."

"That's where you're wrong, sheriff," Barb replied. "It's personal to me and I settle my debts."

"Just make sure you are gone one week from today when I come back," the sheriff said, as he turned and got back into his car.

"We'll see," Barb muttered under her breath. "Maybe you won't be back."

At the public library, Harry waited for the girl, Kat. He didn't know how often she came to use the computer, but he'd seen her here frequently and this is where they had met a few months ago. He had asked her a simple question about computers and saw right away that she was friendly and helpful.

"I'm surprised you didn't know that," Kat said of his question.

"I'm Amish," Harry replied. "All this is new to me."

Soon, they had exchanged first names and told each other more about their personal lives. He told her he had left home on rumspringa and didn't know if he'd go back. His girlfriend had followed a few months later and they were living in a group household with an older boy. Kat said she had left home, too, but for different reasons. She spent the warm summer evenings mostly camping in the hills above Pursuit Lake.

Harry wasn't sure he would find her here this morning, so when she emerged from the women's restroom and sat down next to him, he was pleasantly surprised. Her face looked freshly scrubbed and he caught the scent of soap or lotion – a clean smell. Her hair was tied neatly in a bun. He assumed the library was one of the better places for her to clean up so she could blend with the townspeople.

"Still living in the woods?" Harry asked.

"Yeah, it's not bad in the summertime. I let myself into cabins sometimes when I need food or shelter, but for the last few days I've been lying low."

"You told me once you knew where you could get a bunch of cash," he said.

"Yeah, I do. But I've never touched it and never will. I'm not a thief. It's just something I happen to know."

"My girlfriend and I need to borrow a couple thousand dollars to get a place of our own."

"No way. Why so much? That would be serious burglary."

"We need first and last months' rent, plus a damage deposit. We're in a bad situation. "Sarah thinks we're both in danger and she's probably right," Harry said. "We'll pay you back as soon as we get moved and start jobs."

Harry explained that Sarah feared she would be raped any day now. Their housemate had a gun, and Harry was afraid he might get shot if he crossed their housemate, Tim Wade, and his druggie friends.

The girl listened sympathetically. "I've been raped myself several times by my mom's drunken boyfriends. I don't wish that on anyone."

"I'm sorry," Harry said. "I didn't know. Is that why you're living in the woods?"

"Mostly. I can't go home."

"So can you help us?"

"I'll do what I can; I think you're honest. I know where there's money but I don't think anyone else is aware of it. I don't like stealing, but the money isn't doing anyone any good right now. I don't like bullies and men who hurt women.

"Give me a day or two," the girl said. "Someone's in the house where I found the money, so it won't be easy for me to get in and out."

What is it about vacation that makes a guy eat like this? Shane wondered as he cleaned the last bite off his plate.

On the deck's screened porch that evening, he and Robert had just polished off half an oblong casserole dish of lasagna and a large green salad. The women had shown slightly better self-discipline but certainly did their part, he noted.

"Let's clear these dishes," Robert suggested to Shane. "You women just stay there and relax. Shane and I can handle this."

The two men made several trips to the kitchen, ran some hot, soapy water to soak the dishes, and came back with strawberry-rhubarb pie and a stack of small plates and forks.

"I don't think I can even move, let alone eat any more," Elizabeth said. Marie groaned.

"No rush," Robert replied. "We'll just set this here and visit till someone makes a move toward the pie."

In the distance, Robert noticed low rumbling and booms.

"Is that thunder?" he asked. "Are we expecting another storm?"

"No, it's the big guns at Camp Drum," Elizabeth replied. "When the atmosphere is still as it is tonight, we can hear the Army's live-fire exercises."

"No way!" Billy declared. "I've been reading about it. Camp Drum is a huge Army fort that dates back more than a century. I never thought we could hear it. The winter temperatures there get down to thirty below."

"Now that blows my mind," Robert said. "I didn't know any American military base went back that far. Or got that cold. Are you sure?"

Shane smiled. "I wouldn't go up against Billy on a quiz show. He has a photographic memory."

"It's all in the book I'm reading about Adirondack Park," Billy said. "The fort even held Italian and German prisoners in World War II."

"So tell me what you've learned about Adirondack Park," Robert asked.

"It's even older than Camp Drum. The state was worried that clear-cutting would destroy the forest and water resources, so in 1892 they created the park. It's different from most state parks because it contains about 105 towns and villages. But it accomplished its mission to save the forest."

"You're a walking encyclopedia, Billy," Robert said.

Billy smiled. "Could I be excused to go read some more?" he asked. "Call me when you serve the pie, ok?"

"Absolutely," Elizabeth replied.

Two-year-old Martin already was asleep on a lounge chair.

As Billy disappeared into the house, Shane looked at Robert and Marie.

"I had hoped to get Brad and Irene Haraldsen to join us here, but Brad is still undergoing cancer treatment in Boise. Maybe we can give them a call one of these afternoons." He was referring to the Idaho couple who brought them all together a few years ago at their ranch in Stanley. They hosted the whole group, and the ranch is where Shane and Elizabeth met.

They sat and talked for a while, catching up on Shane and Elizabeth's B&B business on Whidbey Island and Robert's adventures as the governor's bodyguard and driver. Shane could barely control himself when Robert told the story of the governor dedicating a new playground and being mobbed by geese. "I had to chase them off – protect my boss," Robert said. "Nothing in your training prepares you for geese."

Marie shared her stories of raising a two-year-old in Boise. "It's a beautiful city with the most wonderful parks and playgrounds," she said.

"Yeah, if you stay clear of the geese," Robert said.

"I'm so thankful for the city's livability. Martin's favorite is the public gardens at the old railway station overlooking Vista Avenue and the capitol building, where they have a big steam engine on display."

"He's still that same great kid you met last summer," Robert said, "surprisingly easy and mellow for the terrible twos." Marie gave him a long, cold stare.

Shane served dessert, and Billy joined them. Pretty soon Marie announced she couldn't keep her eyes open any longer, and Robert and Shane said the same.

Robert checked the time on his cell phone. "My god, it's midnight. I guess we had some catching up to do."

"You folks go ahead and turn in," Elizabeth said. "I love the evenings here and will sit out on the porch for a few more minutes before I call it a night. Turn out the lights so I can sit in the dark."

Robert and Marie gathered up Martin. Billy needed no coaxing when Shane invited him to bring his book and read for a little while in bed. The lights went dark. Within minutes, the house was quiet and Elizabeth was alone on the porch, with her thoughts. Suddenly, she shivered and felt almost too alone as she remembered the prowler. Was someone out there tonight, watching her? She still felt the old fear at times, after the trauma of a stalker-boyfriend who raped her a few years ago.

She willed herself not to let such thoughts ruin her evening. As her eyes adjusted, she began to notice a few stars and the outline of the far shore. The afternoon thunderstorms had blown over and the sky had cleared. Most of the other cabins and houses were dark, but a light was still on at Aunt Bonnie's. No surprise there, because Bonnie always had been a night owl.

Elizabeth yawned. Across the lake, at a cabin that had been empty for years, a light flashed for several seconds.

Did she imagine it? She didn't think so. But when the cabin stayed dark and she saw no more of the light, she began to doubt herself. The evening was beautiful but the day was catching up with her. She turned and entered the lodge, flipping the lock behind her. Moments later she was in bed with Shane. He barely stirred when she put her arm around him, and soon she was asleep as well.

Shortly after midnight, Sarah LeComte sat in the bow of the canoe, with her paddle across her lap, as it slipped silently through the darkness. She read the shadows as best she could. Every so often, Harry, in the stern, dipped his paddle to push it forward. He ended each stroke with a little twist to steer the canoe away from the low-hanging limbs reaching out from the water's edge. Even in darkness, Harry told her, the shoreline offered better cover from being noticed by any night owls than if they crossed open water mid-lake.

On this muggy summer night, Sarah wore a pink tank top and tan shorts, and purple flip-flops. The air felt sensuous on the bare skin of her long legs, all the way down to her individual toes – a sensation she'd rarely experienced growing up. The shorts were immodest and revealing for an Amish woman under any circumstances but especially in the presence of a male. Curiously, she thought, they were perfectly normal among English teenagers. She knew that her pink, painted toenails were vain but she liked them.

She and Harry had talked about this night for weeks, the exact conditions under which they would give up their virginity. She wanted to do this – get it done so their commitment would be total – yet her emotions were a welter of adolescent hormones and church prohibitions. As the moment drew closer, she knew she was on the verge of a step from which there was no turning back.

Tonight she was seeing another side of Harry. He was cautious and smart, a good boat-handler, having learned the skill at a Mennonite youth camp. He was lean and tall, with the handsome face that comes from high cheekbones. He handled the canoe the same way he moved on foot – with a very light touch. She wondered if he could ever be content driving a buggy on country roads and tilling the soil behind two plodding draft horses, coming home at the end of a long day to a houseful of babies and diapers.

Could she?

Harry had found the canoe in an unattended boathouse, so, technically, they had stolen it. But nobody knew it was missing and neither of them planned to keep it, just use it for a romantic evening they had long planned.

Just then Harry's voice, from the back of the canoe, interrupted her thoughts. "You're awfully quiet up there," he spoke in a hushed voice.

"Thinking about Tim," she blurted. "I think our living situation grows more dangerous by the day. And whatever happens tonight, I can't get pregnant," Sarah replied.

"You're not going to."

"How can you know that?" she asked.

"Tim gave me something for that. I have it in my pocket."

"Where would he get such a thing?"

"You know," Harry said. "Light fingers."

"And where is this place?"

"The far shore. It's a nice cabin right on the shore and it looks like nobody's been around for years. I already scoped a way in."

Sarah knew this whole thing of using other people's cabins was Tim's idea. He'd been breaking into places for more than a year. She wished Tim had just disappeared after he left the Amish community, but he had kept in touch with Harry and convinced him to follow. He had also convinced him it's okay to break into summer cabins.

Harry drew the canoe skillfully alongside the cabin's deck, which was built out over the water. He looped a line around a post and held the canoe snug while Sarah stepped onto the deck. Then he followed.

"I can't see a thing," Sarah declared. "Can't we have a little light? Otherwise I'm going to trip over something and break my neck."

"Okay, but light really isn't a good idea," he replied. "This cabin is supposed to be vacant, so if anyone across the lake sees a light here, it's going to raise questions."

"Just for a second while we climb through the window," Sarah said. "It's the middle of the night and we're clear on the far side from everything else. No one is going to see anything."

Harry hit the switch on a high-intensity, pocket flashlight and held it so Sarah could raise the window and climb inside. Then he turned off the light and followed.

Harry lit a match and held it to a single candle on a bedside table.

"For atmosphere," he declared. "And light. Check out the bed. I fixed it up for us," he declared, pointing to a love nest of pillows. Sarah wrapped her arms around him and gave him a long hug and a kiss. Harry was already reaching for the tank top.

Near the public boat launch, across from the cabin, a second canoe moved silently through the night. The canoeist paddled toward a small cove of reeds and lily pads, intending to conceal the canoe in the vegetation, go ashore and follow the road to a bicycle stashed nearby.

But the headlights of an approaching car suddenly turned night into day. Cars were a rarity at Pursuit Lake at any hour, and it was incredible bad luck to be caught in the open by headlights at night. The car drew closer, an older sedan with a bad muffler – Toyota Corolla, maybe.

She knew the car's lights would sweep right across her hiding spot in the reeds and light up the white canoe as if it were daytime. The reeds provided little cover against those lights.

But inexplicably, the headlights went dark before they could reveal her location. The darkened car rolled to a stop at the launch ramp, reversed, and backed in a half-circle till it faced away from the water. Then the engine went silent.

This made no sense.

The driver's door opened and the dome light came on, backlighting a lanky figure in dark pants and a dark hoodie. He stood and looked around for a moment, listened, then walked to the trunk and raised the lid, activating a second light in that compartment.

The driver reached inside and labored to lift one end of what appeared to be a heavily weighted garbage bag. The load fell to the ground in a heap. The driver took a moment to get a new handhold on the bag, then dragged it through the shoreline brush to the water's edge and lifted one end, then the other, into a rowboat pulled high on the sand. Sarah knew summer people sometimes left their rowboats at the boat launch if they were planning to come back the next day and use them some more. When the load was aboard, the man in the hoodie went back to the car for a cinderblock and something that clinked like chain, and lifted those into the boat as well.

The girl watched as the figure pushed the heavily-loaded boat halfway into the water, stepped aboard and used an oar to shove it the rest of the way free of the beach. Then he sat down and fitted the oars into the locks. The girl felt a new shiver of fear. The man in the rowboat was now facing directly toward her, though the light was dim and he seemed preoccupied.

This was bad. With long strokes of the oars, the rowboat pulled away from the shore toward the far side of the lake, but the girl dared not leave the cover of the reeds till the boat was just a vague smudge in the distance. The occupant's intentions were increasingly obvious.

In time, the rowboat's motion seemed to stop. The girl heard a loud splash and some metallic clinking, and soon the rhythmic thunk of the oars as the occupant began the return trip to his car.

The girl steered her canoe from the reeds and paddled south along the shore, away from what she'd just seen and the sinister figure in the boat. This was enough for one night – way more than enough.

"What's the coffee situation?" Robert asked Elizabeth the next morning when he staggered into the kitchen. He was opening all the cupboards, scanning counters and tabletops, clearly not finding what he expected.

"Well, this is embarrassing," Elizabeth relied. "None of my East Coast relatives are coffee drinkers. This place doesn't have a coffee maker and it sure doesn't have any fresh, ground beans, but I watched how my Dad made it fifteen years ago, if you're desperate enough."

"Anything!" Robert declared. "As long as it has caffeine, I don't care how you make it."

"You're going to eat those words."

"What?"

"I said I'll heat some right now."

Robert sat down in a straight-backed chair and watched Elizabeth pry the plastic lid off a can of Folgers that looked like it had been in the cupboard since World War II. The contents were all stuck together so she shook the can and stirred the grounds with a large spoon. Then she reached for a saucepan and filled it halfway with water, and put it on the burner, and waited as it rustled to life.

When the water reached a rolling boil, Elizabeth scooped several spoonfuls of ground coffee into the water.

"It'll be just a minute," she said, reaching for a mug and setting it next to the stove.

Robert's jaw hung open. The mixture boiled for a moment, then she turned off the burner and poured some black sludge from the saucepan into his cup and handed it to him.

"Coffee up," she declared. "Don't drink the last inch."

Just at that moment, Shane entered the room. "I smell coffee," he said. "Where did you find coffee?"

"Talk to Elizabeth," Robert said. "She'll work a little magic with her tar sands for you," as he moved toward the sink with his cup.

"It's an old family recipe I learned from Dad.

By the way, I'm glad you're both up," Elizabeth said. "I have a little news. Maybe it's nothing, but . . ."

She explained that after everyone went to bed last night, she sat on the porch for a while and let her eyes adjust to the darkness. Except for Bonnie's cabin, all the houses around the lake were dark, but she could just make out the profile of the far shore and the cabin at water's edge that's been empty for years. Sometime after midnight she saw a flash of light from the cabin. It lasted maybe a minute, as if someone were using a flashlight or a lighter to find their way in. After a short time the light went out and she saw no more of it.

"The cabin stayed dark after that?" Robert asked.

"Yes, there was no more light."

Robert turned to Shane. "A lot goes on here at night. I wonder if it was the same prowler you chased from this place. Maybe we should have a look at that cabin later today."

"You go ahead," Marie said. "I'm just at the good part in my book."

That afternoon on the lodge's screened porch, Elizabeth and Marie both read their books. Elizabeth looked up from the page and kept catching Marie stealing glances her way, as if on the verge of speaking.

Elizabeth lowered her book to her lap. "Something's on your mind."

"I have something I want to ask, but I'm not sure it's fair."

"How are you going to find out if you don't ask?" Elizabeth replied.

"I keep thinking about the prowler Shane chased, the light you saw and the other break-ins around the lake. There's quite a bit going on here at night."

"That's true," Elizabeth said.

"Frankly," Marie said, "I could use some excitement. I want to help catch whoever's behind all these break-ins."

"And?"

"We could set up a little two-woman surveillance team, maybe pick up some clues about who's moving around at night."

"You miss your old job, don't you?" Elizabeth asked.

Marie smiled. "I can't pretend I don't." She suggested they take shifts at night, watching both the lake and the house. "If you could cover the first part of the night, I'll take the second shift when it seems like more happens. The boys can watch Martin and Billy. It's not hard; both of them will be sleeping. Sooner or later we're going to see something. If one of us notices activity, we'll text the other one."

"What happens if someone comes here and we corner them? Are we really prepared for that, since neither of us is armed?"

"We'll call the boys. But I want to be sure you are comfortable with this, since police work isn't your field."

"It's just watching. I can do that. I'm not going to chase after anyone."

"Good. If something happens on my shift, I've got the speed and training to deal with it. Any prowler I catch is going to be surprised."

"What about Martin?" Elizabeth asked. "Are you worried about not being there for him if he wakes up?"

"Robert will be there. Martin is my top priority in these pre-school years, but being a full-time, stay-at-home mom is pretty tame for my constitution. As long as we're on vacation and have a little opportunity here, why not get in on the action, eh?"

"I'm in," Elizabeth said. "When should we start?"

"Tomorrow night. That'll give us some time to talk with the boys."

The girl knew that retrieving the old tin with the money would be especially difficult with people in the house. She had already bungled one break-in when she surprised guests she did not know were there. The guy who chased her that night gave her a good scare. The way he moved, and the blinding flashlight he used, implied some police training. So did his ability to follow a trail. The next day he and a woman from the lodge had traced her getaway trail and found her camp in the woods overlooking the lake. She did not want to meet him again.

At 2:30 a.m., the night was moonless, and this time she changed the routine. She'd been eager to try a set of night-vision goggles she'd ordered online with someone else's credit card.

She did that occasionally, ordered something from Amazon Prime and had it delivered to a vacant house a couple of days later, where she could retrieve the package. She always posted a note for the delivery service to make sure they knew someone was expecting a delivery.

So with the benefit of good vision, she approached the compound by canoe as silently as any human can move. She was pretty sure the lodge occupants had secured all the windows after the earlier encounter, but the warped door to the kitchen did not close tightly and was held by just a flimsy, locking latch. She was packing a red LED headlamp for close-up work, and a putty knife and screwdriver to peel back the latch. She wore thin, latex gloves to leave no fingerprints.

Silently, within a just a moment, she was inside.

The lodge was quiet. She stood in the darkness of the pantry for a full minute and listened for the creak of floorboards in the hall above. This time there were none. She had made no clumsy mistakes such as stepping into a galvanized pail in the dark room. She wondered if there were any light-sleepers upstairs, anyone lying awake and wondering whether to make a dash to the toilet.

After a moment, she switched on the LED and scanned the high shelves. The tin was where she remembered. Silently, she moved a chair across the room and stepped up onto it, and reached for the tin. She pulled open the lid and noted the bundles of money inside, and began stuffing them into her pockets. When she had emptied the last of them, she replaced the lid, lifted the tin back to its resting place, returned the chair to its place at the table and headed out the door, pulling it shut behind her, pleased that she'd left no signs of damage or entry. With a little luck, no one would ever know she'd been there.

In the darkness she made her way across the lawn to the canoe, glancing over her shoulder all the way for the pursuer with the blinding flashlight she feared would be right behind her.

She stepped into the canoe, shoved it away from the shore, and silently dipped her paddle into the water. Each stroke was perfection, barely rippling the surface as she gained momentum away from the lodge.

The next morning when the rotary phone in the great room rang, Elizabeth wondered who in the world it could be. Did the sheriff have developments to report?

But the caller was Bonnie next door.

"This is a surprise," Elizabeth declared.

"I wondered if you stayed up late last evening," Bonnie began. "Maybe the boys were working in the boathouse."

"No," Elizabeth replied. "Not too late. We were all pretty tired."

"Then I think the mystery is deepening. I heard something that doesn't make any sense — a big splash about 2 a.m."

"There are beavers in the lake, you know," Elizabeth pointed.

"They don't carry chains. I know a beaver splash when I hear one."

"You heard chains?"

"I'm pretty sure."

"Could you tell the direction?"

"The far side of the lake, best I could make out," Bonnie said. "You know how sound carries over water on a still night. I really didn't think it came from your boathouse, but had to ask."

It was late morning when Elizabeth headed out the pantry door to the compost bin, carrying a pail of apple and pear scraps for the composter. She pushed open the door with her shoulder, and then stopped in her tracks.

The door wasn't locked.

It didn't get much use, and the latch was fussy. Elizabeth kept it locked by habit, and was pretty sure she remembered locking it a day earlier. In fact she was certain. Because it was warped, it wouldn't lock unless slammed, and she had slammed it hard and then tested it to be sure. No one else had been working in the kitchen this morning; no one had used the door. But if a prowler had entered that door, he might have closed it gently to be as quiet as possible, not realizing it needed a slam.

She inspected the hardware. The door showed no damage — not a hint of scuffing or tool marks around the knob or latch. But this was the weak point in the house's defenses and she knew it. If the prowler had come back and used this door, he'd been very, very careful to leave no trace.

"Are you sure?" Shane asked when she told him. "We're all questioning ourselves now, walking on eggshells. It would take a lot of nerve for that prowler to come back and enter the house again with four adults upstairs, especially after what happened the last time."

Then he added as an afterthought, "But just to set your mind at ease, let's look at that cookie tin again."

Elizabeth slid a chair to the cupboard doors, got up on it and reached to the top shelf for the tin. She knew as soon as she picked up the tin that it felt lighter. In disbelief she pried open the lid and . . . nothing.

"It's gone," she said.

"The money?"

"All of it. Gone."

"So now this is grand theft."

Shane checked with Robert and Marie, and Billy, to see if any of them had seen the money. None of them even knew it was there. It baffled him that a burglar had known about the money's existence and where it was hidden. There were plenty of more obvious places for a prowler to snoop before climbing to the top shelf of the pantry and opening an old tin. In fact the whole idea that there was money in the house at all was quite far-fetched.

This burglar apparently had cased the house at his leisure on some previous occasion, probably more than once. But why hadn't he taken the money the first time? Why wait till the house was full of people to come back and risk getting caught? Shane would have to report this to Sheriff Dixon's office, whether or not they had the time and interest to hear about it. This was way beyond simple breaking and entering of an unused cabin.

Shane folded his hands and rested his chin on them, and stared for a moment without speaking. When he finally broke his silence, his expression was serious. The implications of everything that had happened in the last twenty-four hours were ominous. He supposed there could be an innocent explanation for the splash Bonnie heard, and the chain, but couldn't think of one. Much seemed to be happening at Pursuit Lake under cover of darkness.

At the rumspringa house, the day was off to a late start. Sarah and Harry hadn't gotten home till 4 a.m. They lingered in bed and did not emerge from their room till afternoon. After months of living platonically, Sarah was in love with love. When she and Harry finally opened their door and came out to the living room, the house was silent and she hoped Tim was gone for the day.

She busied herself straightening up Tim's mess in the living room while Harry rummaged in the kitchen. She noticed the runner was missing from the hallway.

Then Tim staggered into the room, red faced and rubbing sleep from his eyes. She felt a lump in her throat. Tim's hands fell to his sides and he locked his stare on Sarah.

"Well look at you," he declared. "You're glowing. You can always tell when a cherry's been popped."

Harry started across the room to Sarah's side, but Tim made a fast move and caught him, and punched him hard on the right shoulder, digging his thumb deep into the muscle.

"Ouch!" Harry said. "What's the idea?"

"You're da man. Is she pretty hot? I wouldn't mind some of that myself, now that you've opened her up."

"Back off," Harry snapped, shoving Tim away with both arms. Tim planted his feet and stuck his head into Harry's face. Sarah saw Tim's right hand reach for something in his baggy front pocket. He hesitated, and then came up empty handed and laughed.

"Oh, you have a backbone after all, little man. Did you use the gift I gave you? I don't use those things myself – like to spread my seed around."

Harry and Tim stood inches apart, much too close, and glared, neither one stepping back. Sarah put her arms out to try to separate the two boys.

She felt sick; Tim was capable of anything. She wished Harry would just let him swagger and strut, giving Tim credit for their lovemaking. If Harry pushed Tim too hard, he could lash out with no warning. He seemed unusually edgy and preoccupied this morning. Maybe it was the drugs; she didn't know. But more than ever, she wanted out of this household *now*.

"Come on, Harry," she said, putting a hand on his shoulder. "I need to talk with you in the bedroom." She led him back to their room, closed the door behind them and whispered, "I can't stay under this roof with him one more day. We aren't safe here. Something bad is going to happen."

"Okay," Harry said. "We need money to pay first and last month's rent, and a deposit. I'm talking with someone who can help us. Give me a couple of days to get the money."

"Promise me it's not Tim."

"No, it's not. I would never go into debt to him."

"We can make things work," Sarah said. "I'll take some housekeeping jobs. We can scrape it together."

In the great room, Elizabeth rifled through her grandfather's desk for the phone directory. Not since childhood had Shane used a rotary dial. He dialed each digit and waited for it to *clickety click* its way back to the starting point before entering the next number. This type of dialing took extra time, but the antiquated technology seemed fitting for this place that held onto the past.

When the dispatcher answered, Shane thought her voice seemed tenuous and clipped. "Sheriff," she said.

He identified himself and asked for Sheriff Dixon.

"Andy's, uh . . . not available," she said. "Hey, aren't you the guy from Woody Island who was in here the other day. Right?"

"Whidbey."

"How much do you know? Have you heard anything? I can give you his deputy."

"Know about what?" Shane asked. "Yes, please put me through."

Shane explained to Chief Deputy Hanson that he had been to the office and talked with sheriff a few days earlier about a prowler at Pursuit Lake. Now there were new developments.

"Can I take your number and call back?" the deputy asked. "We have a situation here."

Shane explained he was a fellow law officer. He offered his help if there was anything he could do.

"Not right at this moment," the deputy said, "but I'll get back to you if that changes."

Shane gave the deputy the number at the lodge. The deputy hung up.

Shane set the handset back in its cradle.

"That was strange," he told Robert and Elizabeth, who had both listened to his end of the conversation. "Sheriff Dixon is unavailable – that's the word the deputy used. The deputy says they're dealing with a 'situation' and he doesn't have time to take my report."

It wasn't till afternoon when the phone finally rang, and it wasn't the deputy calling but Bonnie looking for Elizabeth. Shane stood by patiently while the women talked for several minutes, with Elizabeth mostly listening. When Elizabeth finally hung up, Shane asked, "What's up?"

"She said her sources in town report the sheriff is missing. They don't know whether it's some innocent thing or foul play, but no one has seen him since yesterday. He didn't show up for work this morning."

"Holy cow."

"It's complicated because his style of policing is so informal. He and Deputy Hanson don't get along at all. He didn't radio that he was stopping anyone or checking on anything, so no one knows where to look. He's a bachelor and lives alone. He might be just fine but has never dropped out of sight like this, and his department is worried. They fear he had a heart attack out walking."

"Did they check his house?"

"Yes, and everything looks normal. His car is parked in the driveway."

"Well that explains the questions they asked me when I called."

"Absolutely. Let's stop and see Bonnie again, too," he said, turning to Elizabeth. "You said it looked like she was up late. I'd like to find out what she knows about the cabin on the other side."

"Billy is going to play blocks with Martin," Marie announced, "and I am going to kick back and read for a while. The three of you go ahead and check on Bonnie and the cabin," she suggested.

Robert, Shane and Elizabeth piled into the electric boat and headed next door. As Shane steered the boat with one arm on the wheel, he turned around and faced Robert. "There's a certain protocol to this." He motored to a spot in front of Bonnie's cabin, cut power and let the boat drift.

Robert stole a glance at Elizabeth and shrugged his shoulders. "We're stopping. What is he doing?"

Shane faced the shore, cupped both hands around his mouth, and shouted: "Ahoy, Bonnie! It's Shane, Elizabeth and our friend, Robert."

"Ahoy there, neighbors," came the response.

"Permission to come ashore?"

"Granted."

Shane smiled at Robert, who simply rolled his eyes.

Bonnie was in a floral robe this time and was straightening cushions on several chairs as the three visitors came up the path.

"Sorry about my wardrobe but I'm getting a late start today," Bonnie apologized. "My card group left a mess."

Elizabeth introduced Robert, "our Alaska state trooper friend, now an Idaho state trooper and the governor's personal bodyguard and driver."

"How many more of these law officers do you have next door?" Bonnie asked, nodding toward the lodge. "Are you pulling them out of a hat?"

"Only one more," Elizabeth replied. "Robert's wife, Marie, is a former federal wildlife officer. Her fellow agents call her 'the gunslinger' because of her reputation for catching bad guys who resist arrest."

"Dear Lord. Seriously?" Bonnie asked.

Shane nodded. "She's a livewire and you'll like her."

He explained they were curious about the cabin across the lake because Elizabeth thought she saw a light over there last night.

"If you did, it was nothing good. No one's been around that place for several years. The family used to come up from Albany every year. The kids loved this place for the water skiing and fishing when they were little. They played croquet on the lawn with other kids from around the lake."

"It sounds lovely," Elizabeth said.

"It was. I'd take the canoe over there for cookouts. They made a fabulous hamburger, and then we'd sit around and tell stories. I never laughed so hard."

"So why did it end?"

"Nothing is forever. That's the thing about life. You think it'll go on just the way it is, and maybe it does for a while, but in the end, time wins. So you have to hang onto those sweet memories, if you can."

"Where are they now?"

"The parents are both in dementia care. What do they call it? – memory care."

"I'm sorry," Elizabeth said.

"It's a cruel disease, you know – just breaks your heart. I went to see them a year ago but it was more than I could bear. They don't remember the cabin. Didn't know me. They spend their days in wheelchairs, staring at the ceiling, while the TV plays. I don't think they even know who's in the room with them."

"So what's the status of the cabin now?" Shane asked.

"Their kids own it, or they will eventually, but they don't come around. I really don't think either kid likes the place or has any use for it."

"You call them kids. Just how old are they?"

"Oh, probably fiftyish. But you know, the parents always said once you have kids, they're always your kids no matter how old they are. And that's how I remember them – as kids, not adults."

"Well," Shane said, "I think we will run over there in a minute and poke around, and see if we can figure out what Elizabeth saw last night."

"Do you think it's the same person who broke into the lodge?" Robert asked.

"I think it's possible. If it is, maybe he left some more clues for us over there."

By the time they left Bonnie's cabin, a dozen small sailboats were fanning out across the water under blue skies. Shane knew that swimming, sailing and canoeing were all taught at the youth camp; this was one of their activity classes. The run across the lake in the electric boat took only 15 minutes. Shane was growing to love the boat because it was a good deal faster than rowing but also nearly silent, so it didn't call attention to itself like an outboard. Robert and Elizabeth sat back and enjoyed the gentle breeze. Moments later, Shane steered toward the cabin's waterside deck and prepared to secure the boat to one of the deck posts.

"The moss and mildew are scuffed on that board," Robert remarked. "Right there, where you're about to tie up."

It took Shane a moment to detect the subtle marks Robert was pointing to, but he was right. Something had rubbed against the dock recently, right where they were going to tie up. Elizabeth reached for the post and pulled herself out of the boat. Shane threw her a line, which she wrapped around an upright.

Shane made a point of turning and looking back across the lake. As expected, he had an unobstructed view all the way back to the lodge. Robert was already starting a walk-around inspection, checking for unlocked windows and doors. "Right here," he said. "This window is unlocked."

Shane put his hands against the glass to shade his eyes from the sun and peer inside. "Looks like someone's been partying."

"We don't have a search warrant, let me just point out," Robert remarked.

Shane turned back to the cabin and rapped loudly on the window. "Hello. Police officers. Is everyone okay? Does anyone require assistance?"

No answer.

"This doesn't feel right to me," he told Robert, and then announced in a raised voice, "We're coming in to check and make sure no one has fallen or injured themselves." It was an old police trick, establishing the justification to enter premises without a warrant. He pushed up the double-hung window and leaned through it. In a moment he was inside and had unlocked the door for the others.

His eye went right to the queen bed on the sleeping porch. Blankets and pillows were pushed into a rumpled mess at the foot of the bed, not the way one would close-up a summer cabin for the season or even a few weeks.

Robert's nose was tilted up and he was sniffing the air. "What's that smell?" he asked.

"It's driving me crazy," Elizabeth replied. "I think it's fruit. Fresh peaches."

Robert looked around the room, then leaned down and sniffed a candle in a jar by the bedside.

"Scented candle. It's been burned quite recently." Beside it, he pointed out two used paper matches and a matchbook from a café in Crossington.

Shane took a whiff and then straightened up with his hands on his hips. "Someone had a romantic evening."

"I think so," Elizabeth agreed. "And for the record I'm not picking that up," she added.

"What?"

With her shoe, Elizabeth tapped the floor just under the bed. "That."

Shane took a step back and leaned lower to see where she was pointing. There, in the dust, sat a recently-used condom.

""At least they're responsible kids, using birth control. I guess the cabin is making some new memories," Shane said.

"What?"

"Oh, Bonnie and I were talking about all the wonderful memories she had of the family that vacationed here. Said she used to canoe over here for cookouts all the time. We'll leave everything as is and pass these findings along to the sheriff's department. They can contact the owners and let them know they need to secure the place. As it is, they aren't going to be very happy with me letting us in, though I'll personally take the heat for it." Shane knew he'd probably have to do some persuasive talking with the deputy about neighbors looking out for each other's property, Elizabeth's nighttime sighting and her worry that something sinister had happened across the lake.

Shane gave the rest of the cabin a once-over. The toilet needed flushing. Two water glasses in the kitchen needed washing. Otherwise, everything looked as he expected. He herded Robert and Elizabeth out the door, locked it behind them, then climbed back out the window and lowered it.

The puzzle of this place was getting more complex by the day, Shane thought. "We have at least four unconnected events, possibly five," he told his companions at dinner that evening, "except there is a long-shot chance they are all connected."

Robert sat back in his chair and listened, with his hand on his chin. Elizabeth and Marie poked at their food but kept their eyes on Shane.

"We have the prowler I chased from the pantry the night we arrived. We also have, apparently, two lovers who held a romantic tryst in the unoccupied cabin across the lake. We have Bonnie's report of a loud splash that night and the clinking of chain somewhere across the lake. The lovers may be witnesses to that. And now we have the mysterious disappearance of the sheriff, and also of the money from the house."

Robert looked up. "I don't even want to say this, but could there be a connection between the splash and the disappearance of the sheriff?"

Shane stared back at him. "That was the first thought that crossed my mind, too, but it's really a stretch."

Robert continued, "Someone knows something or saw something. We need to get our hands on a witness to the loud splash," he said. "And based on what we've seen so far, the witnesses seem to be moving around at night. If Bonnie is right about the general location of the splash, it was close to the cabin those lovers used, and they may have been there when it happened."

"Then maybe Marie and I can help," Elizabeth said. "We talked and we'd like to start posting a nighttime watch for a while, keeping our eyes and ears open for what happens after dark. It's time to turn up the pressure on whoever is sneaking around here. We'll get you a witness."

"Just be careful," Robert warned. "You know what the sheriff said about the kid who stole a handgun."

"We will," Marie said. "We're just going to be your eyes and ears. When things get dicey, we'll bring in you and Shane."

It would be helpful to have some clue who the prowler was, Shane thought, but he had absolutely nothing to go on. Based on the individual's modus operandi and the camp in the woods, he doubted the prowler was connected to the lovers who used the cabin across the lake. They struck him, potentially, as accidental witnesses.

The prowler's tidy camp continued to puzzle him; it just didn't fit, but it was a lot neater than the mess of evidence the lovers left at the lake cabin. Something about the prowler did not add up. But the lovers – they could know something about the mysterious splash that had everyone thinking the worst. What a tangle of loose ends and coincidences.

It did not escape Shane's notice that Bonnie was a valuable set of eyes and ears who seemed to miss little when she stayed up late. They also needed her connections to the local grapevine. The sheriff, who never had much to contribute, was now out of the picture, as near as Shane could tell, and his chief deputy was preoccupied trying to find him.

It crossed Shane's mind that in addition to a kid with a gun, there was also the possibility that the sheriff was killed by someone for personal reasons. Far fetched as it seemed, Deputy Hanson, for example, could have followed the sheriff to the group household at the end of the day, found no one home, fired two shots at the sheriff in the hallway and set about framing Tim Wade for the murder.

He knew from talking with Bonnie that the sheriff wanted
Hanson out of the department, and Hanson wanted the sheriff's job.
With Hanson leading the investigation, he would be above suspicion.

This was an angle worth considering. Shane realized he couldn't
trust Hanson any more; this was now a Whidbey Island operation – off
the books and unauthorized. That suited Shane, working as a lone wolf
with his like-minded friends.

Elizabeth and Marie started their night watch that evening, with
Elizabeth taking the ten p.m. to one a.m. shift, and Marie watching the
lake and lodge from to one to four a.m. Except for Elizabeth's
persistent fear she was being watched the whole time, she found it
supremely boring. She locked herself inside the screened porch in total
darkness and observed one shooting star, two Earth satellites and a
high-flying jet. In hindsight, she wished they had set this up for two-
person shifts, but they didn't have the backup to do that. And they'd
end up talking with each other instead of focusing on the night.

"Well, that was a bust," Elizabeth said to Marie the next
morning at breakfast. "Nothing."

"That was just one night," Marie replied. "We've got to be
patient, stick with the program, and give it time."

At the rumspringa house, Sarah awoke in a sunny mood. Harry
had come home with bundles of cash, about $5,000. She'd never seen
so much money.

"Where did you get this?" She asked.

"It's better you don't know. For deniability if somebody asks."

"Did you steal it?"

"Absolutely not. I know a girl who loaned it to us."

"Girl? Is this some criminal?"

"Not at all. I trust her and she's honest. She has connections.
It's a loan. We have to pay it back after we get our feet on the ground.
I'll open a bank account in our names and deposit it tomorrow."

"Whatever you do, don't let Tim know about it or find it," she
insisted.

"I'll sleep with it under my pillow."

Harry was still asleep the next morning when Sarah awoke. He
stirred but didn't awaken when she slid her hand under his pillow and
felt for the bundles. They were still there.

She hadn't heard Tim come home last night. That wasn't necessarily unusual, but with all this cash in the house, his absence was a relief. She wondered where he was, and whether they could avoid him today and just quietly disappear from his life.

At the lodge on Pursuit Lake, Shane noticed the canoe was missing from the boathouse. He had been using the electric boat and hadn't paid much attention to the canoe, but now he wondered how long it had been gone. Had the prowler taken it, the same one who took the cash? Someone was targeting the place at will, and Shane felt frustrated and embarrassed he hadn't stopped them.

Climbing the slope back to the house, he sat down at the desk, picked up the phone and called the sheriff's office. Deputy Hanson took a brief report over the phone about the cash and the canoe, and made an appointment to come out and look at the scene, and get a complete statement from Shane and Elizabeth. With no evidence of a break in, the missing money fell into the category of mysterious disappearance. That meant Shane and Elizabeth, and Robert and Marie, were all top suspects now. How much worse could this get?

At the bank, Harry handed the teller five thousand dollars in bundles of hundreds and fifties. "I'd like to open an account," he said. The clerk hesitated.

"Are you transferring this from another bank?"

Harry considered lying about that but thought better. "It's a gift from my parents." Immediately, he regretted this story, as well.

"One moment. I have to get my supervisor's approval."

The clerk took the money, turned and crossed the room to another employee's desk. The two huddled and talked for what seemed too long, then signaled to a third employee to join them. The third employee glanced his way. The teller handed the seated employee the stack of bills and he inserted them into a machine that rapidly counted the entire stack.

Harry wondered if the machine also checked serial numbers against a database of counterfeit or stolen bills. He didn't know the history of this money. Employee number two had left the group and returned to his desk, where he was dialing the phone. Harry wondered if he was calling the police.

How stupid could he be? He had no idea it was this hard to deposit money *into* a bank. He thought they'd just take the money and say, "Thank you." In hindsight, a kid with $5,000 cash was bound to attract suspicion.

Moments later, the clerk returned with a receipt for the cash. "You'll need to fill out some forms for my manager," she said, directing him to a desk at the side of the room.

Increasingly, Harry felt he had walked into a trap.

"Please have a seat," the middle-aged brunette said, looking into Harry's eyes. "This is a lot of cash for a young man to be carrying, and these are very old bills. Have they been stuffed under a mattress for the last 50 years?" she asked with a dead serious stare.

"I guess," Harry replied, laughing nervously, hoping to defuse the tension. He was also hoping like crazy the history of this money was clean. "My parents set aside a little extra for years to help me get an education. I guess they didn't trust banks."

"I see. I'll need some picture I.D."

He was pretty sure she wasn't buying his story. But if her associates had found anything wrong with the currency, he assumed he'd be handcuffed by now.

Harry pulled out his photo ID and library card from his wallet and handed them to the manager. She projected all the warmth of his most stern and severe teacher from elementary school. She took his credentials as and made a photocopy of both sides. Then she handed Harry a thick folder of bank policies and forms for him to complete, requiring him to disclose a mountain of personal information.

What a nightmare. No one in this branch would soon forget him, and that's exactly what he *didn't* want.

When it was all over, the manager told Harry his deposit would not be available for withdrawals until several days had passed, when everything was set up in the electronic system. She handed him a thin checkbook with 10 temporary checks. The first one was numbered 101. He felt like a little lamb, caught up in an English system he didn't understand.

Now, with his deposit frozen for a few days, his $5,000 was useless.

At the lake, Chief Deputy Leland Hanson III sat stone-faced at the kitchen table with Elizabeth, Shane, Robert and Marie, and listened to their story. Unlike the affable sheriff, the wiry and nervous Hanson made no effort at pleasantries. He seemed unimpressed and incurious that he was in the presence of three law-enforcement colleagues – clearly insecure. His tight-lipped, somewhat hostile attitude threw Shane off.

Shane realized everything about their story sounded lame. He couldn't blame the deputy for that. They had no proof the money had ever existed, except Elizabeth's word and Shane's assurance that he'd seen it. He couldn't really explain where it had come from. Any of the four people in the room could have taken it. There was no evidence of a break-in, nor was there any evidence of a missing canoe, though the deputy allowed that it might yet turn up, since it's hard to hide a canoe on a small lake. He expressed less confidence about the money.

Before this "vacation" was over, Shane was determined to show the deputy how real police do things. This was getting personal.

When their business was finished, Shane asked Hanson whether there'd been any progress or leads on the missing sheriff.

"It's an ongoing investigation," Hanson said.

Fine, Shane thought. I'll ask Bonnie.

Electrical Storm

"I'm going over to chat with Bonnie," Shane announced after the deputy had left. The others were setting up a table on the screened porch to play Hearts in the sultry afternoon heat. Marie had promised to teach Billy the card game. Clouds were gathering and Shane surveyed the sky. With luck, a thunderstorm was still an hour away.

Shane climbed into the electric boat, cast off the mooring line and glided out of the boathouse for the ten-minute run to Bonnie's. It crossed his mind that an open boat on a lake might not be the ideal place to get caught in an electrical storm, but he would be quick. Moments later he was in front of Bonnie's cabin, where he completed the landing protocol and went ashore.

"Was that the deputy sheriff I saw over your way?" Bonnie asked. "I can't stand that pompous ass."

"You've got good eyes."

"Binoculars," Bonnie corrected, waving an oversized pair that must date back to World War II. The irony was they were probably better than any of the cheap ones on the market today.

Shane laughed. "You don't miss much, which is why I am here. Yes it was Hanson, and no, I don't much care for him, either."

"Neither did the sheriff," Bonnie said. "Hanson thinks he is Rambo, throwing his weight around. That's not the sheriff's style. Hanson is a career employee of the department, with all the protection of the police union, and of course the sheriff is elected at the whim of the voters.

"It's hard to dislodge a guy just because there are some complaints and you don't care for him. But feelings are pretty raw around here after Hanson knocked the feet out from under a homeless man he was arresting a while back. The poor guy fell on his face and got banged up pretty good. He walked on crutches for weeks afterward."

The mayor, city council and townspeople were divided on what they thought of the chief deputy, Bonnie said. The mayor felt he was a liability to the city, though the council was dived. The chief was not inclined to stand up for him even a little. Several other police officers testified to the city council that they thought Hanson was too aggressive in his style of policing. That "betrayal" from fellow officers struck Shane as extraordinary for a small town. He imagined there were some icy stares back and forth at the office.

The trouble with all these messy personnel issues in city government, Shane knew, was that if the city dismissed Hanson, they could count on a lawsuit that would cost them a lot of money. Their insurance carrier would undoubtedly raise the city's premiums.

"How did Andy Dixon end up with Hanson in his department at all?" Shane asked.

"He's an Army veteran – military police – and was already there when Dixon got elected. You know how it is with veterans – there's a lot of deference to them. He and the sheriff are like oil and water. The sheriff is well liked around here. He has a good relationship with the Amish community and seems to know how to work with the kids. He's a good role model, a good fit for the job."

Shane told Bonnie that he had called the deputy to report the disappearance of five thousand dollars from an old cookie tin in the pantry. It was an awkward meeting because Hanson didn't buy any part of Shane and Elizabeth's story that someone had entered the house and taken the cash.

"Dear lord, that's a lot of money to keep in a summer house."

"It is. And in hindsight, Elizabeth feels rather sheepish about it. We can't prove it ever existed. Apparently, her dad stashed the money in the cookie tin years ago. Imagine what five thousand dollars was worth back then."

"Where in the world did her dad get it?"

"We don't know. This is the first time Elizabeth has been back to this place since he died. She knew the money was there, or used to be there, but never quite got around to removing it. She thought it was well hidden, and I know it was there just a few days ago because she showed it to me. We put it back into the tin and returned it to the high shelf where it was tucked away. In hindsight, that maybe wasn't a good idea."

"You know there was a rumor years ago that her dad might be D.B. Cooper. I never believed it, but her dad drew attention to himself and didn't especially trust banks."

"I know now," Shane said. "Sheriff Dixon mentioned it when he came out to look at the prowler's camp with me."

"Her dad had some odd ideas about financial institutions, and about the end times. Turned his back on the world."

"I'm getting that picture. Seems like there's a lot of non-traditional thinking around here. Hey," Shane asked, "what do you hear from your sources about the search for Sheriff Dixon? Hanson wouldn't tell me a thing."

"They're completely stumped." Bonnie said a member of her card group is a close friend of the sheriff's dispatcher. "They searched the sheriff's house and his car, reviewed all the numbers in his cell phone, and looked at every traffic camera in town. They retraced with dogs where he typically took his walks, and came up with nothing. He has vanished, pure and simple, and it's highly embarrassing to the department. Almost as embarrassing as that five thousand dollars is to you."

"Well, in light of everything that's been happening around here at night, Elizabeth and Marie have decided to post a watch after dark. So they'll be keeping eyes and ears on the lake. We need to catch a break, and sometimes the best way to do that is to force it."

As Shane and Bonnie talked at the dining room table, Shane was sneaking glances out the window. He wanted to stay and talk some more, but the afternoon's puffy, white clouds had stacked up into a tall, anvil-shaped formation with a black base.

Bonnie was way ahead of him. She pointed out the window and added, "Looks like we have a pretty wicked storm brewing. You'd better stay right here till it passes over us."

"I think I can make it.

"I doubt it. That sky looks quite serious," she said, following his gaze. "You're not going to get home ahead of it, so you had better wait it out here."

"I'll make a dash right now. The electric boat moves pretty fast." He pushed back his chair and got up from the table.

"Thank you for the chat," Shane said over his shoulder as he got up and hurried out the door, jogging down the path to the electric boat.

When he got to the boat, he looked back at the house and saw Bonnie shaking her head.

He was halfway home when the first drops hit, and they weren't water but ice – in the middle of summer. Driven by a fierce downdraft, the ice pelted Shane's head and face, stinging his skin in a thousand places. The bottom of the boat turned white as the sleet came faster. The hot day had turned cold. Wind whipped at Shane's shirt and he realized there were whitecaps on the lake's surface. He slouched lower in the boat, remembering that the worst possible place to be on a lake in an electrical storm was an open boat, where the operator was the highest point in all directions. He was suddenly aware of the metal on his body, and pulled off his wire-rim sunglasses, wedding ring and cell phone, and set them in the boat's glove box.

A bright flash lit up the sky and a loud *craaaaaaack-bang* hit the boat at the same instant.

"Oh, shit!"

It was the opening volley in this storm, he knew, to be followed by more. It was super close. Everything was still ok with the boat but Shane knew he was in a very bad place.

He had screwed up, thinking he could outrun the storm back to the lodge when he should have listened to the voice of experience and waited it out with Bonnie.

With each second that passed, the boathouse grew a little closer, but so did his fear that the next lightning strike would be his last. The boat's electric motor wasn't performing as well as he expected; it seemed to be slowing and laboring for the modest speed he was making – growing weak, he supposed, from too much use and too little recharging. He had only one oar in the boat. It would take forever to paddle back to shore if the battery failed. He imagined they'd find his charred remains out here and ask, "What in the world had he been thinking?"

Another flash-bang lit up the sky, followed by a rolling rumble that went on and on. He saw this one hit – a single core descending from the sky toward the lodge, branching into a web of forks. One of them cut the top off a tree in the yard. The top fell to earth, trailing smoke and flames all the way down.

Nothing in Shane's West Coast experience had prepared him for weather like this. He had a lot to learn about Adirondack weather and lightning storms. This was a lesson he'd be lucky to survive.

Two hundred yards to go . . . fifty . . . twenty-five . . . ten. Finally, he was inside the boathouse, under the roof that would deflect any lightning strikes now. He tied up the boat, got out and lay down on the ground inside, shivering in his wet clothes. He would just wait here while the storm raged around him. No need to cross the open yard to the lodge, where the top of that beheaded tree still trailed smoke.

He wondered how the widgeon pilot, Frank Hale, handled weather like this. Hale typically flew at about eight- to ten-thousand feet. These thunderheads could reach fifty thousand. Frank was an old hand; he probably watched the conditions and flew around storms like this, or simply delayed his take-off till it was safe to proceed.

Shane had read somewhere that the average person stands a one-in-three-thousand chance of being hit by lightning in their lifetime. But that includes people living in places where lightning is rare, like Alaska, and the chances are probably one-in-twenty-thousand. In this part of the country, the odds were probably much higher than one-in-three thousand. People who went boating in electrical storms probably raised their odds to one-in-two.

In time, the rain and sleet slowed, the thunder grew distant and the sun came out. Shane watched clouds of steam rise from the earth. A rainbow stretched from one end of the lake to the other.

Dripping water, he got up and walked through the steam clouds to the house, where Robert, Marie, Elizabeth and Billy watched slack-jawed from the deck.

"My god," Elizabeth said. "Tell me you didn't . . ."

"Don't do what I just did," Shane said, walking past the group, dripping wet, and disappearing upstairs without one more word. He needed dry clothes.

Half-a-mile away, the girl watched the rain flow off her makeshift shelter overlooking Pursuit Lake and wondered if she had gotten away with it – the most serious crime she had ever committed.

She'd left no trace of entering the house but had been using the canoe from the boathouse for several days. The canoe's absence was a visible sign she had returned to the property since the night Shane chased her from the pantry.

She hadn't even realized how much money was in the cookie tin till she got back to her camp and counted it.

She would take back the canoe tonight and hoped the lodge guests hadn't noticed it was gone. If they had, she hoped they'd accept its return as a good-faith gesture on her part, putting an end to any further concerns. She needed to distance herself from this place.

Catch and Release

At dinner that evening, Shane was well aware the conversation was unusually subdued. Billy shared some more history of Adirondack Park. Marie talked about the card game. Robert remarked how easy it was to get a smile from Martin, who was sitting in the middle of a disaster area of toys in the great room.

Shane stared at his plate of pasta and said nothing but, "Pass the salad, please."

Finally, he couldn't stand the silent treatment any longer.

"Okay," he began at last, pushing back his chair and setting his napkin next to his plate. "Let's get this out on the table. I did a very stupid and dangerous thing, trying to get back to the lodge earlier today in an open boat when an electrical storm was building. I'm lucky to be alive. But I learned a lesson, and Billy, I hope you don't ever do anything as stupid as I just did."

"Point taken," Robert said. "We are all just immensely relieved you made it back in one piece."

"That's an understatement," Elizabeth added.

"Amen," Marie said.

"The odds of being hit by lightning on the water are extremely high," Shane said, looking right at Billy.

"Now tell us what you learned from Bonnie," Robert continued.

"The search for Andy Dixon is stone cold. That's probably why the deputy is so tight-lipped and edgy. He can't find his own boss and it's supremely embarrassing. I don't know if it's within our power to help with that, but I do know we have five thousand missing dollars and we're on our own with that. My gut tells me we need to catch the prowler I chased from the pantry the first night we were here."

Marie grinned. "That's my department! Elizabeth and I are on it. If anything moves out there tonight, we'll be all over it."

Marie was well accustomed to stakeouts – hours of waiting and watching, fighting to stay awake, followed by minutes of intense action if she got lucky. Otherwise, it was just hours of boredom. She wondered if it was fair to bring Elizabeth into this, who had no police training, but Elizabeth insisted she wanted to help. Not much was likely to happen on the first shift anyway; the activity since they'd arrived mostly seemed to fall in the second half of the night, when Marie would be on watch.

The waiting was a price Marie paid willingly, excited to be on the hunt again as in old times, when she tracked and arrested poachers in Alaska. She played mind games to stay alert, naming the constellations, listening for the sounds of nature, a frog croaking, or the rustle of a raccoon checking the garbage cans.

Elizabeth had reported all clear at shift change. The quarter moon provided only minimal light, but the night was windless and silent. Marie knew Elizabeth had watched the lake from where she felt safest, the screened deck of the lodge. Elizabeth was still wrestling with deep fears after being stalked and raped in Idaho a few years ago. Marie felt enormous admiration at her courage.

More of a risk-taker, Marie was inclined to station herself closer to the water. In the darkness she settled herself in an Adirondack chair in the yard, near the boathouse, where she could listen and watch. The chirp of bats caught her ear. She suspected they were swooping for insects all around her. She had never feared bats and knew they'd do her no harm, but raised the hood on her sweatshirt anyway in case one mistook her hair for a perch. The night was soothing. Whether anything happened or not, it was a privilege to be outside, experiencing this. The hours of darkness were magical; she had always believed that.

The glint of something in the distance brought her out of her happy trance. Had she imagined it? The flash repeated itself and she recognized the rhythm, knew it was a paddle catching the moonlight as a canoeist raised and lowered it. The paddler was just a dark smudge, but the canoe seemed to be coming her way from the direction of the boat launch. She texted Elizabeth: "Canoe incoming. I'm headed to boathouse."

Marie got up from her chair and moved to the corner of the boathouse, where she could hide while she watched. The canoe and its occupant became clearer as they drew closer. She could now see that the paddler was tall and slender, dressed in black, wearing a hoodie. The paddler was coming directly toward the boathouse, apparently intending to beach the canoe inside and come ashore. Could it really be this easy? Marie waited and watched, moving closer to see inside the boathouse. The canoeist paddled right into the boathouse, stepped out and lifted the craft out of the water – first the stern, then the bow –and turned it upside down. Then the dark figure proceeded into the yard, only a few yards from Marie.

"Freeze! Hold it right there!" Marie ordered in her deepest, sternest voice. One thing she had practiced as a wildlife officer was deepening her voice so she could give commands like a man. It came in handy.

The canoeist hesitated, then broke into a run. Several strides later, Marie closed the distance, wrapped her arms around the canoeist's legs, and laid the individual face down on the ground, with a loud *oomph*. Marie pulled a plastic tie from her back pocket and secured both hands, then lifted the canoeist onto her feet.

"Owww, you're hurting me," the canoeist protested.

"My god, you're a girl."

"So are you," the canoeist replied. "Jesus, what is it with you people?"

"I'm asking the questions. What are you doing in our boathouse, with our canoe?"

"Returning it."

"Why do you have it in the first place? Did you break into our house?"

No response.

"You'd better come with me. We need to talk."

Marie marched her roughly up the slope to the house. The girl nearly stumbled twice, but Marie held her on her feet.

"Take it easy, will you?" the girl asked. "I'm bleeding. I've got blood running down my arm."

Marie's text had alerted the whole household. By the time she and the girl reached the porch, everyone was standing there, staring out at the night. Marie marched the girl past the group, through the door, and into the kitchen, where she sat her down at the table roughly, and turned on all the lights in the room. She pulled the hoodie off Kat's head and judged her to be about eighteen.

Marie took a chair directly across from her. "Let's start with your name."

Silence. The girl smirked.

"She's bleeding," Elizabeth said. "Let me clean up those cuts." In addition to the cuts, Kat's face was dirty from being thrown down on the ground.

Marie shrugged. Elizabeth turned and reached for a washcloth, and started running some hot water.

"This will go a lot better if you cooperate," Marie said. "We can do our talking right here at the kitchen table or we can call the sheriff and turn you over to him. Which one is better for you?"

The girl sat there for a moment. Marie sensed she was debating whether to answer truthfully. Then, in a low voice, she said "Kat."

"What?"

"Kat. That's my name. Like the animal, with a K."

"That's your real first name?"

"Yeah. Short for Katarina, if it matters."

"Last name?"

"What difference does it make?"

"I asked you a question."

Elizabeth returned to the table with some bandages and rolled up Kat's sleeve. "Can we undo this zip tie so I can bandage her arm?" Elizabeth asked. Marie snipped the plastic.

The girl stared at the cut on her arm. The bleeding had stopped and Elizabeth was cleaning the crusty blood gently, and dabbing antibiotic on it. Shane and Robert were watching all this, apparently content to let their wives take the lead.

"Ouch!" Kat grimaced.

"Sorry," Elizabeth remarked. "I know this stuff stings."

Kat still hadn't answered the question.

"Brown," she said at length.

"And you live where?"

"My Mom has an old trailer outside Crossington. But she's a drunk and she's getting evicted, so I live mostly in the woods."

"You broke into our house," Marie said.

Kat stared at the floor.

"Yes."

"More than once."

"Sometimes I need food or a place to sleep, especially in the winter."

"That's not all you've taken from us. And you've also entered other cabins around the lake."

"Yeah. Are you calling the police?"

Shane jumped into the conversation for the first time. "I'm not sure. It might depend on how helpful and forthcoming you are."

"I'm answering your questions. Who are you people, anyway?"

"I'm a detective from Whidbey Island," Shane said, "and this is Elizabeth's house. Robert is an Idaho State Trooper, and Marie is a federal wildlife officer."

Kat lowered her head and stared at the table. "Oh god, you *are* the police. I really screwed up. My mom will kill me."

Marie, who'd been playing the bad cop till now, actually felt sorry for the girl, living in the woods with no safe place to call home. She didn't seem a bad person, just desperate and cornered. Elizabeth and Shane had mentioned the books they'd found at Kat's campsite, evidence of a serious, inquisitive mind.

"I'm sorry about the hard takedown a few minutes ago but you ran. Listen, Kat. If you work with us, we'll do everything we can to help you," Marie said. "But we're not very happy about the break-ins. Tell me about your mom. Why are you living like this, afraid to go home?"

Marie was pretty sure Shane wanted to ask Kat some more pointed questions, but thought it was smart to get the girl talking and build some trust. Slowly at first, then more freely, Kat explained about her alcoholic mom and the abusive men she brought home. It made Marie sad because Kat seemed caught in a trap from which there was no good way out.

After awhile, Marie brought the discussion back to the present and the lake. "We think you may know some things, or have seen things, that can help us piece together what's happening here."

"If I answer your questions will you let me go?"

"We may," Marie said. "It depends on what you may have done, and how truthful you are with us."

"Okay."

"The break-in at the cabin across the lake," Shane began. "What's the story on that?"

"That's nothing – just a couple of kids I know. That cabin has been empty for years."

"You know who got into it?"

"Yeah. They're just kids – good kids. It probably won't happen again because they're getting a place of their own. They aren't the first, by the way."

"Do you know their names?"

"Harry, I think, is the guy. I don't know his girlfriend's name."

"People heard a big splash and the clinking of chain the night those kids got into the cabin. Do you know anything about that?"

Kat sat silently a moment, her brow furrowed. "I was on the lake. I heard it, too."

Shane leaned forward. "Did you see anything?"

"I was canoeing. Someone was at the boat ramp, which I never expected – a man in dark clothes, rather lanky in build. He lifted a big bag from his trunk and loaded it into a rowboat, and then headed across the lake. I was scared and stayed hidden. As soon as he got to the other side of the lake, I got out of there. I didn't want him to see me."

"You heard what sounded like chain?"

"Yes."

"What did you make of it?" Shane asked.

"You know. I had a bad feeling about it. I thought I might be in danger for witnessing something criminal that nobody was supposed to see."

At Shane's prodding she described the car and the man in dark clothing with the hoodie. The car was an old Corolla or something like it, she said – whitish or beige.

"Another thing," Shane added. "There's some money missing from this house – quite a lot."

Kat's body tightened. "I don't know. I am not a thief."

Shane fixed his stare on her till everyone squirmed.

"Do you know who does know?" he asked.

Kat shook her head.

"I think you took the money," he said. "I'll just say that straight out. So I hope you'll think some more and come back and tell us the truth, so we can straighten this out. How can we find you if we want to talk some more?"

Kat said she goes to the library most mornings, whenever she's around Crossington, to use the computer and clean up in the restroom. She gave Shane her email address.

"Crossington's a long walk from here. How do you get back and forth?"

"I have a bike in the woods."

"Is it yours?"

"Not exactly. More of a loaner."

"Sit here for a minute," Shane said. "The rest of us need to talk among ourselves."

Shane, Marie, Robert and Elizabeth stepped into the next room. Marie took it on faith that Kat wouldn't try to slip out quietly while they left her in the kitchen.

"She's lying about the money," Shane said. "You could see her tense up and go quiet when I asked."

Everyone nodded in agreement.

"So the question is, do we turn her over to Hanson or do we try to work with her?"

"I shudder to think what would happen to her in Hanson's custody," Robert said.

"Frankly, I think she's more valuable to us if we give her a break for now," Marie said. "She strikes me as basically a good kid. Her life is crummy and she's had some bad breaks. Maybe she's just a better than average con artist, but I think we can bring her around."

"What do you think, Robert?"

Robert gave him the thumbs up.

"Elizabeth, this is really your decision. It's your five thousand dollars."

"I may forever regret this, but I believe in the underlying goodness of human nature. So I say give her the benefit."

Returning to the kitchen, Shane announced, "Okay, we're letting you go. We'd like to talk some more soon, but we're not out to make your life harder."

"Seriously?"

Kat got up slowly and walked to the door, with Marie at her side. Kat paused at the door. Marie held out her arms and gave Kat a hug. "Be safe," she said.

"Thank you," Kat replied. "Thanks for not calling the sheriff." With that she turned and disappeared into the night.

Robert, Shane, and Elizabeth sat at the table for a moment, as Marie rejoined them.

"I hope we didn't just screw up in a way we'll regret for a long time to come," Shane said.

"I know," Marie agreed. "I had mixed feelings about letting her walk out of here, but what choice did we have? My gut tells me she was telling the truth about everything else. I think she knows something about the money but needs time to think about it. I want to believe we'll get the truth out of her eventually. Meanwhile, we now have a mystery man in an old Corolla who threw something into the lake."

"Yep, probably a body, and we probably know who it was," Robert said. "I hope we are wrong."

Shane looked directly at Marie. "Nice work, by the way. Very nice. You've still got the old moves. And you're a smart interviewer."

"Chasing her down got the juices flowing," Marie said. She was wearing the biggest smile Shane had seen in a couple of years. Elizabeth flashed her the thumbs up.

"And now," Elizabeth said, "if you're all satisfied with your morning's work, I'm going to kick back for a little while in splendid isolation and read my book. If I fall asleep, so much the better because it's been an eventful night."

Shane wondered if she were really going to read her book, or whether she wasn't, instead, trying to make sense of her dad's money and the whole D.B. Cooper story. The sheriff had stirred things up, perhaps by design.

Heart to Heart

"Since we're up anyway, I'm going to check Martin's diaper," Marie said. "He makes it through the night most of the time now, but when I get the chance, I like to check. He's at that in-between stage, not quite a boy, but not a baby, either."

The day was off to an early start, but it seemed unlikely any of them would sleep any more now. Too much had happened, and too many thoughts were running through their minds.

It was just an hour later when Marie, plopped into a chair beside Elizabeth with a book of her own. Marie opened it to her bookmark and read a page, then looked up and cleared her throat.

"Yes?" Elizabeth asked. "Let's have it."

"I was just wondering," Marie began, "how you feel about all this."

"All what?"

"All this drama and police activity. It's not really your thing."

"No, I'm not you, or Robert or Shane. I've grown used to a quieter life surrounded by nature, and of course to running a B&B. But I love the three of you to death, and I support Shane in everything he does. I love his commitment to justice. He's the best man I've ever known, which of course is why I married him. Sitting here this morning on the deck, I'm a happy person."

"Seriously?"

"Absolutely. More power to you – to all three of you."

Marie smiled. "I hope you aren't just saying that."

"It's funny you were worried about me," Elizabeth said, "because I've been worried about you. Please don't hate me for saying this but I think you are badly conflicted about motherhood."

Marie looked down at her book and was silent a moment. "You're perceptive."

"Sometimes I think it's my curse."

"I love Martin. You know that. But I desperately miss the challenge of police work. I don't know how I'm going to get through the next few years till Martin starts school. All I think about is the excitement of the chase."

"I could see it in your eyes when you captured Kat," Elizabeth said.

"Yes, and you could hardly call her a bad guy," Marie replied. "More of a delinquent. Still, that was my first real chase since Martin was born!"

Elizabeth didn't reply.

"Do you think I'm a good mother?" Marie asked. "I worry about that all the time."

"I've never seen you neglect Martin in any way," Elizabeth said, choosing her words with care, Marie thought. "I can see he's a handful to manage. When it comes to motherhood, I'm no expert. I had it pretty easy and skipped over those tough, early years with Billy because he was already a grown boy when he and Shane came into my life. I didn't have to give up very much to be his mom. And in fact he still has a mom, Judy, so maybe my job is to be more like a friend than anything. I'm careful not to overstep my role with him. As Martin gets older, you may find you share some interests, much as I've discovered with Billy."

Marie let the thought sink in.

"What about Robert?" Elizabeth asked. "How is fatherhood going for him? Do you think he'll stay in his job as the governor's driver?"

"That's a good question. You get right to the heart of things. He dotes on Martin. He took the job with the governor partly to get into something safer now that we are a family. It's his dream job in many ways but a little tame for his constitution. I suppose we both miss the challenge of our old jobs, which got our hearts racing a little more."

"I understand completely."

It was just noon when Shane rounded up the group and sat down at the old rotary phone in the great room. He knew it was two hours earlier where he was calling. He laboriously dialed eleven digits and waited as the line clicked and crackled, and then the phone rang three, four times. He imagined the different switchboards and circuits through which this call wound its way.

"Brad Haraldsen," answered the baritone voice on the other end of the line. The connection to Stanley, Idaho, was bell clear and Shane thought Brad's voice was surprisingly strong, considering he was a cancer patient fighting for his life.

"Brad, it's your old buddy Shane. I'm here at Pursuit Lake, New York, with all the usual suspects."

"By gosh, I wondered if you'd dropped off the face of the Earth."

Shane pictured his friend Brad, who had always reminded him of Ernest Hemingway, both as a writer and as a rugged outdoorsman living in the wilds of Idaho.

"How are you feeling?"

"Like a zombie," Brad said. "This lymphoma makes me so lethargic it takes an hour to decide whether to get out of a chair. But I've learned to appreciate the birds in the yard and the deer and other animals that come up to the house. I'm glad to be home, looking out across the valley with the mountains all around us. Nature is the best medicine. I think the treatments are helping. It's just a long road. So how are things at the lake?"

"We have a situation here," Shane said.

Brad laughed.

"I never doubted you would," he said. "Hang on just a sec. I'm going to put you on speaker so Irene can get in on this."

"I'd do the same but we don't have much technology here at the lodge," Shane said. "So I'll pass the phone around the room before we're done. I'm speaking to you on an old rotary desk phone that weighs about ten pounds."

"Hello Shane," came Irene's voice. "Good to hear from you. I haven't seen Brad smile like this in weeks."

"Enough about me," Brad interrupted. "Let's talk about you. What's going on there?"

Shane explained about the prowler he chased the first night, the break-ins around the lake, the missing money, the big splash with the clinking of chain, the lovers in the empty cabin, the homeless girl Marie tackled, and the sheriff nobody can find.

"I have to give you credit," Brad said. "You've got yourself in the middle of an unholy mess. Have you shared this with the local authorities?" Brad asked.

"Not exactly all of it. The chief deputy is a jerk and my relationship with him is strained. Our neighbor here at the lake calls him the Rambo type. Hanson made it pretty clear he doesn't need or want outside help, especially mine."

"Fine, then," Brad said. "You're on your own, which is how you work best anyway."

"It's a team effort, you know. You should have seen Marie take down that runner the other night. Actually, it was dark and nobody saw it but Marie, but the victim was very humbled and subdued when Marie marched her into the kitchen with her hands tied behind her back.

"I should clarify that it was a teenage girl who lives in the woods. Elizabeth patched up her cuts. Marie and I questioned her, but it was Marie who really built a relationship with her. We think the girl knew more than she told us, but we let her go. Marie even gave her a hug."

"Wow, I'll bet that came as a surprise," Brad said. "What are you going to do if there's a body on the bottom of the lake?"

"I don't know. I honestly don't know. We have two witnesses who heard the splash and some clinking of chain. We know roughly where to look. If we can find the lovers who spent the night in the cabin nearby, we may learn more."

"How clear is the lake?"

"Pretty clear. Maybe too clear. Billy likes to ride in the bow of the boat and watch for fish. The lake is maybe twenty to thirty feet deep. The angle of the light and cloud cover makes a big difference in how far down you can see. In places I think you could see all the way to the bottom, and if there's a body, I really don't want him finding it."

"No. You can't have that."

"If you have any thoughts about all this in the next few days, give us a call," Shane said. "Now I'm going to pass the phone around so the others can say hello."

"Hey, before you do that, is Billy close by?"

"In the other room. We can get him."

"Do that, because someone just walked into the room here who would like to say hello."

Elizabeth brought Billy to the phone and handed him the receiver. "It's Brad and Irene, in Idaho."

"No sir," came the voice on the other end of the line, so loud Shane could make out the words even without a speaker. "It's Bolivar, the chief cowboy around this place. How are you doing, Billy? Do you need reinforcements?"

"Yes!" Billy exclaimed.

The second Shane heard Bolivar's voice, memories came flooding back of the wonderful adventures Billy had with Bolivar on Brad and Irene's ranch two summers ago. The swaggering cowboy with the black beret instantly adopted Billy for the entire visit, taking him fishing and canoeing, panning for gold, and teaching him the harmonica.

"He's the son I never had," Bolivar always said, and it brought a smile to Shane's face.

Billy told Bolivar about the amphibious airplane, the electric boat and the old house with all its books.

"It sounds pretty tempting," Bolivar said, "but when you get done in New York, come out to Idaho and we'll have some real fun. I'll show you some of my best, new, secret, gold-panning spots on the Yankee Fork River. Nobody knows but me. People think the gold-mining days are over, but they don't know Bolivar. I found one nugget so big I had to hoist it into my truck." Billy's face lit up with joy.

At the rumspringa house, Sarah and Harry were puzzled. They had seen Tim and his old Corolla only once in two days, very briefly, when he was cleaning something in the entryway. That was good – in fact, couldn't be better – but Sarah was pretty sure he'd be back. She was still anxious to get away from this place. She wondered if Tim had left town. Most of his clothes were still in the house, but nothing of value.

The rental contract was in Tim's name. At month-end the landlord would expect the next month's rent. Tim always had plenty of money. By the time rent was due, she and Harry would be gone. Maybe Tim was already gone.

That was just as well because Tim had apparently removed the runner from the hallway. Whatever he spilled on it must have been something he couldn't clean. Imagine that – Tim cleaning *anything*. Now he just had to explain it to the landlord and pay for it.

Harry and Sarah had identified a couple of furnished houses on the edge of town that seemed suitable to rent. They'd either have to wait until the bank made their funds available or else convince the new landlord they had the money but he couldn't cash their check just yet. It sounded pathetic, she thought.

What would it take for Tim to disappear? A girl? An overdose? Jail? Whatever it was, she wanted to be gone before he came back.

Confession

The call to Brad and Irene raised everyone's spirits, and Billy was ecstatic about talking with Bolivar. Shane had his second wind now, confident he could break the case with a little more work. "I'm going into Crossington for a bit," he told the others. "I'll be back in a few hours."

Kat, the prowler, had said a young Amish boy named Harry was one of the lovers who spent the night in the cabin across the lake. He often used the computers at the public library.

When Shane walked into the building and saw who was sitting at the computer kiosks, he was dismayed. An older man, who smelled like manure, had stuffed his bedroll and pack under one of the desks and had his head down by the keyboard, apparently sleeping. Another patron was talking to himself about alien signals interfering with his sexual function. Shane wondered what it was like to be a librarian, going into this field because you love books, and ending up having to manage the homeless and mentally ill patrons who simply seek shelter in a warm place.

Two young schoolgirls sat as far as they could from both men at the opposite end of the technology area. Shane meandered behind them. They were looking at websites about Florida and Bermuda. An older woman with trifocals angled her head to read an email on a computer screen. Shane surveyed the other library patrons and saw no one remotely fitting the description of the boy Kat called Harry.

He selected a book from the shelves about inns of the Pacific Northwest and settled into an overstuffed chair to wait and watch. He was pleased at the nice write-up about the Eagles Inn B&B. But waiting for Harry could take a while.

Three hours later he declared defeat. There was no sign of Harry and none of Kat, either. He wondered if Kat had fed them a tall tale the other night. Maybe she was a better liar than he thought. On the other hand, she hadn't said she and Harry went to the library every day. Shane drove home discouraged but also mindful this was the nature of police work. Sometimes you get lucky. Sometimes, you don't.

The last thing he expected was what he found when he drove up the long driveway to the lodge in the old GMC and parked. An old bicycle was propped against the porch, and there, on the veranda, were Marie, Elizabeth and Robert, having tea with Kat. Martin was hanging from Marie's leg, apparently determined to hold on like a human ball and chain as long as he could. Marie tried to ignore him.

"Pull up a chair," Marie said. "Kat has been filling us in on some things you'll want to hear." Marie turned to her. "Go ahead and start at the beginning again, if you don't mind."

Kat's eyes darted back and forth among the others as if searching for approval, but avoided Shane. He sensed she wasn't comfortable with him.

"Take your time," Shane said. "I know this isn't easy."

Kat took a moment to compose herself. She sipped some more tea, put down the cup, stared at it, turned the handle a bit, and then looked up at Shane, right into his eyes.

"You asked about the missing money," she began, "and I lied. I regret that and know I'm in some serious trouble."

"We could see it in your eyes, and the way you tensed up," Shane remarked.

"But you let me walk out of here."

"We felt you were basically honest. We were hoping you might think about things and eventually tell us more."

"That blows me away. No one has ever given me a break like that. You don't even know me."

"But we are getting to know you. Your friend, Marie, here, is a pretty good judge of character."

Marie nodded.

"I took the money," Kat said.

"Five thousand dollars is a lot of money," Shane said. "That's grand theft – a felony. It's guaranteed jail time."

"I know. It wasn't for me but some friends who promised to pay it back – and I believe they will. That's why I didn't admit it. I've never done anything like that before. I was planning to put it back before you knew it was gone.

"Who are these friends and why do they need that kind of money?" Shane asked, rocking back in his chair and looking at the ceiling. He turned and studied the faces of the others around the table.

"It's a couple who are in danger from their roommate."

"What kind of danger?"

"The girl is afraid she'll be raped. The boy could be shot."

"Why do they need the money?"

"To move out of the house they're sharing with the other boy and rent a place of their own."

Shane thought for a moment. "If we tell the sheriff, there's no question you're going to jail. I'm not sure we need to do that. Honestly, we are winging it, here. If we can find another way to resolve this without making things worse for you and for ourselves, I'm all for it."

Kat explained more about the couple – a boy named Harry and his girlfriend – Amish teenagers on rumspringa. "I don't know their last names – can you believe that? I stole five thousand dollars and gave it to someone whose last names I don't even know. They're the lovers who entered the cabin across the lake."

"So they're the ones who heard the splash when the body went into the lake," Robert concluded.

Elizabeth leaned forward and pushed her teacup to the side. "Let's talk about this. I'm thinking out loud now. That five thousand dollars has sat in that cookie tin for years. Nobody but me knew it was there till I showed Shane recently. My dad put it there, showed it to me, and then died, and never used it for anything. So if that money could do some good, and get paid back, I think Dad would be happy."

"Are you sure?" Shane asked her. "This is grand theft and we have no guarantee Harry and Sarah will ever return it. Nobody loans money this way – it's not done."

"On the other hand," Robert said, "it could work. It's far-fetched but not impossible – not like any law enforcement work I've ever done, but it's creative. I think we'll need to meet this couple, get a feel for who they are. This whole idea is built on a lot of trust."

"Oh god, do you think so?" Kat asked. "I just wanted to come clean and do the right thing, but I was afraid my next ride would be in a sheriff's car. This will work; I'll make sure it does. Harry and his girlfriend are honest people. You can trust them."

"Who's going to talk to them?" Robert asked.

"Let me do it," Marie replied. "Better yet, Kat and I can do it together."

"I'll try to find Harry," Kat said. "Give me a little time."

Bottom fishing

"My life is a mess," Kat confessed to Marie two days later. "There's nothing for me here. That's part of the reason it took me a while to find Harry. My mom's being evicted from her trailer and she's in a rage, threatening to get even with the sheriff."

"It's just bluster, though, isn't it?" Marie asked.

"I'm not sure. When she gets drunk she could do anything. She's got a gun and won't listen to anyone. I tried to talk to her but she scared me. I don't know what she thinks she will do, or where she will go.

"Anyway," Kat continued, "Harry was a little hard to find because he and Sarah are getting ready to move tomorrow to their new rental place across town. We can see them at their old place this afternoon at two o'clock if you like. I thought that would be more private for us to visit than at the library."

Marie and Kat piled into the old Suburban and headed for town. Marie found the address and it was typical of the places kids rent as group households anywhere, old and in need of paint and repair, with an un-mowed lawn and overgrown shrubbery. But inside, the house was surprisingly clean and presentable. Harry and Sarah obviously had been doing their best to get the house ready to turn over to the landlord. The condition of the interior gave Marie an unexpectedly good impression of them.

Kat introduced Marie and explained that they had met under complicated circumstances. "I was trying to return the canoe I borrowed to their boathouse the other night and Marie ambushed me." Harry's eyes shifted back and forth between the two women.

"It was actually a good thing because I ended up having quite a talk in the kitchen with everyone, and they were not what I expected. They listened and were kind, and did not call the sheriff on me. Even though Marie dumped me face down in the dirt when I ran, we're working things out."

Marie noticed Harry kept his eyes on the floor.

Sarah laughed. "I'm sorry," she said, putting her hand over her mouth. "I'm trying to picture that. But why are you telling us this?"

"Because they know I gave you the money, the five thousand dollars," she said, turning to face Marie.

"Which is a felony," Marie said. "Kat could go to jail. But none of us want that. We talked and what we want to do is to come up with a solid plan for you to repay it over time, so it's an honest-to-goodness loan with a proper repayment plan."

Harry and Sarah both nodded. "We never wanted to get Kat in trouble," Harry said. "She was trying to help us. We can repay some of it right now because it didn't cost us five thousand dollars to get into this house. He reached for his little checkbook and wrote Marie a check for two thousand dollars.

"This is the first I heard of where the money came from," Sarah said. "Harry wouldn't talk about it."

"It was for your own good," Harry said, looking at Sarah.

"We can work it out," Marie remarked. "I also understand you spent some time in the cabin on the far side of Pursuit Lake a few nights ago."

Sarah's face turned red and she looked down at the floor.

"That's true," Harry replied.

"What we want to know is whether you heard a loud splash nearby while you were there."

"Yeah. I was surprised and looked out the window to see what it was," Harry said. "The cabin was dark so nobody knew we were there. I saw a guy in a rowboat, just a black figure. After the splash, he started rowing back across the lake."

"That's helpful," Marie said. "Was there anything about the splash that seemed odd?"

"I heard the clink of metal, like chain. That didn't seem normal at all."

"Roughly where did you see the rowboat?"

"Toward the outlet stream. Like the length of a football field from the cabin."

"This really helps. We have several other witnesses but you were the closest."

"Do you think there's a body in the lake?" Harry asked.

"We don't know. We'd like to find out," Marie said. "But let's talk about you for a few minutes."

Marie said she understood Harry and Sarah were giving English life a try on rumspringa and had found themselves in a bad situation with their older housemate.

"Tim," Sarah said. "Tim Wade. He was a friend once when we all lived together in the Amish community, but he's changed. He and his dad didn't get along. He has a wicked temper and is experimenting more and more with drugs. The sheriff has been to the house a couple of times talking to him. I'm really scared he plans to rape me, the way he looks at me and belittles Harry. He'd do it on a whim. That's why I'm so desperate to get out of here."

"You think he's dangerous?"

"Absolutely," Sarah said. "I'm sure of it. He and Tim got into a shoving match over me the other day. He's got a gun and he showed it to me. I thought he was going to pull it on Harry when they jostled, but he changed his mind. I saw him reconsider."

"Where is he now?"

"We don't know. He disappeared and hasn't been back, thank god. He doesn't lift a finger around here, though he did remove the runner from the hall before he left. That was weird. We're still scratching our heads over that."

The comment intrigued Marie. "Mind if I have a look?"

Marie got up and walked to the hall, with Harry, Sarah and Kat following her.

"Was the rug stained pretty badly?" she asked.

"Not really," Sarah said. "I don't think it was that old. It was actually in pretty good shape."

"Does it smell like bleach to you here?" Marie asked.

"I guess so, now that you mention it," Harry said. "But Sarah was using bleach in the washing machine."

"No, what I'm smelling is closer than that. There's a stain on the floor here," Marie said. "Something soaked all the way through to the flooring." She continued to inspect the hall, her eyes systematically scanning up and down the walls of the narrow corridor, finally landing on one spot about four feet from the floor. She leaned closer and studied what she'd found.

"Were these two holes always here?"

"I never noticed," Sarah said. "Did you?" she asked Harry.

"Not really. To be honest I never paid much attention."

"Well, the splintering appears fresh and I think the sheriff's department may want a closer look," Marie said.

"Bullets," Sarah said. "That's what you're thinking."

"Yes," Marie replied. "Don't do any more cleaning. We've got to alert the sheriff."

"Oh god," Sarah said. "Tim is going to kill us."

"Come and get me with the Suburban," Shane said when Marie telephoned him with what she'd learned and found. "I'd like to talk with Deputy Hanson face-to-face. This is too important to keep to ourselves any longer. But tell Kat she's free to go. We don't need to drag her into this any deeper."

Two hours later, Shane and Marie sat across the desk from the deputy. Hanson held his ballpoint pen in his right hand and clicked it absently against his metal desk drawer. It was driving Shane mad but he forced himself not to bring it up.

Shane outlined what he had. "We've been working on tracking down what happened to our five thousand dollars," he said, "and have uncovered some other things that may shed light on the disappearance of the sheriff."

"Ok," Hanson said, glancing at his watch. "I'm listening."

"Witnesses saw a solitary figure in a rowboat cross Pursuit Lake from the boat launch the other night. One witness saw the man load something bulky into the boat. There was a loud splash and the clinking of what sounded like chain. I have a pretty good idea of the general area where the splash was centered."

"That's a pretty thin lead," Hanson said, putting his pen back into his pocket and leaning forward. "Did you get a description?"

"Not really. Thin and tall. Dressed in black. Driving what looked like an older, white Corolla."

Shane continued, "Earlier today Marie interviewed a young Amish couple here in town whose housemate disappeared two days ago. You may know the housemate's name, Tim Wade."

"I do. The sheriff and I were keeping an eye on him."

Marie picked up the story. "The young couple are afraid of Tim and are moving out of the house today. He drove a Corolla. They mentioned Tim had a gun, and had removed a rug from the hallway, which seemed quite unusual, so I looked around. There's a stain on the floor. The hallway smells of bleach, and I found two fresh holes in the wall that I think were made by bullets. Given that the sheriff is missing, and given his history with Tim Wade, this got our attention."

Hanson leaned forward in his chair, then stood and reached for his hat. "What's the address? I'll need a complete written statement from you both as soon as you can provide it." He turned to his dispatcher. "Get someone with a forensic kit over to this address. I'm headed there now."

"Can we tag along?" Shane asked. "We know the kids pretty well, Harry Roush and Sarah LeComte. Nice kids. They're pretty shaken up."

"Ok, but stay out of the way."

Within an hour, it was clear that someone had been shot in the rental house. Hanson dug two bullets from the wall with his jackknife and dropped them into a plastic baggie. His forensic specialist used a prepackaged mixture of aqueous Florescein in a spray bottle to check the floor and walls. It revealed blood spatter all over the wall where Hanson recovered the bullets, consistent with two shots exiting the body on that side. He searched methodically for additional bullets in the hallway but found none. Then he did a walk-through of the house for additional evidence, but found nothing.

The entire hallway had obviously been washed with bleach, but Florescein reveals latent blood presence nevertheless. A large pool of blood was evident on the hardwood floor, where the body presumably fell and rested until it was removed, along with the carpet. Hanson made arrangements to saw out a section of the floor for DNA testing. Shane looked out the window and noticed another officer taping off the front door as a crime scene.

"My guess is that the shooter dragged the body out the back door on a tarp," Marie said, "and backed his car to the end of the driveway to load it where he wouldn't have an audience."

"That's what I'd do," Hanson said, turning to Harry and Sarah. "It's a good thing you're moving to your new house today," he told them, "because no one can enter these premises now till further notice without our permission."

"I guess we know now why Tim hasn't been back," Sarah said.

Shane looked directly at Hanson. "What's next?" he asked. "The lake?"

"I think so," Hanson said.

It was Billy who noticed the zodiac from the porch. He was watching the lake with binoculars when he saw the orange craft with a big outboard motor, and the word POLICE printed boldly across the pontoons on both sides. It was heading for the far side of the lake from the vicinity of the boat launch.

"There are two men in police jackets on board," he yelled, staring through the binoculars. "This is big!"

Elizabeth joined him and watched the craft speed away.

"Hard to say," Elizabeth remarked. "Maybe they're just training."

Billy wouldn't take his binoculars off them. Shane watched, too, and after awhile, when the zodiac reached the vicinity of the outlet stream, it slowed and drifted to a stop in its own frothy wake.

"They're throwing a big contraption with hooks into the water," Billy said. "I know what that means."

"What?" Elizabeth said.

"They're looking for a body."

"Oh my god, no," Elizabeth remarked. "What makes you think that?"

"I wasn't born yesterday."

Shane stifled a laugh. "He has a point, honey."

"This is gruesome," Elizabeth said. "Shouldn't we turn our attention to something more wholesome?"

"I'm not missing a second of this," Billy declared.

"Then maybe we should all pull up some chairs and watch together," Shane suggested. "Make it family viewing."

Elizabeth glared. "You are sick."

"There's no TV here," Shane shrugged. He knew there'd be hell to pay for this later.

Shane watched the men pay out the line till it went slack. Then they raised it several feet till the line went tight again. He assumed they were adjusting their hooks to be just above the lake bottom, where they would snag anything half-suspended that might be floating in that area.

Pretty soon the zodiac started to creep forward, much more slowly than before. This looked like the tedious part of the job, running a grid pattern as best they could, back and forth, from their starting point outward. No doubt they had global positioning on board to help them keep a tight pattern so they didn't miss any areas. This could take them a while, but Billy showed no sign of giving up.

"What's so interesting?" Robert asked as he and Marie came out to join the others on the porch.

"They're looking for a body," Billy blurted, pointing across the lake. "Wait till I get back and tell my friends."

"Seriously?" Robert asked. "And you're all watching this together as a family?"

Elizabeth gave Shane another icy stare.

"Billy's going to watch it whether we do it together or not," Shane said. "So I thought I'd watch with him."

"Well, then, we'll join you," Robert said. "I'm kind of curious, myself."

Elizabeth and Marie went for refreshments. Shane suspected they were huddled in the kitchen, plotting revenge or some strategy to break up this sick male obsession on the porch. But they returned with cool drinks and chips. Shane estimated an hour had passed since the search began. The zodiac kept working its pattern, stopping occasionally to raise the hooks and clear aquatic plant material, waterlogged branches or mud from the array.

Shane was reaching for chips when he realized the zodiac had stopped entirely and was backing up. Both men were pulling hard on the line, which hung straight down from the side of the craft. They were laboring, making slow progress. One of the men was on a walkie-talkie. In the clear water of the lake, he imagined they could already see what they were pulling toward the surface.

Moments later, something pink broke the surface alongside the boat. "Okay, that's enough Billy. They've found their man. Let's give that man some privacy now as they pull him from the water. No one deserves what happened to him."

Shane knew Billy hadn't seen much, but it was enough. The party mood was broken. Billy's face had turned somber, as if he were close to tears.

Shane put his arm around Billy. "I'm sorry you saw that. What we do as police can be very rewarding at times," he said, as they turned toward the house. "We help people, and that's what I like best about it. But the job is also very sad and upsetting at times. We see things nobody really wants to see. Pulling a body from a lake is one of them. Those officers in the zodiac aren't having a very nice day, but sometimes it's part of the job. People want to know what happened. Now that they've found that guy, his friends and family will have the answers they need to find peace."

"Did you know him?" Billy asked.

"I'm not sure. If it's who I think it is, yes, I did know and like him. He was a very nice man. It's not right what happened."

"Did you catch the guy who did it?"

"Not yet but we will. We're pretty sure we know who it is. Marie is working on this, too, and she gets a big part of the credit. They wouldn't have checked the lake if we hadn't urged them to do it."

"Cool," he said, smiling again. "Good for Marie."

Shane was especially curious how this development would be reported in the news, so he made a point of tuning the lodge's old, floor-model, A.M. radio to the local station that evening at news time. The radio was an antique, full of glass tubes, but the sound was surprisingly clear after a full minute of warm-up. The opening bulletin didn't disappoint him.

County sheriff's deputies today recovered the body of missing Sheriff Andrew Dixon from the waters of Pursuit Lake. Chief Deputy Leland Hanson III said his officers recovered the body from a depth of about 30 feet. It was weighted to the bottom with chain.

"We've been systematically working this case around the clock ever since the sheriff disappeared, and this break was the result of old-fashioned police work. We've also identified where we believe the sheriff was murdered and are looking for a suspect. We hope to have him in custody soon."

Shane wasn't surprised Hanson said nothing about the visiting law officers who handed him the critical tips on a silver platter. Hanson was feathering his own nest, positioning himself to run for sheriff in the next election as the officer who got results.

This high-profile case was a gift from the gods if he could just stay in control of it. If it was the sheriff they had pulled from the water, then so much the better, because Hanson's worst enemy was gone.

Billy had listened to the radio bulletin with Shane and wanted to know what would happen next to the body he'd watched pulled from the lake.

"Well, Shane said, those men on the boat zipped the body into a heavy plastic bag to transport it back to Crossington."

"Then what?"

"I'm pretty sure they took it to the county coroner's office. The chief medical examiner needs to look at it carefully and be sure of exactly what killed him."

"Won't it be obvious?"

"No, sometimes it isn't. Sometimes what seems obvious isn't actually how someone died in a crime. It's very important to know exactly what happened."

"Oh," Billy said, apparently satisfied for now.

Meanwhile, the question on Shane's mind was where to look for Tim Wade. They had strong probable cause to believe he murdered the sheriff. Shane assumed the sheriff, walking home a few evenings ago, must have seen Wade near the house or perhaps stopped to see if he was home, and ended up in an altercation in the hallway in which Wade got to his weapon faster than the sheriff did. They would never know the full story unless they caught Wade and he told them how it unfolded.

Wade was on the run now, especially after the news that the murder scene had been found and the sheriff's body had been recovered. Shane tried to imagine where an eighteen-year-old would take cover. Tim's money wouldn't last long. He could ask his drug pals for help, but it was debatable whether they'd want to take the risk of bringing the police down on themselves by helping him. It was clear that he also knew his way around Pursuit Lake.

Shane shuddered at that thought, but there was a certain logic to it. After finding the body in the lake, the authorities would expect Wade to be as far as possible from this place, not hiding right under their noses. He might be hoping to let the search cool before showing his face publicly again.

Scenarios

If Kat was right, the car Tim was driving the night he dumped the sheriff's body into the lake – if it was Tim at all – was an old Corolla. It seemed to fit the description Harry and Sarah gave of the car he drove around town and parked at the rental house. If he happened to be hiding in one of the unoccupied cabins around the lake, there were plenty of good places to conceal it, Shane knew. Nearly all the cabins had narrow, weed-filled driveways where no one ever drove except the property owners on rare visits to the lake. It was food for thought, but at this point he wasn't planning to go door to door.

Instead, this seemed like a good time to let Chief Deputy Hanson carry the effort for a while with his old-fashioned police work, and for Shane to devote his own attention to vacationing with his family and friends. He didn't like or trust Hanson, and wanted to wash his hands of the whole affair.

Meanwhile, Kat had dropped out of sight after setting up the meeting for Marie with Harry and Sarah that broke open the case. She was probably preoccupied with her mother's eviction. Notwithstanding Kat's obvious rejection of the choices her mom had made, Shane wondered how strong the bond was between them. Love-hate relationships can be surprisingly hard to break.

Shane and Elizabeth still needed to set up a formal repayment plan for the rest of the five thousand dollars with Harry and Sarah, but they had the couple's new address and email, and still had some time to sit down with them before heading back to Whidbey Island.

"I've been thinking about Kat," Elizabeth said. "She's too bright for the predicament she's trapped in. I have some ideas on how we can help her break out of this go-nowhere life. I haven't worked out the details yet, but hang on because I'll have more to say about that soon."

"I'm all for it," Shane said. "She's a bright kid with a good heart and I think she could make something positive of her life if she could just catch a break."

When the phone rang at the lodge the next afternoon, Elizabeth took the call.

"Did you hear?" Aunt Bonnie began. "They found Tim Wade's Corolla."

"Really? Where?"

"In the woods outside Foreston. Every inch of it was wiped clean and there was nothing in the trunk. Not a shred of blood evidence or fingerprints. They're looking for fibers."

"How do you find out these things?" Elizabeth asked. "There's been nothing on the news."

"I have a source close to the sheriff," Bonnie replied. "That's all I'm going to say. I thought Shane might like to know."

"I'm sure he will."

"Hanson impounded the car and is still processing it and keeping a lid on the news for now."

Shane had been lingering near the phone as Elizabeth talked. As soon as she hung up, she turned to him with the news.

Shane couldn't stop playing with scenarios in his mind. He wasn't surprised Hanson was keeping the car under tight wraps. What if Hanson had followed Sheriff Dixon to the rumspringa house and quarreled with him? After shooting him in the hallway, Hanson could have loaded the sheriff's body into Tim's car, sank the body in the lake and then dumped the car in the woods, wiping it clean as he did so. This would effectively frame Tim Wade for the murder and establish that he was on the run, setting up a believable scenario for Hanson to kill him in an attempt at capture.

Unfortunately, it didn't fit. The suspect that Kat had described seeing was tall and lean. Hanson was a shrimp, for lack of a more delicate word.

Nevertheless, Wade, realizing he was the chief suspect, would have no choice but to flee and hide out. Hanson, for his part, no doubt was hoping to find Wade before anyone else and silence him so there wouldn't be any trial. This would explain why Hanson hadn't released the name of his suspect to the public. At this point it was impossible to know the truth but one thing was certain – Shane did not trust Hanson. And he wanted to find Wade before Hanson did.

Then again, Shane wondered about Harry and Sarah. They seemed like nice kids but were frightened and cornered in the house with Tim. Was it possible Tim had attacked Sarah, and Harry had risen to her defense? Tim seemed to take special delight in mocking Harry, and had made no secret of his sexual interest in his girlfriend. If Harry had gotten Tim's gun, he could have shot Tim.

It stuck in Shane's mind that the two young people had cleaned the rental house exceptionally well. This seemed completely out of character for young kids. He'd noticed the strong odor of bleach when he visited. They knew their way around Pursuit Lake, and certainly had access to Tim's car. Harry was tall and lean, like the individual Kat observed dumping something into the lake. Pretending to be witnesses to the loud splash and clinking of chain gave their story an air of credibility that might just be a clever deception.

A good cop keeps something else in mind, too. It might be none of the above.

Trigger Happy

The sun was well over the horizon and growing hot when Tim Wade awoke. He rubbed his eyes and face, stood up, stretched his arms over his head and arched his back. The day already felt muggy, but at least it had been a warm night for sleeping out. Tim had lain in the grass on a hillside overlooking Pursuit Lake, an area he knew well from his many cabin-prowls.

Now he was hungry and his joints ached. He'd picked up a few bug bites. He had finally slept after two days on the run. The woods were the only place he felt reasonably safe from Deputy Hanson. By now Hanson had shaken down every drug dealer and user Tim ever knew in Crossington and Foreston for leads on his possible whereabouts, and checked every bus, cab and Uber in the region for people matching his description.

He'd like to go back to the rumspringa house for food and more clothes, but it was out of the question. He would break into a cabin instead.

He had jettisoned his cell phone as soon as he realized deputies had been to the house and established a crime scene. The police would be trying to triangulate his location from the phone. A radio would be helpful for some news. All he had now were the clothes on his back and the comforting bulk of the semi-auto pistol in his pocket.

Choosing a cabin was the next thing. He did not want to be anywhere near the boat launch or the youth camp, and the activity they generated. Most houses and cabins on the west side of the lake would be occupied. But his old standby on the east side, an isolated cabin right on the water, had been vacant for years. It had some sentimental appeal, too, as the love nest he'd recommended to Harry and Sarah.

He could get there on foot or by boat. It was a long hike on foot, but getting there overland would be less likely to attract attention. So he would ignore his growling stomach and walk. Besides, he liked something else about the cabin. He had a far-fetched idea how to get completely away from this place, and the cabin was situated right where he needed to be for that.

"I'm going next door to see Bonnie," Shane announced that morning after finishing a breakfast of eggs scrambled with broccoli, and hash browns.

"Again?" Elizabeth asked.

"She's the best source I've got about this place."

"I thought you were going to focus on vacation for a while," Elizabeth pointed out.

"I thought so, too," Shane said, "but you know how I am once I get ahold of something. I need some information to help us plan our next move."

"Us?"

"Yeah – all of us – you and Robert and Marie. Aren't we in this together?"

"True," Elizabeth replied with just a note of hesitation in her voice.

"Things are getting interesting," Shane said. He tucked a map into his shirt pocket that a real estate company had distributed of the lake.

Moments later, he was out the door and on his way to Bonnie's in the electric boat.

On Bonnie's kitchen table, Shane unfolded his map. It showed fourteen cabins and houses, the youth camp, the outlet stream and the beaver lodges in the inlet area. "Let's talk about this," he said, "because I'd like to know the best place to hide if I were a kid on foot, on the run. No doubt Tim Wade knows all this already."

Bonnie studied the map for a moment.

"If I wanted to totally avoid people I think I'd pick one of these three on the east side," she said. "The west-side cabins are mostly occupied in the summertime, but the east-side cabins sit empty. They're harder to get to and the owners simply aren't around for various reasons. If you were careful, you could shelter in these for weeks and not be noticed. Of course they all have good access from the water."

111

Shane asked Bonnie what she knew about the families that owned each of the cabins around the lake, and she filled him in. He was amazed at her recall – her memory for detail about names and family history.

"What about the road to these?" Shane asked, pointing to a dashed line on the map that led to the east-side places.

"Unpaved and unimproved," Bonnie laughed, "with deep ruts that'll break an axle if you rush it. More of a driveway than a road. It's just a weed-grown, dirt track wide enough for one car. Snow sits on it ten feet deep all winter and nobody plows it as they do the west-side road. So it takes forever to melt in the spring, and then it's a muddy mess. Nobody even tries to drive there till it hardens up in the summer."

"Well this guy will be on foot, unless he stole a car," Shane said. "And he'll be traveling light except for a semi-auto pistol. He may be the guy who murdered the sheriff."

Bonnie gasped and raised a hand to her mouth.

"But we don't really know that for sure. He has a history of assault and drug dealing, but at this point he may just be a scared kid on the run from Deputy Hanson. He's probably hungry and tired. If he were to break into those cabins, would he find any food?"

"Not much. Next to nothing, I'd say. But why would he come here? Why not Foreston or Crossington?"

"I don't know that he will," Shane said. "It's just a hunch on my part. He knows the lake. The hunt for him in town is way too hot. Hanson probably has the bus system and other public transportation sealed off. The kid's friends are being harassed and they're scared, as well. He needs to get away and avoid contact with anyone who could betray him to the police."

"Well," Bonnie said, "the nicest place over there is the love nest where those kids had their tryst the other night. The other two places are practically shacks, probably full of rodents and bats, and in bad repair from neglect. If he's really hungry, he's going to have to take some risks and go foraging for food because I doubt any of those places have even a can of beans in the cupboard."

"That's what I think, too," Shane said. "We're going to watch the lake like hawks, especially at night, and we'll need your eyes and ears as well."

Shane was mindful that a good detective always operates with a theory – a scenario – based on what he knows. With this, he takes his best guess of what's coming next. His theory might be completely wrong, but without a working hypothesis he'd be powerless. If his assumptions were right, he'd be one step ahead of the suspect. The job came down to imagining himself in the other guy's shoes. What would I do if I were him?

He really had no idea if Tim had fled to the lake. He was an entirely different personality and might not be thinking rationally. Or he might add up the situation differently. He was a drug-user, which adds a layer of unpredictability to everything he did. Shane couldn't modify his theory to include that – irrationality was beyond him. But taking everything into account, the lake made sense to him.

Shane thought about his dad, who had also been a cop. He'd lived into his nineties and died of old age in hospice care. In his last days, Shane's dad had retreated into memories of his career, merging real and imaginary. To be honest, it was mostly the latter. His mind couldn't differentiate between cases he'd worked on and episodes of police dramas he'd watched on TV. When Shane visited him, his dad talked of Matlock as a personal friend. Shane played along. In hindsight it wasn't a bad way to go, comforted by his friends in this imaginary world.

Perhaps if Shane were lucky, he'd do the same when his time came – leave this world and ease into the next one while reliving the job that he loved so much.

Shane didn't want to frighten Bonnie, but needed to be honest about his thinking, so she could prepare for the worst that could happen if it came to pass.

"I could be way off base," Shane said. "But if he's over there, and he's hungry, he will have to come this way to find food, probably by boat and probably after dark. Leave your porch light on so it's obvious that you're home. And keep in close touch with us. If you hear or see anything, let me know right away."

"I will."

Bonnie thought for a moment and then added, "I think I'll load a couple of shells into my husband's twelve-gauge," nodding toward the bedroom. "If you hear a couple of loud booms in the next few hours, don't give it a thought. It'll just me letting the neighbors know there's a trigger-happy old lady around here with a shotgun."

Flashbacks

Tim studied the pictures on the refrigerator – a teenage girl jumping her wake on a water-ski, a boy fishing from a rowboat, a little dog cuddling with them on the sofa. The photographs depicted a wholesome, idyllic childhood – English family life as he had once imagined it. There was a picture of the father, he supposed, painting the cabin; another of the mother with a platter of roasted turkey – normal people leading normal lives.

The photograph of the mother with the turkey made him remember his own mother, whom he knew only briefly when she was alive. She seemed a saint looking back – beautiful and gentle, hard working, devoted to her husband and son.

He poked around the cabin. A metal rack held some kindling for the wood stove, cut and split maybe twenty years ago. A utility closet held an old broom, a croquet set and a kite.

He could see this cabin had been a happy place before it became a forgotten place. A magnetic calendar showed the entire year 1994. He supposed that's about when the pictures stopped, because the colors were washed out with age. In a frame in the kitchen, a simple quote gave him pause: "A life lived for others is a life worthwhile."

He imagined the woman of the house had put it there and that she lived by those words. He could imagine his mother living by those words, though he, himself, couldn't relate to living for others. His whole life had been about just living at all – avoiding the beatings, surviving, and running. He wondered how different his life would have been if his mother had lived.

In any case, for the family that spent summers in this cabin, something had made time stop. What had happened to these people that simply froze their lives?

Imagining others' lives was something he did often when he broke into houses and cabins. It didn't change anything; he just wanted to understand what propels a life one way or the other.

He had made a mess of his – done bad things. He could blame the drugs but they were really just an excuse, something to numb the pain. The seeds of what he'd done went back much further to his father and his temper. Things hadn't worked out – not in the Amish community and certainly not among the English. Now he was a hunted person and he was pretty sure how this would end . . . unless his getaway plan worked.

He'd had women but never a girlfriend. He had slept last night in the bed where Harry and Sarah made love. It was a luxury after the previous night on the ground. He kept his pistol under the pillow in case there were any surprises, but the night passed without incident. He felt limited by the lack of a cell phone or radio, wondering what was happening in the search for him.

He would die soon. Maybe today; maybe next week. Police could be outside right now, closing in. He wondered if his father would feel anything – be sad he hadn't done more to love his son. Maybe in the end it didn't make any difference.

He looked out the window from behind a curtain and didn't see anything. Going from cupboard to cupboard in the kitchen, he found one old can of stew but no opener, and some stale coffee, which he heated and drank gratefully. The sell-by date on the stew was ten years ago, but that was the least of his concerns. For a can opener he used his jackknife. Balancing the point of the blade just inside the rim, he pounded the knife with a hammer. With effort he loosened enough of the lid to pry it back and extract the stew. It would hold him till he found more food and planned his next move. It would probably have to be by boat, at night.

Robert and Shane puttered in the boathouse, checking the trickle charger on the electric boat and bailing water from the bilge. The sleet that had fallen on the boat had long since melted and accumulated several inches deep under the floorboards as water.

"The next time we use this boat, I want it fully charged," Shane said. "Not half dead like it was during that electrical storm."

"Oh, admit it, Shane; you secretly enjoyed that little drama. You're a risk-taker."

"I was scared out of my wits."

"You can't let go of a bone once you get your teeth into it. I've seen that time after time."

"I admit I love the chase."

"I never really asked how you ended up a cop," Robert said. "But there's plenty of opportunity to be scared in this work."

Shane laughed. "Maybe I like it *because* I'm a risk-taker. I did some things in college that were well outside the comfort zone of my family. They were not how I was brought up. I didn't say much about it, but I saw a side of life my parents and brother probably never experienced and wouldn't approve of. They're much more traditional and religious."

"So what did you do?"

"Drinking and women," Shane said, "a lot of both. And the more I studied, the less I liked any part of religion. My brother never indulged in any vices. I had relationships with a lot of different women. In hindsight I wonder what it gained me compared to, say, my brother who married the only woman he ever dated and has been happily married his entire life."

"Well, you found Elizabeth and I'd say that's a pretty good outcome."

"Point taken. In the end I found a woman who was very wholesome and traditional, whose intellect and interests challenged me. So I went back to my comfort zone in my personal life. But maybe the wild years taught me some things about human nature that I've been able to bring to my job."

"In any case," Robert said, "it sounds like you were the rebel in your family."

"Very much so. In fact mom often called me that – the rebel. Of all her children, that was my nickname."

The two men went about their chores in silence for a few moments, and then Shane asked.

"What about you?

Robert looked up and thought for a moment.

"I was the sober one; that was how I rebelled. The village lifestyle was mostly subsistence. Kids went to school for a few years and started to dream, and then got pulled back into a life of hunting and drinking, and snowmobiling. There was so little daylight in the winter. Boredom and depression were almost unavoidable for adults, along with domestic violence."

"It had to be hard," Shane agreed.

"There was so much alcoholism, I don't know how I avoided it. Maybe my parents would have been more comfortable if I'd become a drunk like everyone else in the village, but I saw the pain it caused and swore I wouldn't give in to it. So I got out the minute I could. The smart ones did that; I wasn't the first or last."

"I can't imagine the strength it took to break the cycle, get an education and move on to become an Alaska State Trooper," Shane said. "No doubt as a native you had to prove yourself over and over to your fellow troopers," Shane said.

"Some were a little slow to embrace diversity, you could say," Robert laughed. "I had to be a little tougher than my persecutors. But little by little, they came around."

"So I was going one direction at that point in my life; you were going the other. Somehow we both came out of it ok. Deep inside us both, we had a life force that overpowered everything else."

Robert put down the coffee can he was using to bail water from the bilge and looked up. "I haven't heard it put that way before; maybe that's a good way to explain it."

A moment later he continued, "So," he asked, "do you think he's over there?" He nodded across the lake.

Shane shrugged. "It's impossible to know. It's just my theory. I think he *could* be. If I were Tim, the lake is where I would head to drop out of sight. But honestly, he could be anywhere. If he's there, and armed with that semi-auto, I really don't want to take any chances with our safety – with any of us. It just isn't worth it. His reputation is all about violence, and this isn't our fight. It's Leland Hanson's fight, not that I trust him one bit."

"So for now we keep an eye on things from a distance," Robert remarked.

"Yup. We mind our own business."

"Listen to you," Robert laughed. "You know," he said, raising his eyebrows, "there is one other thing we could do."

"What's that?"

"Walk the road. Maybe pick up his trail. If Bonnie is right that those cabins are not used any more, and the road is overgrown with weeds and grass, and if he got there by walking, he will have left a trail. I'm a pretty good tracker."

"I know. And I think that's a darn good idea."

"It would tell us if someone has gone that way. Tracking is Marie's specialty, too," Robert said. "We need to take her. It's pretty important to her self-esteem."

"Absolutely," Shane agreed.

Capsized

Robert, Marie and Shane left on their walk a little after noon. Elizabeth stayed behind with Martin and Billy. She told Shane it was about three miles by road to the east-side cabins. Shane guessed if someone had recently traveled the road ahead of them, they'd know it long before they covered the whole distance.

The walk felt strangely like a race, Shane thought. Marie moved to the front and took long strides and deep breaths, swinging her arms in big arcs. She smiled broadly. Robert hustled to keep up, twenty feet behind, all the while staring earnestly at the ground. Shane followed ten feet behind Robert, watching them both and trying to adopt a "normal" gait.

"We should go walking like this more often, for the fellowship," Shane suggested in a feeble attempt at humor that apparently went over Marie's head. Robert scowled. The west-side road soon gave way to the east-side road, if one could call it that, just a one-lane dirt track. Some of the weeds were three feet tall.

"Right there," Marie said, stopping abruptly and pointing ahead while she waited for the others. "See those broken weeds?"

Robert and Shane reached her position and looked at the flattened ground cover. "How do you know it wasn't a deer?" Shane asked.

"The stride is short, like a man walking. Look around. There are no hoof prints anywhere on this road," Marie replied. "Deer put a lot of weight on their small hooves. If a deer had done it, we'd know. There are more broken weeds and clumps of grass beyond this. Those marks were made by a person with shoes that matted down the ground cover with every step he took."

"How long ago?" Shane asked.

"Recently. A day or two," Marie said. "The grass hasn't straightened up yet." Robert nodded his agreement.

Shane felt for the Glock in his pocket. "So now we have our answer. The next question is, do we follow the trail further or call it good?"

"We don't know which cabin he's in, though we can guess," Marie said. "If we keep going a little more, we can see which driveway he took. But it's really up to you."

"Then in the spirit of caution, let's call it good," Shane said. "We know what we came to find out. The closer we approach his hideout, the greater the risk. Finding him is one of my goals, but keeping us alive and healthy is even more important. He's scared and has already killed one person, as far as we know. With nothing to lose, the next will be easier."

With mixed feelings, Shane turned and led his group back.

"We had him," Marie grumbled, staring at the ground.

They were halfway back to the lodge, screened by trees from the lake, when Shane heard the amphibian approach. The widgeon made a circuit around the lake while Frank Hale no doubt looked for swimmers, boats, logs or other floating objects that might be in the way of landing. Then he descended and dropped behind the tree line. Shane pictured in his mind the plane touching down in a rooster tail of spray. Seconds later, from the sounds, he knew Hale was taxiing toward the youth camp, perhaps to drop off a passenger. One by one, Hale shut down the engines. Several minutes later, Shane heard two loud bangs in rapid succession.

"Did something backfire?" Marie asked.

"Gunshots!" Robert shouted.

"What in the hell?" Shane replied.

The three of them broke into a run.

Within seconds, Shane heard one of the amphibian's engines sputter to life, and then the other. The engines accelerated to what seemed like full power and the pitch changed. After a minute they went quiet again.

Five minutes later, Shane, Marie and Robert reached the lodge, winded, after running all the way. Elizabeth and Billy were standing on the deck, looking toward the lake. The amphibian was sitting a short distance from the youth camp and Frank Hale was standing in the nose hatch, studying the horizon with his hand shading his eyes.

"Boy oh boy, did you ever miss something," Billy screamed.

"What happened?" Shane asked, looking at Elizabeth.

"I didn't see it but Billy did," she replied.

"What did you see, Billy?" Shane asked.

"The airplane just sank a boat that was chasing it."

"What? Slow down. Explain what you mean."

"I watched the plane come in and land. It taxied toward the youth camp, shut down and dropped someone off. The pilot was closing the door and getting ready to take off again when a man in a little boat came rowing toward it. He got pretty close before the pilot saw him. He was yelling something and waving what looked like a gun. The pilot ducked down and closed the hatch and the man fired a couple of shots at the plane. I guess the pilot was mad because he started the engines and revved them up. He put the plane into a turn. All that wind and water caught the boat and knocked the man out of it, and the boat flipped over and sank."

"What about the man?"

"He took off swimming toward the other side."

"Did he still have the gun?"

"I don't think so. He was swimming as fast as he could with both arms. I think he let go of the gun when the boat overturned."

"Good work, son," Shane said. "That's an excellent report." Shane turned to Robert and Marie. "This is a break – a big one. If Tim Wade lost his gun in that attempt to hijack the amphibian, then we don't have to worry about getting shot if we try to approach him."

"But we may have a different problem," Marie said. "Frank Hale no doubt is on the radio right now to the FAA, and they're on the phone to the sheriff. Deputy Hanson and his troops are going to be all over this place. If you were trying to get to Tim before Hanson did, it just got a whole lot harder."

"On the other hand," Robert pointed out, "who is to say the guy in the boat was Tim? As far as Frank Hale and Deputy Hanson are concerned, it was just some crazy guy with a gun. I'm not sure that changes much, but Hanson may not connect the dots."

"We can hope," Shane said.

Thirty minutes later, Hanson's black SUV came up the driveway. Shane stood on the porch as the deputy got out, put on his wire-rimmed sunglasses and smoky bear hat, and swaggered up to the house.

"What the hell happened out here a while ago?" Hanson asked. "Did you see it?"

"Afraid I didn't," Shane said. "I was off on an exercise walk with two of our guests."

"So the plane wasn't coming here?"

"No, I think it dropped someone at the youth camp. My son watched the whole thing from the deck here."

Hanson asked Billy a few questions and then left for the youth camp. Shane noted the amphibian remained just offshore from the camp where it had been for the last hour since the incident. The pilot was looking over the entire plane, the engines especially, while he waited. No doubt he couldn't leave until he gave a statement to the sheriff's office.

"Hanson doesn't seem to be doing much with this," Robert observed. "I guess he sent two officers up the east-side road to look for the swimmer, but it's a pretty half-hearted response."

Tim Wade sat on the grassy shore across from the youth camp. He could see the amphibian still sitting out front and a black SUV parked by the beach, no doubt from the sheriff's department. Tim didn't think he had hit the plane; he had fired to make the pilot stop. The pilot's reaction in starting the engines and swamping the boat had totally surprised him. If no one found any slugs in the airplane's hull, so much the better, because it would be just that much less evidence that the shots were fired from his gun.

The hot sun was drying his clothes and he'd soon be ready to get on the move again, minus the gun. That was a huge loss. He had botched the whole hijack attempt and drawn attention to himself that would make everything harder. Whether he could go back to the cabin was debatable. The search didn't seem very inspired. Maybe they didn't even connect him with the cabin. Two deputies had walked past his location a short while ago, but they were talking about sports and appeared indifferent to looking very hard. He was frankly surprised this was such a non-event, or appeared to be.

Meanwhile, he was famished.

"I am so damn mad," Bonnie said when she called that evening. "I am just furious."

"What's wrong?" Elizabeth asked.

"After that little drama with the airplane, and after all the deputies left, I caught a ride into town for some grocery shopping. Figured the excitement was over for one day. But when I got back I'd been burglarized! No one has *ever* burglarized me. They must have seen me leave."

"Oh no," Elizabeth said.

"I should have left the radio blaring to make it seem like I was home. They took my little transistor radio, a backpack and a whole bunch of canned goods. And my can opener. The backpack was probably to carry it all."

"I'm so sorry."

"Oh it's worse than that," Bonnie said. "I'm afraid we are royally screwed now because they also took my husband's twelve-gauge and a box of shells."

"Have you called the sheriff?"

"No, but I think I'll have to talk to that twerp," Bonnie said.

"I'll tell Shane."

"Was it him?" Robert asked.

"It had to be," Shane replied, "and he's incredibly brazen to strike so soon after the airplane fiasco. The heat's barely off and he's already rearmed himself. With the battery-powered radio he can finally get some idea of what's happening in the search, and with the food he can keep going for a while in one of the vacant cabins. He's tenacious."

"And hungry and desperate," Robert added. "He's going to end up dead."

"I think you're right, and if it happens we may never know the truth about who really killed the sheriff."

"You still think it might have been Hanson?"

"The pieces fit. That's all I'm saying. And I haven't ruled out Harry and Sarah as killing Tim Wade. Motive, means and opportunity – they all had them."

"A sheriff makes a lot of enemies," Robert mused.

"And so did Tim," Shane added.

Marie had walked into the room at the beginning of the conversation and was standing a few feet away, listening. "We need to get to Tim Wade before Hanson does," she said. "That needs to happen soon, and I think the ideal time to do it is when he's asleep," she said. "Tonight."

"And how do you suggest we do it without a shootout?" Shane asked.

"We take the road and sneak up on him after dark. He's had a big day; he'll need to sleep. If we go to three different windows and hit him with bright flashlights, and yell 'freeze' simultaneously, he'll be so disoriented I don't think he'll pick up the gun. I think he'll wet his pants and surrender without making a move."

"Or start blasting holes in the cabin walls," Shane said.

"Assuming we apprehend and interrogate him, then what?" Robert asked. "Do we turn him over to Deputy Hanson?"

"Maybe that depends on what he says."

"We're going to be interfering big time in a police investigation," Robert said.

"I see it as trying to recover the items stolen from our elderly neighbor," Shane said. "We suspected someone was squatting in the cabin across the lake. When Aunt Bonnie's cabin was burglarized, we had a feeling it was this guy, so we went looking. One thing led to another."

"Hanson won't buy it," Robert said, shaking his head.

"But if Tim Wade has some information about Hanson's possible involvement in the murder, we'll be on solid ground not turning over the star witness to him. We'll turn him over to the state police for safe keeping."

Silent Witness

At one a.m., Robert, Shane and Marie left on the one-hour hike to Tim Wade's presumed hideout. Talking among themselves, they had agreed that two o'clock would be the best hour to spring their surprise, when Wade would most likely be asleep. All three carried bright flashlights for the moment of confrontation; Shane carried the only firearm, his Glock. He hoped it would be enough if things went bad. He wanted to apprehend Wade without resistance.

Since most of the road was well out of sight of the cabin, the three found their way comfortably with their flashlights. But right away Marie noticed something different. "Cars have come this way," she said. "More than one. These wheel tracks weren't here the other day."

"What do you make of it?" Shane asked.

"I don't know. Did Deputy Hanson send any cars up the road when he was looking for the swimmer?" she asked.

"I don't think so. He sent two deputies on foot, but I wasn't aware of any patrol cars coming this way. It's a pretty poor road anyway. Maybe I didn't give him enough credit," Shane said. "Maybe he put two-and-two together, thought about where the swimmer was going, and decided Tim must be hiding in one of the east-side cabins."

"It could be one car coming and going," Marie said. "Or more than one car coming but not yet leaving."

Shane wondered if the owners of the "love nest" cabin might have driven to the lake to secure things after getting his report of a break-in several days ago. If so, it was colossally bad timing. They had walked into an ambush.

At that instant, gunfire ahead shattered the stillness. "That's no twelve-gauge. Those are automatic weapons," Shane yelled. The firing lasted maybe fifteen seconds, and then stopped.

"I think we're too late," Marie said.

At the cabin, deputies were already stringing "Police – Do Not Cross" tape. Lights, powered by a generator, illuminated the cabin. The front door and several windows were shattered.

A deputy recognized them as visitors who were vacationing at the lake. "I'm sorry," he said. "This is as far as we can let you go."

"What happened?" Shane asked, pulling out his wallet to show his badge and ID. It was a nonsensical question because he already knew.

"We tried to arrest a murder suspect. He reached for his weapon and we put him down."

"Is Deputy Hanson here?" Shane asked.

"He's inside, with the body. It's pretty bad in there. "

Shane shook his head.

He did not hang around to talk to Hanson. "There's nothing to say to him," Shane told Robert and Marie. Let's get out of here.

"Do you think Tim was a murderer?" Marie asked.

"I don't know," Shane replied. "He did some bad things – violent things. But whether he went so far as to murder the sheriff, I don't know. Sometimes kids start down a pretty bad road when they're working out their place in the world, and then later they pull their lives together, and end up doing good. Everyone deserves that chance."

"It pisses me off," Marie said on the walk back to the lodge. "We know this was murder – first the sheriff and now Tim Wade. Hanson was behind one or both of those deaths. Now we may never know. And of course he won't let us look at the scene – which, I suppose, I wouldn't, either, if the tables were turned. But he's making sure he has plenty of time to control the evidence and everything the coroner sees."

"There has to be an internal investigation," Robert pointed out. "They have to reconstruct exactly what happened, in what sequence. If the officers fired first, with no provocation, it could come out in the report."

"What are the odds of that?" Marie asked. "Hanson is the boss and you know how the blue wall works. Those officers will stick together with one story. You know that. Hanson will make sure of it. And he'll make sure the evidence backs him up."

"Let's think about this," Shane said. "There must be another way. Sometimes even a wall has a crack in it if you can just find it."

It was just midmorning – the start of another sunny day – when Kat showed up at the lodge with a backpack. No one was stirring except Elizabeth, who took one look and invited her into the kitchen for eggs, hash browns and bacon. Elizabeth thought Kat looked pretty rough, as if she'd slept in her clothes for a few days and hadn't been able to clean up. She had always been thin as a rail, but Elizabeth thought Kat had lost a few pounds.

She watched Kat eat the eggs greedily and clean every bit of her plate.

"I miss my B&B," Elizabeth said. "Haven't had any guests to pamper except Robert and Marie, so it's fun to have you here this morning."

"Do you think I could stay here for a day or two?" Kat asked. "I can sleep on the sofa or floor. Things are worse than ever at home."

"What's wrong?"

"Mom's getting evicted. She and Steve are at each other's throats. Steve is moving out, and Mom will be living in her truck in a couple of days. I called and she said to come get my stuff because otherwise it's all going to the dump."

"What a mess," Elizabeth agreed.

"There's nothing for me here," Kat said. "Nothing to go back or forward to."

"You are always welcome with us. If you'd like to freshen up in a few minutes, there's a bathroom just down the hall," she said, nodding in that direction. "When Marie gets up she will be delighted to see you."

Elizabeth asked Kat if she was pretty worried about her mother.

"Of course," Kat said. "She's my mom. She's drinking herself to death. If she would just stop drinking, maybe she could start to climb out of the hole she's dug for herself. But that isn't going to happen. She'll hook up with some other loser, some abusive man, and repeat the cycle all over again."

"You have to really hit bottom to give up an addiction," Elizabeth said. "In your mom's case, I don't know where bottom is. I don't know how you can help her – how anyone can. Maybe the shock of losing her home and living in her truck will do that."

"That trailer is not much to lose," Kat said. "It hasn't been a 'home' in a long time."

Elizabeth filled in Kat on the reason the others were sleeping late. "They are exhausted and depressed because they had a plan to apprehend Tim Wade this morning without violence, and really thought he could explain what happened to the sheriff. Deputy Hanson got there first with overwhelming firepower and made sure that didn't happen."

Kat listened attentively in silence. Finally, she offered, "Harry Loush knows more than he's saying."

"Why do you say that?"

"The story he's been telling publicly is that Tim was gone when he and Sarah got home the morning after the big splash at the lake. But I happen to know Tim was still there when Harry and Sarah got home. Tim told Harry privately that he was still at the house when Hanson shot his boss, and he was pretty shaken. Tim shared the story of what happened with Harry."

"That's huge," Elizabeth said.

"I didn't want to drag Harry into this, but it's not right for Hanson to gun down Tim and cover up what happened at the house. Maybe Harry can help your husband find out the truth."

"Who's in the bathroom?" Marie asked when she staggered into the kitchen in her robe.

"It's Kat," Elizabeth replied. "She showed up here a couple of hours ago looking pretty rough. We had a good talk while I made breakfast for her. She wolfed it down. She said some things about the Tim Wade case the rest of you will find interesting."

"Well then I'd better roll Robert out of that bed because we're both pretty depressed, and this sounds like something he needs to hear."

"Give Shane a shout, too. He can't hide under those covers forever. I'll start some more bacon and eggs. The smell of bacon usually gets things going around here."

Within minutes, the whole group was gathered 'round the table, with Robert and Shane looking just as rough as Kat when she arrived. But Kat was now looking much better. Billy was already dressed and gone outside, looking for adventure. Martin was atop his high chair, surrounded by a floor covered with scrambled eggs, hash browns and other food he had thrown as far as he could between bored bites of breakfast.

"Kat's going to stay with us for a few days," Elizabeth announced. "Things are complicated at home, as if they could get any worse than they already were."

"We will love to have you," Shane said.

Kat explained about the eviction. Then Shane nudged her to the topic of Harry Loush and what he had learned from Tim Wade.

The table went silent. Robert and Marie leaned forward and put down their forks. Kat looked down at her plate, then up, and swept her eyes across everyone at the table.

"Tim told Harry that Deputy Hanson shot the sheriff."

"Based on what?" Robert asked.

"The sheriff apparently was walking home when he saw Tim go into the house, so he followed and knocked on the door. Tim said it was just bad luck and bad timing that the sheriff saw him at all.

The sheriff and Tim had a conversation about the gun the sheriff had heard Tim was carrying. At some point Tim handed the gun to the sheriff and they talked about whether Tim had a permit, which he admitted he didn't."

"So how did Hanson get involved?" Shane asked.

"Hanson showed up during this conversation and joined the two in the front entry hall. Hanson seemed to have a big chip on his shoulder about something the sheriff had said to him earlier. The conversation got heated and Tim said it was clear the two men didn't like each other at all.

The sheriff told Hanson he had everything under control and Hanson could leave. Hanson asked to look at the gun, and the sheriff handed it to him. Seemingly on impulse, Hanson turned and fired two shots into the sheriff, and he fell to floor, dead."

"Holy cow!" Marie declared. "That's as callous as it gets."

"There's more," Kat added.

"After Hanson shot the sheriff, he wiped the gun with his handkerchief, handed it back to Tim to get his fingerprints on it, and ordered Tim to clean up the scene and dispose of the body. He essentially blackmailed Tim because of his drug dealing, and told him they could either be on good terms or bad, and that Tim knew what this meant. Tim was well aware he was being framed but had no choice. Hanson told him what to do about the runner and the bleach, and suggested Tim dump the body into the lake where it wouldn't be found for a while."

"Tim told Harry he was getting out of there and they'd never see him again."

"My god," Shane said. "It all makes perfect sense. I just wish we had a way to prove it."

"We'll work on that," Marie said, smiling broadly and turning to Kat. "You've done us a huge favor."

"I owed you one," Kat replied.

"I need to make a phone call," Shane declared, pushing back his chair. He walked to the office and called Bonnie, next door.

"I know you have a source in the sheriff's office," he said. "Do you think you can get the names of the sheriff's deputies who participated in the raid this morning with Tim Wade? I need to know a little about each one, and whether your source thinks one of them might have enough conscience to talk with me honestly about what happened. I'm not looking for the official story but the real story of how Tim Wade died."

"That's a tall order," Bonnie said. "People's lives and livelihoods are on the line."

"I know," Shane said. "No one wants to rat on his boss or his friends. But maybe there is someone who's really upset about the death of the sheriff, and who sees what Hanson is doing, and is feeling very conflicted. That's the person I need to find."

"I'll give it a try. I'm good but I don't know if I'm *that* good."

Bodice-Rippers

Acting sheriff Hanson lost no time publicizing his version of events in a press conference for the county's newspaper and radio station. Shane heard it over the local station as he stood by the radio in the great room of the Pursuit Lake lodge.

A team of sheriff's deputies led by Chief Deputy Leland Hanson this morning surrounded a house at Pursuit Lake where murder suspect Timothy Wade was hiding. He is believed responsible for the recent death of Sheriff Andrew Dixon. Hanson said his officers entered the house about 2 a.m. and confronted Wade, who was asleep, ordering him to surrender.

Ignoring orders to raise his hands, the suspect instead reached for a nearby shotgun and officers opened fire in self-defense. Wade was pronounced dead at the scene.

Hanson expressed pride in the professionalism of his team, saying they followed correct procedure and used the utmost restraint, firing only when the suspect left them no choice.

The chief deputy says this closes the books on a sad chapter in county history. The sheriff was the first law officer in the county ever to lose his life in the performance of his duties. Hanson said he was proud his department could solve the crime against one of their own, and bring the suspect swiftly to justice.

Shane knew what Hanson meant by justice – don't take him alive. The officers no doubt felt they were avenging the murder of their sheriff in a way that Wade couldn't weasel out of with years of appeals to avoid the death penalty. Hanson's whole account was neat and tidy, Shane thought, except that it wasn't quite as neat as Hanson described. Shane hoped to set the record straight on that soon.

Kat had entered the room as Shane listened to the press announcement. "That isn't right," she said. "Tim didn't kill the sheriff. Hanson did. And I highly doubt Tim reached for his gun."

"With your help, we're going to get Hanson," Shane said. "We just need a little more time to locate a witness in law enforcement who can corroborate some of this."

"You think you can find one?"

"It's surprising what you can find if you look hard enough. Every time I think we're blocked on this investigation, something opens up. Hanson is not well liked. He's made plenty of enemies. We just need to find one of them who's ready to talk, and we've got someone working on that.

"Hey," he said. "This looks like a good day for some boating and fishing. Do you feel like a boat ride with Billy and me?"

"Why not?" Kat replied. "My whole life is crazy. I can't remember the last time I did *anything* just for fun."

"Then we'll fix that today."

An hour later, with three fishing poles and some worms in a can of moist earth for bait, the trio headed out in the electric boat. Elizabeth had loaned Kat a stylish white sundress and broad-brimmed hat. Marie had equipped her with large, round sunglasses. Shane thought the transformation was stunning. She was a beautiful young woman.

"Where to?" Shane asked Billy.

"The outlet stream."

"Ok, then you take the wheel and drive us there," Shane replied, moving to the back of the boat with Kat so Billy could sit in the captain's chair.

They were making good time, almost silently, across the lake. "This is fun," Billy declared, making a gentle "S" curve just to try out the steering. Kat trailed her hand in the warm water, smiling and soaking up the breeze.

"Do you think the outlet will be a good place to find fish?" Shane asked.

"Probably not, but I just want to see it," Billy said. "The inlet area might be better for fish, where they will bunch up more. That's where the beavers are, too, so I'm saving the best for last."

"That's pretty shrewd of you," Shane observed as they cruised past the cabin where Tim Wade had died in the shootout. He didn't think Billy knew about that. He wondered if Billy realized they were passing close to the place where the sheriff was pulled from the water. Most likely he did, but his mind was on other things this morning.

"Everything in this lake is mostly just scrap fish and spiny rays," Billy said, "so I don't think we'll catch anything we want to eat, but it'll be fun to try our luck. This lake gets a lot of acid rain, so the fish and plants don't do very well. I guess we can always bury the fish in the garden to build up the soil."

Kat looked at Billy with her head cocked. "How in the world do you know so much?"

"I read a lot. Since we got here I've been studying about Adirondack Park and the effects of heavy industrialization of the Eastern states on the lakes, especially."

"I love books, too," Kat said, "but you amaze me for a thirteen-year-old. Have you read any astronomy? That's one of my interests – the stars and planets."

"Yes, I love it. When I was in Idaho, we looked though a telescope at the moons of Jupiter and the rings of Saturn. The night sky there is very clear. The whole area is now a national Dark Skies Preserve."

"Cool."

"Elizabeth is a little bookish, too," Billy said. "It runs in the family – all the excessive nerdiness."

Shane laughed, and then Kat joined in. Shane realized it was the first time he had ever heard Kat laugh.

Billy took them a short way into the outlet stream before deciding it was too narrow and shallow for the boat. He reduced speed and made a gentle U-turn, and then set his course for the inlet area. Shane realized he needed to spend more days like this with Billy. Kids grow up fast, and these precious days together are the memories one cherishes for a lifetime.

Billy chose a spot near a beaver lodge, close to some clumps of reeds, and brought the boat to a stop. They watched a beaver swim toward the lodge, eyeballing them, and then slap its tail and dive. The three of them baited their hooks and dropped their lines into the water. Shane didn't think they'd see any more of that beaver today. Billy watched with interest, but took it in stride. Shane knew Billy had already seen beavers at Redfish Lake in Idaho.

The water here was only a few feet deep and Shane could see the bottom in several places. Within a few minutes they were all playing fish. One by one they landed small bullheads and threw them into the fish bucket.

"This doesn't seem real," Kat said, "this whole day. I haven't had a day like this ever," she said as she dug her fingers into the bait can for another earthworm.

"I don't have many days like this, either," Shane said. "Not nearly enough."

When they were all satisfied with their catch, they put away their poles. Shane turned to Billy and said, "Okay, captain, take us home. When we get back to the boathouse, just kiss the boat up to the dock gently."

"How was it?" Elizabeth asked when the three boaters came trudging up to the deck with their fishing poles.

Billy showed off his bucket of bullheads. "We found the fish," he said.

"We're not eating those," Elizabeth said, screwing up her face.

"Thank god," Shane muttered. "Billy was a very fine captain today. He did all the boat handling and also knew where to find the fish."

Kat smiled. "It was a perfect day to be on the water and let our cares melt away."

"We all need that," Elizabeth agreed. "I think that's why this place exists and attracts so many people back, summer after summer. It's an escape from the cares of the world."

"Except that this summer it's been the focus of some unusual cares," Shane said. "I think we're getting toward the end of that, but I've been preoccupied with it and have neglected the relaxation piece. Billy and Kat helped me rediscover that. Everything about this day was a joy."

Together, the group walked up the steps and into the great room, where they found Robert and Marie reading books.

"And how was your day?" Shane asked.

"Whoo. Steamy," Robert replied. "Marie is teaching me how to sit still and read a book. But all she brought with her are trashy novels. Have you read any of these romance novels?" he asked, holding up a paperback with a woman on the cover, showing a lot of flesh. "They're pretty torrid."

"You should be more like Billy. He reads to improve his mind," Shane said.

"Not my thing," Robert said. "This is my new genre."

"I can see that," Shane agreed. "It the book business that's called a bodice-ripper."

"Well, I'm getting ideas from it."

"You're on vacation," Elizabeth added. "It's ok to get ideas."

"I'm getting embarrassed," Marie said. "I'm a little shy, you know." Shane noticed her face was beet red. "Shouldn't we be solving a murder or something?"

"In due time," Shane said. "We're on a little break here, having some quality time."

"By the way, Kat, you look very fetching in that summer dress," Marie added, changing the subject entirely.

"It's the new me."

"Well, the new you is beautiful."

Just then the big rotary phone rang. Shane picked it up and heard, "What the hell is going on there?" It was Brad Haraldsen, calling from Stanley, Idaho. "I'm not getting any news."

"Well, several of us are just back from fishing and caught Robert reading trashy novels."

"I thought you were up to your necks in crime."

"We are, but we're getting it cleaned up. There's just one loose end now. We're trying to prove the deputy sheriff murdered his boss and blackmailed someone else to dump his body into the lake."

"Jesus, is that all? You call this a vacation? I thought you were chasing cabin prowlers."

"We were," Shane said, "but it escalated. One thing kind of led to another."

"What does the blackmailed guy say?" Brad asked.

"Not much, because the chief deputy permanently shut him up in a shootout here the other day. We're looking for someone in the department who will tell us exactly what happened when they cornered the suspect. My guess is that the deputy told his men to make sure the suspect didn't get out of there alive."

"That's entirely possible," Brad agreed.

"Luckily," Shane continued, "we have a pretty good idea how the deputy murdered the sheriff earlier because our deceased witness told someone else what happened before the chief deputy got a chance to silence him."

"But tell us about you? How are your treatments going?"

"Ok, I guess, but it's a seesaw process. Some days I feel almost human, like today. Other days every muscle aches and I barely have the energy to get out of a chair. I get light-headed and short of breath. It's not the lifestyle I had in mind, but it's the one I've got. I don't know what I'd do without Bolivar to run the ranch. He's carrying almost the whole load now, and he does it cheerfully."

"And how is Irene? This must be hard on her."

"Oh, I'm sure it is. She drives me to appointments and makes nutritious meals that keep me going. And worries, of course. I wish we could both turn off the worrying because it doesn't change anything – just saps our energy. We need to get some help for both Irene and Bolivar. But I also wish to hell we could be with you at the lake, getting in on this fun you're having."

"Well, we think of you constantly and ask ourselves, 'What would Brad do?' If you were here you could write a book about this place and the adventures we're having. I'm learning about the East. The other day I nearly committed suicide, crossing the lake in an open boat in an electrical storm. I won't do that again. You should see the afternoon thunderstorms we get. Unbelievable!"

"Well, take care of yourself and give our love to all the others. And be careful with electricity."

Shane was still smiling at Brad's closing advice when the phone rang again. This time it was Bonnie.

"Is something wrong with your phone?" she asked. "All I get is a busy signal. I've been dialing your number for the last ten minutes."

"Just talking with an old friend out West, my partner in solving several crimes in the past."

"I've got a name for you. Do you have a piece of paper?"

"I don't need one."

"Yes, you do."

"Ok, hang on." Shane put down the phone and found a note pad, and scrambled through desk drawers to find a pen.

"Let's have it."

"Peter Stoltzfus."

"Spelling?"

Bonnie spelled it slowly for Shane, then repeated it when he got tied up in knots halfway through. "Where did you go to school, anyway?" she asked.

"You couldn't find some other name?" he asked.

"Stoltzfus is a good, Amish name," she said. "The deputy grew up here in the Amish community before he opted out on rumspringa. That's why my source thinks he's a good bet for you."

"Yeah, I see the possibilities," Shane said.

"Bad as we know Tim Wade was, Peter has a built-in understanding of the pressures of Amish life on teenagers. We think he's probably feeling pain about the summary justice Tim Wade got the other day in the raid.

She went on. "Tim was young. He still had time to turn his life around, but Hanson made sure he never got that chance. Peter is the best we can do in that group. My source says several of the others are pretty convinced they did the right thing, settling a score for their sheriff. Peter is a gentler soul, more like Andy Dixon. In fact, he was a great admirer of Sheriff Dixon."

"That's good information, Bonnie, very good. You and your source did us a big favor."

"Just get that arrogant creep, Leland Hanson."

Inside Man

Shane decided to sleep on the question of how to approach Stoltzfus. It had to be a private conversation, away from the sheriff's department. He didn't especially want to call Stoltzfus at work and have others in the room know he had called. And he needed to minimize the telephone contact – just enough to ask for a private meeting. Anything he said on the phone needed to be short and unspecific.

By morning, he knew what he would do. He sat down at the phone, picked up the receiver and dialed the number.

"Sheriff," answered the dispatcher.

"Officer Stoltzfus, please," Shane said.

"May I tell him who's calling?"

"It's a confidential, private matter. I'd rather tell him directly." He wasn't sure the dispatcher would accept this, but the next words he heard were, "One moment."

The extension rang and a baritone voice answered, "Stoltzfus."

"Officer Stoltzfus, my name is Shane Lindstrom and I'm a sheriff's detective from Washington state, vacationing at Pursuit Lake. I'd like to meet with you privately, away from the office, without drawing the attention of your fellow officers. Would you be willing to do that?"

There was a long pause on the line.

"That's an unusual proposition."

"The circumstances are unusual – a criminal matter. I'm trying to be as discrete as humanly possible."

Shane had a feeling the officer would not be able to turn him down, in the face of such an intriguing question.

"I could do that. What is your badge number? I'd like to verify that. And your location?"

Shane gave him the information and Stoltzfus suggested a time later in the morning when he would stop by.

When the deputy's police cruiser came up the driveway Shane was waiting on the porch. The car rolled to a stop and Stoltzfus took a moment to check his computer and gather some materials before opening the door. He stood up and put on his hat, and Shane was immediately struck by his height, at least six-foot-two, and his no-nonsense bearing. He had kind eyes and made a good impression. Shane stepped forward and shook hands with him, and then introduced the officer to Elizabeth, Robert, Marie and Kat Brown, explaining that Robert was an Idaho state trooper assigned to the governor's detail, and Marie was a former US Fish and Wildlife agent.

"This is a distinguished group."

"I might ask our friend, Kat Brown, to join us because she has some important background on what I want to discuss with you, if that's okay."

"Fine with me," Stoltzfus said. "I still don't know why I'm here."

"We'll get to that momentarily," Shane said.

Shane led him to the table on the porch and they all took seats around it. The relaxed, open-air setting and birdsong belied the seriousness of the occasion. Shane explained that he wanted to talk about the police operation the other morning that took the life of Tim Wade. "Do you know much about Tim?" Shane asked. "Maybe you know he was brought up in the Amish community, and had left to live among the English, and had gotten into a lot of trouble in the last couple of years."

"Yeah, it upsets me when someone from our community gets into so much trouble, because I always think we failed them somehow. I still think of it as my community, though of course I'm English now. From a law-enforcement perspective, Tim wasn't one of our favorite people," Stoltzfus said. "He was a pretty screwed up kid."

"He may have murdered Sheriff Dixon," Shane said, "but we're not sure."

"Wait a minute," Stoltzfus said. "Two things. First, I don't think there's much doubt about that, and second, how did you and your friends get involved in all this?" he asked, scanning the faces at the table.

"I'll start with your second question first," Shane said, explaining that the very first night he and Elizabeth stayed at the lake, they had a break-in at the lodge. Subsequently, there was another. They set out to catch the prowler and eventually Marie did, and it turned out to be Kat.

Stoltzfus looked at Kat. "I know your mom," he said, shaking his head. "We've been out to her trailer many times. And there have been some other prowling and truancy issues," he said.

Kat smiled but said nothing. Since the night Marie captured Kat, Shane said, Kat has become a good friend.

"Even after we caught Kat, the cabin prowls continued," Shane said. "Kat provided information that led us to a young Amish couple who used the cabin across the lake as a love nest. That's the same cabin where Tim Wade was hiding."

"The significance of the Amish couple is that they were the closest witnesses to the splash when Sheriff Dixon's body was thrown into the lake."

"Okay," Stoltzfus said.

"Kat was on the lake that night and observed the man who dumped the body – just a shadow in a rowboat because it happened in darkness. She couldn't identify him but did see the car, an old Corolla, and noted that the man was tall and lean, which fits with Tim Wade's profile, among others. When we heard that, coupled with some additional information, we started thinking Tim was the murderer."

"Okay."

"Now here's where it gets interesting. The young Amish couple were living in a rental house in Crossington with Tim, whose behavior increasingly frightened them. He was dealing drugs and had a violent temper. One of the roommates told Kat that he and his girlfriend came home to find Tim cleaning the entryway with bleach and removing the runner. Tim confessed to one of his housemates that Sheriff Dixon had followed him home and confronted him about a semi-automatic pistol he was carrying."

"That makes sense," Stoltzfus said. "I know Dixon was concerned the gun would be used in a violent crime if he didn't get it out of Wade's hands."

Shane continued. "According to what Wade told his roommate, Deputy Hanson showed up and asked to look at the gun. The sheriff handed it to him and Hanson shot the sheriff with it twice, point blank, right in front of Wade."

"Dear god. But do we really take Wade's word on this?"

"Well, here's the thing," Shane continued. "You probably know, as other people, that Dixon and Hanson couldn't stand each other. So it's plausible that it happened the way Tim said."

Stoltzfus conceded that the department was divided about whose style of policing was best for the community. Hanson was the tough guy, and this appealed to some of the gung-ho deputies. There are always people who go into police work because they like power and guns. Dixon took a much gentler approach, more of a community-policing style. Speaking personally, Stoltzfus said he always leaned toward Dixon's approach because he got people to trust him and work with him.

Shane went on to explain that Hanson blackmailed Tim into taking the sheriff's body to the lake and disposing of it – essentially implicating him. With Tim as the only suspect, nicely framed by all the evidence at the rental house, Hanson was in a good position to arrange for his death in a shootout with arresting officers, effectively closing the case.

Stoltzfus looked at his hands for a long minute.

"It's quite a scenario," Stoltzfus said, "but I'm not sure you can ever prove it. I'm not sure what the truth is. And I'm not sure where I come into it, either."

"Well, first of all, you know what happened in the raid. What were your instructions from Deputy Hanson?"

Stoltzfus hesitated. "I'll tell you as a fellow officer, in confidence, but this is strictly off the record."

"Understood."

"You know how these things go. Wade wasn't coming out of there alive. Hanson told us Wade was armed and dangerous, and had killed before. Our job was to get justice for the sheriff – swift and sure. There wasn't going to be any court case, or years of prison and appeals. So we basically went in there shooting and it was all over in a few seconds."

Shane remarked that to his way of thinking, this added to the argument that Hanson had something to hide.

"So what do you want from me?" Stoltzfus asked.

"I'm hoping you'll tell the truth about Wade's death at the internal inquiry. Depending on what you say, it may be possible to force Hanson into a lie-detector test that will blow this case wide open."

"If I speak up, I'll be finished in this county. I'll be a pariah among the other officers. Even with the union defending me, there will be no way I can continue to work in the department."

"Well, just think about it. Keep your eyes and ears open around Hanson. He may slip up and say something about what happened at the rental house."

Stoltzfus nodded. "And what about you?"

"We're going home in a few days and I suppose this will all be behind us. We've taken this about as far as we can. Whatever happens with Hanson's career and the future of law enforcement in this county, it won't be our problem. Personally, I hope I never see the guy again. It galls me to think an officer of the law can do something like this and get away with it. If we're right, Hanson has two murders on his hands. What's to say he won't do it again the next time someone stands in his way?"

Stoltzfus nodded, pushed back his chair and got up slowly.

"He's going to run for sheriff, you know," Stoltzfus said.

"That's what I heard."

Stoltzfus shook hands with everyone and walked out to his car. "I'll keep this between us," he said, opening the door and lowering himself into the driver's seat. He set his hat on the passenger seat at his side.

Shane watched the car disappear down the driveway and wondered if this was the end of things. Sometimes you catch the bad guy. Sometimes you don't.

"Now what?" Kat asked.

"I'm not sure," Shane replied. "We've planted a seed; now we wait and hope."

The deputy's car had just disappeared from view when the phone rang. It was Aunt Bonnie, wanting to know about the conversation.

"He's a good guy," Shane said. "Thoughtful and forthcoming. But we put him in a pretty tight spot with our unproven allegations about his boss. He did confirm what we already thought, that Tim Wade didn't have a chance in that raid. I can't quote the specifics of what he said, but it doesn't take much imagination to guess."

"So now what?" Bonnie asked.

"That's what we're asking ourselves, too. We're at a dead end unless something gives in the police investigation of the raid. I doubt Hanson will ever tell anyone what really happened to the sheriff, but you never know. He hated the sheriff so much he might get drunk and say something. Stoltzfus could be the key to uncovering what happened in the raid, depending on where his conscience leads him, but there's a high price to pay for challenging the official account. Hanson wants to be sheriff and the community will have to decide whether he has the personal qualities they want in that role."

Shane told Bonnie that Frank Hale was coming in the widgeon tomorrow for Robert, Marie and baby Martin. He would return the next day for Shane, Elizabeth and Billy, "and possibly one other passenger."

"Who's that?" Bonnie asked.

"We hope it'll be Kat, but she doesn't know yet."

Fresh Start

"Are Harry and Sarah in danger?" Kat asked at lunch. "Tim told them his version of what happened – that Hanson killed the sheriff. So they are the closest witnesses now."

"I wish I could say they aren't," Shane replied, "but it's possible. On the other hand, Tim's version of events is getting out in the community now. The rumor is spreading that Hanson might have had a motive to kill the sheriff and silence Tim. So if something were to happen to Harry and Sarah, it would cast a lot of suspicion on Hanson. I'm sure he's aware of that. I gave officer Stoltzfus the whole picture, too, so he'll be watching Hanson closely."

"But right now, Hanson is getting away with everything."

"Right now that's true. I think there's a good chance justice will catch up with him, but I don't know how soon – tomorrow or a year from now, or five years. We've taken this as far as we can on our vacation."

Kat stared at her plate, her eyebrows furrowed. Shane knew she was pretty upset they hadn't been able to close the case against Hanson. She had hoped Harry's report of talking with Tim would do it. Shane was frustrated, too.

He interrupted the silence. "On a completely different subject, Elizabeth and I have a proposition for you, if you'd like to hear it. Elizabeth has all the details."

Kat lifted her eyes toward Elizabeth with some skepticism, even as her body stayed hunched over her plate.

"Come out West with us," Elizabeth said. "Fly home with us tomorrow."

"You mean like a little vacation?"

"No, more like permanently," Elizabeth said. "Start a new life. You could stay indefinitely, get a job, maybe finish your high school diploma and go to college."

"Seriously?"

Shane jumped in. "There isn't much for you here but homelessness and hiding out. We've been talking about this. We'd like to see you get a fresh start and make a real life for yourself."

Elizabeth explained that their good friends, Brad and Irene Haraldsen, have a beautiful ranch in Stanley, Idaho, and need help because of Brad's health. "We've told them and their ranch foreman about you. It would be a lot of responsibility for you, and a leap of faith for our friends to trust a young woman with a history of petit crime."

"I wouldn't let you down," Kat said. "I would never do that."

"Brad and Irene are pretty excited," Elizabeth continued. "You could go there at least for starters," she said. "You'll love the Basque foreman, Bolivar, and he'll teach you a ton of things about horses and the outdoor life. Irene is a horse-lover and artist. She said you can live in the ranch house with them and they'll pay you a wage to work there. If you want to know what a great guy Bolivar is, just ask Billy.

"I don't even know what Basque means."

"It means he's a total character, believe me. The Basques come from a region of Spain. Many of them fanned out across the West to work as shepherds and cowboys, to raise money to send back to their families in Europe. But some, like Bolivar, stayed and settled here.

"Cool."

"Robert and Marie live just a few hours away, in Boise, so you won't be far from them. Boise is a lovely, small city on the Boise River. And Shane and I are just an airplane ride away on Whidbey Island. I can always use help with my bed-and-breakfast, if you find that ranch life is not for you."

"This is incredible," Kat said, with a big smile. "This is a lot to digest."

"We know it's sudden," Elizabeth said. "But you have no future here that I can see. It may be time to make a big change. Come with us to Whidbey Island and then we'll take you over to Idaho so you can see the situation there, and you can decide if you want to give ranch life a try."

Kat looked out at the water as the widgeon taxied up lake to get the longest possible takeoff run. Shane sat in the right-hand seat beside Hale, an extra set of eyes to help Hale scan the sky for other aircraft. Elizabeth and Billy sat behind them, and Kat in the rear. The sky was blue and the morning air was cool, which Shane said would give them more lift for the takeoff. Something was ending at this moment in Kat's life, and something else beginning. She was going on faith now, leaving for a faraway place with people she had just met, but felt that she trusted.

Hale made his turn at the end of the lake and opened the throttles. The engines roared and the plane started to accelerate. Kat thought at first it was making more noise and spray than progress.

"Come on, baby. Come on, come on," Hale coaxed as the amphibian pushed a big wave across the water with its bow. It seemed to be sitting very low in the water. As Kat looked out the side window next to her, she watched the float that hung down from the wingtip. At first it dragged in the water, but after while it rose clear of it – one less connection to the place she was leaving. Through the windshield she could see that the youth camp at the end of the lake was growing closer. The widgeon would need to get airborne soon. Kat wondered if Hale always talked to his plane. She supposed it was like a wife to him; he was essentially married to it.

"Alright, that's more like it!" Hale said, with relief in his voice. "We're on the step now."

Elizabeth turned and explained that the aircraft was now riding much higher in the water on just a small piece of its hull, reducing drag. It would pick up speed and break free soon. And if not, Kat thought, we will all die.

Just at that moment, Kat noticed the water outside her window was falling away. She hadn't even felt the plane rise into the air. They passed low over the youth camp and Kat saw kids looking up and waving. She waved back, never imagining she'd be in this place, in the sky looking down at the little world that had been her whole life for years, the cabins she'd broken into and the hiding places in the woods where she'd made her camps. Hale began a slow turn to the west over the forest as the plane climbed higher and higher, and in a moment Kat's world was gone.

*

Elizabeth explained the flight to Syracuse would take about thirty minutes. They were flying over dense green forest, peppered with blue lakes, large and small. Soon, the view below gave way to houses and roads, the outskirts of an urban area. Shopping centers and strip malls appeared. Within moments they were circling an airport that struck Kat as quite large.

Hale was on the radio, something about "downwind" and "final," descending and turning, lining up with the runway. Hale tapped Shane's shoulder and pointed toward a tiny dot in the distance and Kat heard him say into his radio, "Yes, we see him. We have visual." The ground seemed to be rising up to meet them. They crossed yellow markers and were over the pavement now, and plunked down hard. The widgeon bounced roughly on rubber tires, with two screeches and puffs of blue smoke.

"Sorry about that but I wanted to catch the end of the runway so I could take the first turnout," Hale said to Shane. "This gets us out of the way of the big guys." He turned off the runway and taxied toward a tie-down area for small aircraft near the terminal. Behind them, a United 737 was just touching down right where they'd just been.

When Hale opened the door, a wave of heat hit them all. They climbed out, shook hands with him, gathered their suitcases and began the labored walk to the terminal. The smell of this place struck Kat as hot asphalt, not the sweet fragrance of the woods on a warm day. This would be a brutally hot day in Syracuse, well over 100 degrees with high humidity. She imagined there would be afternoon thunderstorms, again but they'd be long gone. The odor of kerosene hung heavily in the air as jet aircraft came and went from the loading gates.

An hour later they were squeezing into their seats in one of them. Kat had never flown on any aircraft before. After riding in the widgeon, this jet with all the families and fussing kids seemed cramped and claustrophobic. Today she would travel thousands of miles over the entire expanse of the nation, over prairies, farms and mountains. She wondered about the people living their lives on those farms in the heartland. Were they happy?

The flight attendant closed the front door with a loud thunk and made a safety announcement. Air vents in the ceiling hissed loudly and Kat adjusted hers to blow directly on her. The jet engines started and something pushed the plane back from the terminal, and they began taxiing toward the end of the runway. After a short delay, the roar of the engines grew intense and the aircraft began to speed down the runway, lifting into the sky.

The pilot introduced himself on the intercom and announced they would climb to a cruising altitude of thirty thousand feet. She could see less and less detail on the ground. Little by little, the minutes passed and Kat lost interest in the flatlands below. She could see barns and irrigation circles, but not much else till, hours later, the pilot announced they were already descending through Snoqualmie Pass into Seattle. From thirty thousand feet, they could actually descend into the Cascade Mountains. Things were suddenly interesting again.

Nothing could have prepared her for her first view of Seattle, a vast and beautiful city sprawling farther than she could see, surrounded by lakes and inlets of the Pacific, and a whole string of volcanic peaks dominated by the magnificent Mt. Rainier, with its glaciers and ice fields. Ships and ferryboats criss-crossed the bay by the waterfront.

On the opposite side of Puget Sound from the Cascade Mountains, another snowcapped range rose into view.

"Those are the Olympic Mountains," Elizabeth said.

None of it seemed real. Their plane circled out over Puget Sound and Elizabeth pointed to a landmass in the distance. "That's Whidbey Island."

A few minutes later the plane touched down and taxied quickly to the terminal. Stewardesses opened the forward door and everyone stood to retrieve luggage from the overhead bins. The aisle filled instantly with people and no one moved. Kat felt claustrophobic.

When the crowd ahead finally cleared, they poured off the loading ramp in a river of humanity milling inside the terminal, and then crowding around the baggage claim carousels. Kat had never seen anything like the carousels, never seen so many people before, nor heard so many languages. She didn't care for this. It was already growing hard to remember Pursuit Lake. Soon they boarded a shuttle bus for the last leg of the trip to Whidbey Island.

"This will take about an hour," Elizabeth said. "We have to pass through the downtown area and continue north to a little town called Mukilteo to catch a ferry to the island, and then we'll be almost home. A friend will pick us up at the shuttle stop." Kat looked out the window, in a spell. Things were looking better and better, as the world outside grew wilder and wilder. When they reached the ferry and she looked across at the forested island on the other side, she knew this was going to be ok.

"This will just be a twenty-minute crossing, a short hop across the water," Elizabeth said when they drove onto the ferry.

"Can we get out and walk around on the boat?" Kat asked.

"Absolutely."

Kat rushed up the stairs and out to the viewing area on the bow, so she could breathe the marine air and watch the island draw closer. Emotions were welling up in her now – a mixture of excitement and also the realization she was impossibly far from home. She wondered if she'd ever see the East again, ever go back to her mom and the familiar life she'd left behind.

When they pulled up in front of The Eagles Inn Bed and Breakfast, Kat felt she'd arrived in paradise. Lush evergreens and firs surrounded them. She gazed at the bay, where sailboats bobbed at their floats and a few glided across the water, leaning into the breeze, their sails full. Birdsong filled the air. She listened and watched, inhaled the fragrance of the trees, speechless. A yellow-and-black butterfly fluttered through the air and landed on a purple-flowering bush a few feet from her. Birds came and went from a feeder in the yard.

"This must be a little overwhelming, this day," Elizabeth said.

"It is. My head is spinning. I've never traveled more than a few miles from home."

Elizabeth showed her to her room. "Take your time," she said, "and when you're ready we'll get together on the porch and unwind from our day with a glass of wine."

Dinner ended up being cheese and crackers, along with their wine. "We'll hang out here at the B&B for a few days, and then fly to Boise so you can see Robert and Marie again. They'll give us a lift to Brad and Irene's ranch in Stanley. It's entirely different from Whidbey Island but I think you will like the Wild West setting overlooking the Salmon River. I know you like wide open spaces. If it turns out you don't care for the ranch, you can always come back to Whidbey Island with me and help out here at the inn."

"You're being awfully nice to me."

"It has a way of coming full circle," Elizabeth said. "A few years ago when my brother was murdered on the Alaska Ferry, it shattered my whole world. Brad and Irene made a special effort to look me up at my home and offer their support. In fact they invited me to visit them at their ranch, which I did. That's where I met Shane and became part of this group of friends you've gotten to know. In the midst of my grief and sadness, something wonderful happened in my life. I think that's what we all want for you, someone with the potential to turn her life completely around."

"Tell me about your brother. Did they ever catch the person who murdered him?"

"He was a pilot for an Alaska bush airline, riding north on the Alaska ferry to pick up his airplane in Juneau. The people who owned the airline were involved in smuggling, and my brother wanted out. When he learned that Shane was on the ferry, he tried to set up a meeting with him, but my brother's bosses had him murdered. Shane, and Robert and Marie, caught them."

"Do you think Shane will ever get Deputy Hanson for the two murders?"

The question surprised Elizabeth. After this long day of travel, covering thousands of miles, Kat's thoughts were still on the unfinished business back home.

"He isn't someone to let things go. But hey, something else just crossed my mind."

"What's that?"

"We need to take you shopping to get some nicer clothes for your wardrobe."

"Maybe a sun dress like that one you loaned me at the lake?"

"Absolutely! And some mysterious dark glasses so you'll fit in with Marie and me."

West

"I've been nosing around," officer Stoltzfus told Shane when he phoned him at home later that week. "One of the other deputies overheard a loud argument between she sheriff and Hanson on the afternoon of his murder."

"Interesting."

"It is, but of course it doesn't prove anything, just that tensions between them were high. Apparently it was quite heated and Dixon asked Hanson to resign. Hanson is impulsive and has a wicked temper. He flatly refused and walked out."

"It all helps tighten the noose of circumstantial evidence around Hanson," Shane said. "If we can find some more officers with doubts about Hanson and convince them to join with us, we may yet crack this case."

"Hanson's been throwing his weight around more than ever since you left, badmouthing the former sheriff, and it's wearing thin with some of the other deputies. Dixon had many friends. Hanson didn't like having you and Robert Yuka looking over his shoulder. Now that you're gone, I think he feels a little more free to do things his own, heavy-handed way."

"How did he turn out to be such a tyrant?" Shane asked.

"The story I heard is that, because he was a small kid, he was bullied in school. His nickname was Shrimp. He didn't do well in class or sports and his dad considered him a wuss. So he made up his mind he would go into law enforcement and become somebody with power, so he could prove something to all the people who didn't believe in him. He enlisted in the Army and became a military policeman, which gave him the training to move into this line of work when he went back to civilian life."

"Are his parents still living?"

"I don't think so. He's an only child and I believe they're both deceased."

"Well," Shane said, "I appreciate that you're continuing to look into this. I'm still hoping we can get justice for Andy Dixon and Tim Wade."

At dinner that evening, Shane filled in Kat on what he had learned from Stoltzfus. "It's not enough to nail Hanson yet, but it adds to the pressure. I think Stoltzfus will continue to dig into the two murders."

"Good. I was afraid you were just going to drop it now that we're back here in Washington, and you're getting back to your normal routines."

"No, I'm going to stick with it as long as there's any chance at all we can get him," Shane said. "Guys like Hanson get overconfident. That's when they slip up."

Elizabeth gave Kat three nights to get a feel for the island and the inn. Then she booked tickets to Boise. "Let's go see Robert and Marie, and get you over to the ranch. We'll leave Shane here and the two of us will have a little getaway of our own."

"I'd like that," Kat said. "This is heaven on earth, but what you've said about the ranch really intrigues me, too."

The flight to Boise took barely an hour. As they circled over the city, Kat could see it was in a beautiful setting on a tree-lined river at the foot of the mountains, but much smaller than Seattle. The terrain here looked arid, quite different from Puget Sound. The plane landed and taxied to a stop at the terminal. By the time they reached baggage claim, Marie was waiting with Martin to greet them.

"Robert is off with the governor today, driving him somewhere, so I'm your welcoming committee." She gave Kat a big hug, and then did the same with Elizabeth. "It's just a short hop to the house," she said.

"I've flown so much and seen so much of the country in the last few days, I barely know where I am," Kat said, "but this is a beautiful place."

"I think so, too," Marie agreed. "It's a comfortable city and we'll take you past Boise State University while you're here, just in case you decide you want to go to school there someday," she smiled. "Bolivar's daughter, Dakota, goes to school at Boise State. I should clarify it's his secret daughter. It's a long story but Dakota's mother doesn't want it known she had an affair with Bolivar long ago."

The next morning the three women, and Martin, climbed into Marie's Toyota Highlander and left for Stanley via the mountain route, through Lowman. Marie carefully strapped Martin into a child safety seat in the center of the back seat. He seemed happy to have a view.

"This isn't the only way to Stanley," Marie said. "Some people prefer the less mountainous southern route across Camas Prairie and through Ketchum and Sun Valley. Snow often closes this route in the winter, so I like to take it in the summer when I can. We have some good scenery this way." Kat thought it would be hard to find any view in this state that wasn't out of this world.

Four hours later they rolled into Stanley. The sign said population 68. "That's the permanent population," Marie said. "In the summer, it's way bigger as hundreds of campers and outdoor enthusiasts converge on this area." She pointed out Mountain Village Café, where Bolivar's daughter waited tables in the summertime, and the Salmon River, better known as the River of No Return.

When she turned up the long driveway to the ranch, Kat leaned forward and unrolled the window. Sweet, fresh air poured into the car. Purple wildflowers lined the roadside, and horses grazed in lush pastures lined with white fences. They passed a barn and some tidy outbuildings. The ranch looked down on the valley and the little town of Stanley, with a view that stretched for miles.

Towering over everything, the snowy crags of the Sawtooth Mountains rose steeply to frame the valley. When they reached the ranch house, an older couple and a younger cowboy got up from Adirondack chairs on the deck.

Marie pulled the car to a stop and they opened the doors. The group from the house descended the steps to greet them. Marie noticed Brad walked more slowly now, with a cane. He had said over the phone he was unsteady after his latest round of treatments with a chemical that was known to cause neuropathy. She watched closely to see if he staggered sideways but couldn't catch him at it.

"Marie and Elizabeth, it's good to see you again," Brad declared. "I'll bet your passenger here in the sun dress is Kat Brown. We've heard a lot about you. I'm Brad Haraldsen and this is Irene, and our dapper friend here in the beret is Bolivar, our ranch foreman."

"Billy's friend," Kat said.

"Indeed he is," Brad replied.

Bolivar turned directly toward Kat, removed his beret and bowed, declaring: "It is an honor and pleasure to welcome you, Ms. Brown. I am at your service."

Kat shook his hand. "You're going to have to explain about Basques to me," she said, "because where I'm from, the local population is Amish."

"Oh believe me, that is a job I can cheerfully handle. Do you like horses?"

"I don't know. I don't have any experience."

"You'll be riding like Annie Oakley in no time." The image made Kat smile.

"Come on inside," Irene said, "and let me show you the ranch house. I fixed some lunch for us, since you've had a long drive. We can do some talking while we eat."

Kat hesitated and brought up the rear. Marie could see she was still taking in the view in all directions. The snowcapped mountains were so close she could reach out and touch them. Marie imagined that for Kat, this was a dream come true – like nothing she'd ever seen.

Irene showed Kat to her room so she could get settled. A plush quilt covered the log-style bed, which she assumed was aspen or cottonwood, two trees Elizabeth had pointed out on the drive from Boise. The bed looked so cozy, Kat flopped down on it just to try out the bounce. Watercolor paintings of horses and wildflowers hung from the walls, no doubt some of Irene's work. Cushy rugs begged for bare toes.

"If you decide you want to stay here a while, we might divide your time between helping Bolivar with the outside chores and helping Brad and me in the house," Irene said. "Sometimes it's hard for me to take a full day to drive Brad to his appointments in Boise, so I might have you do some of that."

"You're an artist," Kat said to Irene, her eye landing on watercolors on the wall."

"I'm addicted to painting. I've been doing it for years."

"And you're a writer?" Kat asked Brad. "I think that's what Shane told me."

"Yes, I was a journalist before I retired. That's how Shane and I got to know each other. I was looking for the truth about a journalist friend who died mysteriously, and Shane had a hunch it was murder. We teamed up to solve it and have been friends ever since."

"Maybe you can tell me about it on the drive. I don't know what I'm going to do with my life but I've been thinking I'd like to write."

"You won't be sorry. And when we drive, you can tell me all about Pursuit Lake and what's happening there. Shane told me a little about the deputy sheriff and the two murders."

Irene shooed the group to the table, where she had laid out a lunch of chicken salad and fresh-baked bread. "Just help yourselves."

Kat looked at Bolivar. "So what would my job be outside, with you?"

"Well, he said, we have two dozen horses to feed and groom, and they need exercise. I'll need to teach you to ride. We clean their stalls every day and spread fresh hay. Sometimes we repair fences and ranch equipment. And sometimes we just sneak off to have breakfast in town or go fishing in the mountains."

"So that's where you go when I can't find you!" Irene declared, laughing.

"If all I did was work, I'd be a boring fellow," Bolivar said. "Now that I might have a partner in crime, it'll be more fun than ever."

"Whatever you are, boring is not the word that comes to mind," Irene replied.

Kat was silent, her eyebrows furrowed as she weighed all this. After a moment she turned to Elizabeth. "I think I like it here. I still want to spend some time with you on Whidbey Island, but right now I'd like to try the cowboy life."

"We'll take good care of you," Irene said.

After lunch, Marie and Elizabeth said their goodbyes and started back to Boise. Kat and Bolivar headed down to the barn so Kat could get acquainted with the horses.

Harry Loush fumbled with the keys to his back door. He thought he had left the porch light on, but it was dark when he got back to the house after working late, and he could only feel for the right one, and try it in the lock. Sarah was babysitting for a professional couple and wouldn't be home till later.

In the darkness, something shifted in the shadows and Harry made out the profile of a figure in a dark hoodie. In an instant, the figure kicked the legs out from under Harry and he went down hard. Fists and feet followed, working their way up and down his ribs, knocking the wind out of him. Harry felt a rib crack. He tried to protect his head and groin, with little effect. The figure knew just how to place the blows.

"You've been talking out of turn," the figure said. "That has to stop. If it doesn't this is only the beginning. Next time we'll come for Sarah." The figure walked away and Harry lay there for several minutes, fighting for breath. He hurt all over, and bled from cuts on his head and face.

After while, he pulled himself into a crouch, and later still he struggled to his feet. He didn't know how long he had been on the ground, but he didn't want Sarah to find him like this. He fumbled some more for the key, shaking so hard now he could barely hold it in his hand. Finally, he found the lock and opened the door. He sent straight to the bathroom and started to clean himself up.

On the steps of the county courthouse, Peter Stoltzfus stood before the microphone. A crowd of some 150 sheriff's deputies, city police, state patrol, citizens and news reporters looked on. Given the sensational nature of what they knew was coming, statewide media also showed up.

"Today, I am announcing my candidacy for sheriff," Stoltzfus said. *"I do this after sober reflection, mindful that many of my fellow citizens are not happy with the lone candidate running on the ballot to replace Sheriff Andy Dixon.*

"Serious questions have arisen about the candidate's role in the death of the sheriff and also of the chief suspect, a young man named Timothy Wade. I was part of the raid in which Wade died, and don't think his death was necessary. We'll know more about that when we get the findings of the official inquiry. Many of my fellow officers join me in this conclusion. In light of all this, I felt I had no choice but to offer the citizens of our county an alternative, one who shares the philosophy and approach of our late sheriff. If you feel the same, I ask for your vote."

"Did you get the news?" Aunt Bonnie asked when she telephoned Shane at the inn. "Stoltzfus is running for sheriff. He made a big announcement today on the steps of the courthouse, in front of a row of American flags, and it's front page news all over the state, given the controversy over Leland Hanson."

"That's phenomenal," Shane said. "That changes everything. Stoltzfus didn't say a word to me about it, but I'm proud of him."

"Yes, and there's more. Someone beat up Harry Loush the other night when he returned to his house after dark."

"Is he okay?"

"He will be, but he's hurting. Some of Harry's friends are demonstrating with signs today in front of the sheriff's office. They're blaming Hanson."

"Wow, that's going to be a photo op for the state media."

Shane was struck by the irony that Hanson was running for election as the tough guy who solved the sheriff's murder. But before this was over, Stoltzfus might get the credit as the low-key deputy who solved it. The more Hanson tried to put a lid on things, the more the lid blew off. The Stoltzfus announcement was the crowning touch.

Leland Hanson poured himself a vodka neat and drained the glass down his throat. The liquid burned and he poured another. He wasn't sure how long he'd been sitting at the rough pine table, nor how many drinks he'd had, but he was dizzy and light-headed – close to passing out. Right now he just wanted to numb himself – drink himself unconscious or to sleep. The collection of empty bottles at his feet suggested he was close to his goal.

He'd owned the cabin north of Foreston for eight years. It was in a copse of trees at the end of a dirt road, behind a locked wooden gate, four miles off the highway.

No one else knew about it, and it's where he came when he needed to get away and think. After pulling his car through the gate, he stopped on the other side and swung it shut behind him, snapping the padlock. Then he got back into his cruiser and continued up the overgrown road.

The one-room cabin would be cozy under normal circumstances — a single bed, a table with two chairs, a pot-bellied stove, and a small sink that passed for the kitchen. In the corner, behind a curtain, was the toilet. There was no hot water. No shower. No cell service. He kept the cabin stocked with a few cans of stew to heat on a one-burner gas stove, and plenty of alcohol.

On the table next to the now-empty vodka bottle sat Hanson's Glock pistol. From time to time he picked it up to inspect it, then put it down again.

He didn't know how things could be worse. A rumor had started — he didn't know where — that he'd murdered the sheriff and Tim Wade. It had spread through the county and especially his own department, and he was powerless to stop it. He couldn't fathom why people were so eager to believe an unproven rumor. The contempt of his fellow officers was palpable.

He pushed back his chair and took a step toward the nearby bed. His legs folded beneath him and he fell forward, landing face down. He remembered nothing more.

When Shane reached Stoltzfus by phone that evening, they had a lot to discuss. "This might be a good time for you and Robert Yuka to show your faces in Crossington again," Stoltzfus said. "I think it might really shake up Hanson, after everything else that's happened this week. He's embattled on every front now, not talking with anyone because he doesn't trust anyone. His campaign is completely off balance. All his media coverage is negative and he has pulled his ads. People are tearing down his yard signs. The wall of silence about the internal investigation into Wade's death has broken."

Shane agreed it was the right time to let Hanson see them again. Their presence in Crossington might be just the touch needed to push Hanson into a crisis. As soon as he put down the phone, he dialed Robert in Boise.

"I'll ask the governor for a few more days off," Robert said. "He knows we're on the trail of a murderer and getting close. In fact it's such a big story he even read an article about it in the local newspaper here."

"I'll get some time off, too. We'll meet in Syracuse and rent a car. I think we're close to breaking this case."

In Crossington, Shane and Robert checked into an upstairs room in the Snooze Inn, a budget motel on the outskirts of town. Stoltzfus had recommended it as the place police stayed when in town on business. Management treated police well and gave them a fifteen percent discount on the room and meals.

The room was clean but outdated, with twin queen beds topped by threadbare bedspreads. On the dresser sat a big, old-fashioned, boxy TV.

Shane went to the window, opened the drapes and looked at the view, which was the parking lot. He could see their car and he liked that – always liked being able to see where he was parked. Only a handful of cars were scattered across the lot, which Shane took as a sign that their motel should be quiet tonight. The clerk had told them the rooms on either side were vacant and he'd try to keep them that way unless they got a late surge of guests. A long hallway ran the length of the second floor outside their door.

They opened their suitcases and started unpacking. A light rap on the door told them that Stoltzfus had arrived. He greeted them with the news that Hanson was taking some time off to reassess his campaign. "Unfortunately, no one knows where he is."

On that note the three law officers left for the Bucky Beaver Café next door to discuss strategy over dinner. Shane figured it must be a good place to eat because several police cars were parked out front – city police, sheriff and state patrol.

They had just settled into a booth when their perky waitress appeared with coffee and menus. "Evening, Sarge," she greeted Stoltzfus. "Gentlemen." All three men turned their cups right-side up and she filled them from a full carafe. "Do you need some time to think or are you ready to order?" Shane could tell this was a place where most people were in a hurry and didn't need a menu.

"What's good here?" Shane asked.

"I'm going to have the Police Special," Stoltzfus said.

"Make that two," Robert added.

"Three," Shane chimed in. He saw the waitress scribble "PSx3" on her pad as she got on her way. Shane turned to Stoltzfus and asked, "What's the Police Special?"

"Chicken fried steak with mashed potatoes and gravy."

"Does that come with anything green?"

"You can get a side of canned green beans if you ask. Most people don't."

"Don't say a word to Marie about what we had for dinner tonight," Robert asked Shane. "She's trying to make me eat healthy."

"Same here," Shane remarked.

Stoltzfus laughed. "I eat like this all the time. The Beaver is essentially the police café."

"Every town has one," Robert said. The conversation went silent for a moment.

"So here we go again," Shane said. "First the sheriff disappears. Now, his deputy. What do you make of it?"

"I think Hanson is severely depressed," Stoltzfus said. "My guess is that he's contemplating suicide. Wish I could say I feel bad about that, but honestly I don't. If it happens, it happens. It'll make things simpler from a trial standpoint."

"If that's true, our presence here may be the last straw," Robert said. "But how are we going to let him see us if he isn't around?"

"We can always call a press conference for the newspaper and radio station, and give them an interview. One way or another, he will find out fast."

Woodpile

Kat watched the blue digits on the clock flip ahead to 5:00. She was already wide-awake under the warm comforter, wishing she could just stay there. But she willed herself to throw back the bedcovering and swing her legs to the floor. She wanted to have breakfast and be ready to leave by 6 a.m. for Brad's cancer treatment in Boise.

In her previous life as a homeless kid in the woods she had not done much driving, but she had a driver's license and Irene had given her several lessons in Brad's Jeep Cherokee since she arrived at the ranch. She knew this day of being Brad's driver was an important chance to prove herself to Brad and Irene, and show them they could trust her. Kat thought the driving lessons had gone well, and Irene complimented her on her steadiness behind the wheel.

Kat was just finishing her oatmeal and fruit when Brad came into the kitchen. He popped two slices of bread into the toaster, poured a cup of black coffee from the carafe, and selected a banana.

They planned to take the mountain route that Marie liked. Traffic would be light and it was a straight shot into Boise that avoided freeway traffic. Brad said he didn't know how many hours his appointment would take, but probably four or five. With travel time it would be a twelve-hour day, maybe more. Brad needed to have labs drawn first. His oncologist would see the results forty-five minutes later and decide whether to go ahead with treatment.

Irene gave them both a hug, wished them a safe drive and a good day, and they were on their way. They descended the winding driveway from the ranch to the highway and turned west. Kat was struck by the contrast between this idyllic, natural setting and the highly artificial world of cancer care. A moment later the little village of Stanley fell away in Kat's rear view mirror and they were in the wilderness.

She wondered what went through Brad's mind on treatment day.

"What are these treatments like?" Kat asked. "I don't know anything about chemotherapy except for the stories that people suffer nausea and feel terrible afterwards," she said.

"Nausea hasn't been an issue for me," Brad replied. "I don't feel especially bad after a treatment, but I'm terribly sleepy. They give me pre-meds that affect me in various ways and make it difficult to drive. I receive a pretty stiff dose of prednisone and Benadryl, and an anti-nausea drug that lasts several days. The Benadryl, especially, makes me profoundly sleepy but the prednisone wants to keep me awake. So it wouldn't be a good idea for me to attempt a four-hour drive after sitting in the chair and getting filled full of medicines."

"What is it like, knowing you have cancer? Just hearing that word – it must be terrifying."

"It's a shock the first time you hear it, but there are really two parts to the experience," Brad replied. "You get treated for the symptoms, so you focus on that. For me the worst symptoms so far have been fever and chills. I had night sweats until I'd received several treatments of the drug.

"Eventually those symptoms ended, making my life much better. But I've also had a furious itch, which, I understand, is called The Hodgkin's Itch. It's so deep there's nothing you can do to stop it. This also has gotten better, thank goodness. Mostly now I just suffer from profound fatigue and apathy, not really having the ambition to do much but look out the window."

"I can't imagine it," Kat said, "when you're used to being active, and using your mind to write."

"Nobody really can. You look like a normal person, and people think you are, but you aren't. In any case, that's the 'symptom' piece. I wanted to tell you also about the psychological piece. Once you get cancer, you pretty much know it's going to kill you. It'll be cancer or some complication of it, such as pneumonia. So you no longer think of your life as an endless story, where there's always tomorrow if you waste today or spend months feeling sorry for yourself. You start thinking about what you've done today, what you've done with your life, and what your legacy will be. Nobody wants to die, but on the other hand it's nice to have a little time to put the finishing touches on your life."

"Is there a chance these treatments will push the cancer into remission?"

"I suppose there's always a chance, but not a big one. Since this is a stage four recurrence of the lymphoma I had a few years ago, it's quite serious. The drug I'm taking definitely is shrinking my Hodgkin's tumors, so that's good. With each treatment I feel stronger and clearer headed. But when the drug stops working, then the cancer will come back, and that's bad. So I look at it as buying some time. I've learned how precious time is to all of us, because we only get so much of it. But you're lucky. You've got your whole life ahead of you – many good years – so I hope we can help you get a new start out here in Idaho."

"I hope so, too. I am grateful to all of you for taking a chance on me."

Brad asked Kat how Robert, Marie and Shane had become so involved in the murders at Pursuit Lake. Kat told him it all started when she broke into the lodge, thinking it was empty, but it turned out Shane and Elizabeth were there. Shane chased her off but she snuck back two additional times for different reasons, which eventually led to Marie capturing her.

Kat said she personally witnessed Tim Wade dumping the sheriff's body into the lake, though at the time she didn't know either of their identities. She introduced Shane to some Amish kids she knew, Harry and Sarah, who were much closer witnesses to what happened that night, and who also happened to be Tim's housemates. Harry told her Tim confided that the deputy had shot the sheriff in their house and blackmailed Tim into disposing of the body. Then the deputy organized a raid to silence Tim.

"Wow, that's a tough one for Shane because there is no living witness to dispute the deputy's account," Brad said.

"True, but it's widely known in the community that the sheriff and deputy couldn't stand each other. A witness in the sheriff's department said they argued heatedly the day of the sheriff's disappearance. Tim's account is believable, and on top of that the deputy is widely disliked for his tough guy style of policing."

"Do you wish you were back there?" Brad asked.

Kat drew a sharp breath. "Not for a moment!" Then she added, "Well maybe just long enough to see how this ends. I had to leave my Mom, but it wasn't hard. She's an alcoholic who's made a wreck of her life, and doesn't want to get better. So there's nothing I can do to help her."

"That's hard," Brad said. "I can't imagine how you feel, knowing what your mom has lost because of the alcohol. Look at the price she has paid for it – driving her own daughter out of her life."

A tear rolled down Kat's face and she wiped it away with the back of her hand, hoping Brad didn't see.

At the hospital, Kat parked in the underground garage and rode the elevator with Brad up to the oncology department. She wondered if hospitals were all like this, cold and impersonal, with their polished floors. She'd never been inside one since she was born.

The waiting room was full of people, mostly older but with some younger patients as well. She had no idea infusion therapy was such a big part of medical care. This was where many people reached the end, she knew. Some people gained a second chance, a few more years; others essentially had no hope. Knowing Brad would be here for several hours today, she decided to do some walking in the neighborhood and get lunch while he met with his doctor.

Brad and Kat both carried cell phones so he could call if he needed her back sooner. Kat dialed Irene at the ranch to let her know they had reached the hospital and everything was fine.

Four hours later, Kat got the call. She pulled the Cherokee around to the loading zone. Brad walked out the front entrance with the assistance of a nurse, who handed him off to Kat. "I'm fine but a little unsteady. I might start walking sideways, so I'll hang onto your arm so I don't fall over."

Kat loaded him into the passenger seat, and Brad adjusted it into the reclined position. "I'll probably do some sleeping on the way home," Brad told her.

"Just relax and close your eyes," she said. "I'll try to avoid the bumps, and when you wake up from your nap, we should be coming up the driveway to the ranch house." She pulled smoothly away from the curb, conscious this was an important assignment, one of the best things she'd done in her life. She liked the way this was working out. For the first time in memory, she was doing something important for someone else.

Moments later they were leaving Boise behind and climbing into the mountains, past Lucky Peak Reservoir and the last pockets of population. It was a peaceful evening for the long drive home; she was looking forward to it. Kat snuck a glance at Brad and saw that his eyes were closed. She was alone with her thoughts.

She went back in time. Warm memories washed over her as she relived the day she started kindergarten with her new dress and lunchbox. She could still name most of her goofy classmates. She took a rug to school for naptime, but nobody slept. She stifled a giggle when she remembered Byron, the boy who always unrolled his rug next to hers and made her laugh. The teacher separated them but he made faces at her from across the room. Where was he now?

Her mom was young and beautiful in those days, working in an office in Crossington and coming home every night to the trailer, where her dad worked hard to clear the land and plant their garden. He talked of his big plans for their farm. They would sit on the sofa and relax before dinner with a beer – one or two, not many – and her mom would sink into his arms and they'd flirt. It was a happy time. Sometimes Kat joined them on the sofa in one big pile of bodies.

Both her mom and dad came to school and met the teacher. "Kat is a pleasure to have in class," the teacher said. "She gets an 'A' in citizenship. She is thoughtful and kind to others and everyone likes her. She works hard and always learns her lessons."

Soon the teacher started reading to the class and Kat got her first book – Dick and Jane. She was soon hooked on reading, a love that only grew as she discovered the faraway places she could go in the pages of books.

At home, something was changing so gradually she could barely see it. Her mom worked later. Her dad drank more. Sometimes nobody made dinner. Kat started scrounging for her own lunch.

When her parents were together, they yelled at each other. Kat hoped it was a phase, something that would pass, but it got worse. One day her dad loaded his truck and said, "That's it." He gave Kat a hug and drove out of their lives forever. She was devastated.

Her mom drank more and grew distant. She lost her job in Crossington. Her health declined as she ate junk food and gained weight. She got angry at Kat for no reason and punished her arbitrarily. There was nothing to eat. Her mom brought men home from the tavern. Kat skipped class, shunned the men and then simply left to live in the woods. By the time she was sixteen she did like her dad, left home and never went back.

She shivered and returned to the present. There was nothing for her in those memories. Her life was here and now. She'd been driving for hours. The evening was just approaching sunset as the Cherokee climbed the last big mountain pass on the way into Stanley. Brad was still sleeping in the passenger seat, and Kat had been focused on driving smoothly and consistently.

As the highway started its climb to Banner Summit, at more than seven thousand feet, Kat found herself behind an old pickup truck loaded high with firewood. She slowed to forty, thirty, then twenty-five miles per hour. The truck was laboring to climb the hill.

It would be nice to get around this decrepit rig that looked like an accident waiting to happen, but there were no good places to pass, and Kat's overriding goal was to get Brad home safely. So she gritted her teeth, dropped back hundreds of feet, and matched the truck's speed. They'd start down the other side pretty soon and then the truck would go faster. The truck was hugging the centerline, which made her nervous. On the pavement's outer edge, next to the guardrail, the terrain fell away a thousand feet to the valley floor.

When things went to hell, it happened so fast she barely saw it. An oncoming truck came around a curve too tight and too fast, and the pickup driver swerved sharply right to avoid a collision. Both vehicles fishtailed as the drivers fought for control. Firewood tumbled from the pickup and bounced end-over-end down the highway toward her.

The oncoming truck shot past her on the left, just missing her car as the driver finally regained some control. The old pickup braked and pulled over to the shoulder. Kat slowed smoothly and did the same, turning onto the shoulder a safe distance from the firewood, her heart pounding.

She turned on her emergency flashers. The driver of the oncoming truck that caused it all was long gone down the mountain.

Brad stirred from his sleep and sat up. "What's happening?" he asked.

"Quite a bit," Kat said. "Two trucks ahead of us nearly hit each other and one of them lost a load of firewood, but I was staying well back."

"Thank god," Brad said.

"I don't like to tailgate, especially when I'm behind a load like that," Kat said, pointing to the firewood all over the highway. "Life is too short." Then she excused herself to go meet the driver and help him gather up his load from the highway.

A throbbing headache awoke Hanson. He didn't know how long he'd been lying on the floor. It must be afternoon, he assumed from the angle of the light outside. He'd apparently fallen and struck his head on a corner post of the bed, judging by the blood on the post, and passed out. He sat up slowly and reached with his hand to check for a cut. Crusty blood covered his forehead and nose. He took a moment to inspect the rest of himself for injuries. Aside from bruises on his arms and ribs, he seemed okay, but the hangover was excruciating.

He was still trying to decide if he had the courage to do what he'd come here to do. He wondered what people were saying about him in Crossington. Carefully, he stood up, bracing himself with a hand on the bed as he made sure he wasn't going to fall again. He'd brought a little transistor radio with him to use in checking the news, and was curious now to see what they were saying.

At the sheriff's office, Shane and Robert sat on the edge of desks with other deputies and state patrol officers who crowded the room. Stoltzfus stood in the front of the room and addressed the group.

"Most of you know Shane Lindstrom and Robert Yuka, visiting officers from Washington and Idaho." He nodded to the two men. "They helped identify Hanson as a suspect in murdering Andy Dixon, as well as fingering him for having arranged the death of the only witness who could implicate Hanson, Tim Wade. I asked them back to help us put pressure on Hanson to turn himself in and answer some questions."

"But in the meanwhile," Stoltzfus continued, "Hanson has disappeared and we don't know if he's on the run or suicidal. So we need to get out and find him as soon as we can."

The memory was vivid, just another variation of others Hanson had relived over the years growing up. The diminutive seventh-grader with the white, knobby legs and horn-rimmed glasses stood by the wall of the school gymnasium as his classmates chose up sides to play dodge ball. One by one, the taller and more athletic kids chose one-another for team one or team two. When both teams were finished with their selections, Lee was still standing, by himself, against the wall. He hated team activities.

His physical education teacher, a macho ex-marine with a crew cut, said, "Over here, Lee. You'll be the ball boy. If somebody loses a ball into the stands, your job is to chase it down and pass it back to the team that lost it."

It was humiliating.

The teacher, Mr. Thrasher, blew his whistle and the two teams commenced play. Then Thrasher stepped outside for a Camel. The irony of this was not lost on Hanson. More than one of his teachers was a role model for the opposite personal habits of what they taught. Hanson hated the hypocrisy. He wanted to report these teachers, but no one in a position of authority cared in the least.

Within moments, a ball hit one of the players on the shoulder and bounced far up into the bleachers, out of sight and out of reach.

"Ball boy! Ball boy!" the teams chanted. "Hurry up, ball boy."

Lee ran up the steps two at a time, searching frantically underneath and behind benches. The ball had bounced several times and vanished in the maze of seating twenty or thirty rows up into the stands. He got down on his hands and knees, trying to see in the shadows below the benches. Had it fallen through an opening to the floor twenty feet below? The chanting from the teams grew louder and more impatient. Finally, he found the ball and tossed it back to the floor, ending the uproar.

Mr. Thrasher, having finished his smoke and stubbed out the butt, came back into the gym, asking what the hell the yelling was about. "Your ball boy, here, made us all stand around while he took several minutes to retrieve the ball from the bleachers," said the captain of the football team, who was also a prominent Christian in the student body.

"Is that true, Lee?" the teacher asked. "Let's see some hustle, ok?"

Hanson hated everything about high school. All the popular kids belonged to cliques. The good-looking girls worshipped the athletes as if they were gods. The athletes were doted on by coaches and fawned over by classmates. He had watched overweight coaches pull the best athletes out of class for some pet project that had nothing to do with learning. They made no effort to reach out and include people like him in anything fun. He was invisible and always would be. He had carried the resentment within him for years.

To go up against a self-professed Christian was even harder. Hanson knew that in a week or two, Thrasher would send him out to the playground with a pail to pick up cigarette butts, all Camels. He wondered what would happen if the Christian complained about a coach or teacher. They'd listen, he was pretty sure. Everything in life was rigged.

Hanson took a swig of vodka from the bottle. What was happening to him now just seemed like an extension of high school, with the disintegration of his campaign for sheriff. He switched on the transistor radio for the local news.

Authorities said today that an internal inquiry into a sheriff's raid at Pursuit Lake found that murder suspect Timothy Wade died as the result of an unlawful order issued by the acting head of the department, chief deputy Leland Hanson. It's a devastating indictment of the once leading candidate for sheriff, to succeed Andy Dixon.

The investigation found Wade had not resisted arrest, as originally reported, but was shot multiple times by officers when he sat up in bed, unarmed. The only firearm in the room, a double-barreled shotgun, was several feet away, propped against the wall, according to officers who were present in the room. It was later determined that someone had moved the shotgun to the bed in an apparent attempt to make it look like Wade had been a threat to the arresting officers.

Meanwhile, two law officers from out-of-state who helped break the case are back in Crossington this week to assist local authorities and question officer Hanson. They are detective Shane Lindstrom from Washington and Idaho State Trooper Robert Yuka, of Boise.

The deputy, the first candidate to declare for sheriff, abruptly announced yesterday he was taking a break from his campaign and has not been seen since.

Hanson was furious. He blamed Lindstrom and Yuka for every bit of this. He could feel their unseen hand directing every development in the complete collapse of his plans.

The question weighing on him now was whether, in some careless moment, he had ever told anyone, at any time, about this getaway cabin in the woods outside Foreston. He was pretty sure he hadn't. But if he had, it was only a matter of time till Lindstrom and Yuka found out and came looking for him. He wanted some time to work out what he was going to do.

"Does he own any secondary real estate around here?" Shane asked Stoltzfus as they huddled to plan their next move. "I'm thinking of a hunting cabin or vacation place – somewhere he could drop out of sight for a while."

"Not that I ever heard of," Stoltzfus said. "He wasn't one to share a whole lot about his private life."

"It's sad," Robert added. "Underneath the bluster, he's a pathetic figure. He has to be a lonely guy. He just doesn't have any friends, it seems. You wonder how he got that way."

"Well, let's check county property tax files," Shane said. "Maybe we'll turn up his name paying taxes on an additional property, and that would give us a place to start."

Back at the ranch in Stanley, Brad was praising Kat as they sat together at lunch with Irene. "You really showed me something on that drive back from Boise," he said. "You showed judgment and maturity beyond your years."

Kat's face turned red. "Maybe it's all the practice I got prowling cabins. I learned to be cautious, always thinking ahead to what could go wrong."

"Caution makes a good driver – concentrating on the road and thinking ahead. I won't hesitate for a moment to ride with you next time."

Kat was pleased. Now, she just needed to impress Bolivar this afternoon. He'd been showing her how to slip an apple to a horse and make soothing sweet talk while she saddled it. "Your tone of voice means everything to the horse," he said. "Be reassuring, and kind. The biggest thing is to adjust the straps snugly so the saddle doesn't flip upside down and dump you in the dirt when you attempt to get on."

Yesterday he'd gotten her up on top of a mare named Sugar Plum just to sit there for a few minutes. Kat wasn't used to being so high off the ground, at the mercy of a large animal that could flick her off like a pest if she didn't establish rapport and gently show it she was in charge. "She has a sweet disposition," Bolivar said, "so I think this is a good horse for your first ride." Kat and Bolivar hadn't ridden together yet, but she had a feeling it would happen today. She kept the image of Annie Oakley in her mind.

She finished her lunch, pocketed an apple, and headed for the corral. Bolivar met her outside the barn and tossed her a white cowboy hat.

"What's this?" she asked.

"Your hat."

"Seriously."

"Absolutely. You have to look the part, Miss Katarina," Bolivar said. "Black for me; white for you. That way, we'll keep our hats straight. Now, let's get out there on the trail."

"Where are we going?"

"Up on that ridge, Annie Oakley," he said, pointing. "There's a nice view of the ranch and the whole valley from up that way."

In hindsight, Hanson knew his impulsive decision to murder the sheriff had been a mistake. He understood this now, even though it seemed, at the time, like an opportunity that had fallen into his lap, and that he might not get again. The sheriff was going to fire him. If he had waited for that to happen, it would have been the end of his career. The rumspringa house was the perfect place to frame a well-known troublemaker. Andy Dixon had done him a huge favor by going there to talk with Tim Wade.

Hanson had covered his tracks credibly by implicating Wade, but he could see he had pushed his luck too far by eliminating him as a witness with the raid. Wade had already told Harry Loush what actually happened, and this had gotten back to Shane Lindstrom. He, in turn, had found someone within the department whose conscience was troubling him, and it had all steamrolled from there.

Hanson reached for the bottle. The Glock pistol still sat on the table in front of him. He put down the bottle and picked up the pistol. He flipped off the safety and held the gun up to his head, to his temple and to his mouth. Then he put it down and reached for the bottle again.

What was the point? Life was just a series of disappointments, unless you were Andy Dixon or Shane Lindstrom. Life for them was charmed – everyone loved them. Hanson had never had a girlfriend, nor any friends at all except a few misfits and outcasts like him. He imagined Lindstrom had had his choice of women. He was probably a big frat man in college. Hanson had limped through high school with C's and D's, and barely kept his head above water in community college, where he took criminal justice courses. He had never been able to study. When his college grades fell short, he enlisted in the Army, going into the military police specialty.

The sheriff's department was the one place he fit in. His methods were harsh but he got respect. No one understood how important that was to him.

Now, he knew, without an iota of doubt, what would come next – trial and prison for the breach of procedure that led to Tim Wade's death, and maybe even the murder of Andy Dixon. Both would be unbearable.

Irene watched the two riders trot their horses up the trail to the brow of the hill, hooves kicking up swirls of dust. Leading the way was Bolivar in his trademark black hat, looking like the Cisco Kid. Kat followed in a white hat, her lean figure an extension of the horse she was riding. He was already calling her Annie Oakley at dinner. Irene smiled proudly as she watched Kat sit tall in the saddle, handling her horse with poise and confidence. Bolivar had taught her well and no doubt was showing off his student where Irene and Brad could watch. Kat was learning the ranch life fast.

Irene had enjoyed the view from that overlook a thousand times – verdant, green pastures, purple Camas wildflowers, willows and aspens, and the Salmon River winding its way toward the sea. The valley and its backdrop of jagged, snowcapped peaks never failed to enchant her. She envied Kat, seeing it for the first time from the back of Sugar Plum. Her heart would be full.

Elizabeth and Marie were right about Kat – she was a bright and responsible woman, not what one might expect of a cabin prowler and feral daughter of a trailer-trash, alcoholic mother. Kat needed and deserved a new life, far from the dead end of home, and this ranch was like a confidence course for adulthood. Irene wished Elizabeth could share this moment, since she had approached them with the idea of offering Kat a fresh start.

Brad joined Irene at the window and put his arm around her, and watched. Irene was glad she and Brad shared the same ideas about helping people turn their lives around.

"You know," he said, "you think a lot about your life when you get down toward the end. Everyone leaves a legacy. You want yours to be positive. I look at Kat out there, and at our friends Shane and Elizabeth, and think these are the best things I've done in my life. Nothing else comes close."

"Here it is," Stoltzfus said as he brought up Hanson's property tax file on the computer. Shane and Robert gathered behind him and looked over his shoulder. "This is almost too easy. He owns a small cabin on the outskirts of Foreston, several miles up a private road."

"Then that's where I'd start," Shane said. "It sounds like a perfect hideout. Do you feel like a drive?"

The three officers selected a couple of additional firearms from the department's gun safe – a rifle for Robert and an assault weapon for Stoltzfus, along with a supply of ammunition. Shane had his Glock. They also took a set of long-handled bolt cutters and a megaphone, in case they might need to hail Hanson from a distance. Shane wondered if Hanson might be waiting for them, either with intent to kill them in an ambush, or to commit suicide-by-cop. He was obviously in a highly emotional state, capable of anything.

At the turnoff to Hanson's property, the padlocked gate was their first obstacle. Stoltzfus snapped off the padlock with the bolt cutters and they started up the narrow, earthen drive. It was obvious that another car had been there recently because it had left clear tire prints.

They were still half-a-mile away when they smelled the smoke.

"That's pretty acrid and it doesn't smell like vegetation," Robert said. "It's black – which suggests building materials. If it were somebody burning trees and brush full of moisture it would be white."

"I have a bad feeling," Shane commented.

The cabin, when they reached it, was just a smoldering foundation, with collapsed walls and roof. The grass around it had burned itself black in a perimeter of several feet before the flames died out. The officers got out of their car, weapons ready, and fanned out to the nearest cover in a crouching stance in case Hanson was hiding nearby in the woods. But after a brief check of their surroundings, they concluded he was nowhere around.

173

"Do you think he set the fire and then took his own life?" Stoltzfus asked.

"If he did, we should find some remains of his body in the embers," Shane said, "but that won't be easy." Portions of the foundation and floor were still burning, and most of it was too hot to check closely. The roof had fallen on top of the floor. They took several minutes to poke at what they could reach without equipment to move the collapsed roof.

"What's this?" Stoltzfus asked, prodding at a shiny glass pile with his shoe.

"Vodka bottles," Robert declared. "Empties."

"How do you know they weren't full when the fire started?"

"The caps are all missing, and they didn't get hot and explode. They're still intact. Someone was doing some serious drinking."

"I don't find anything and I don't smell flesh," Shane said. "His body could be under all this smoldering debris but it'll take a proper investigation to look for it and rule his death in or out. I'm inclined to think he burned down the cabin and then drove away."

"There's no sign of his car," Robert added. "We know there are tire tracks coming up the driveway. He probably drove here in his department cruiser and left the same way as well."

Stoltzfus scowled. "So he's out there somewhere with his service pistol, planning his next move, perhaps feeling more cornered and more threatened than ever."

"That's how it looks," Shane said. "We missed him by an hour, give or take. But let's get a forensic team up here to go through the ashes, just in case he's under all this debris."

The sign, in large red-and-black letters, read EZ Guns. It dominated the façade of the cinder block building with bars on its windows and doors. The man in black sat in his car outside the strip mall on the outskirts of town and watched customers come and go. He sat in the passenger seat, not the driver's seat. It was an old police trick. No one thinks twice about a passenger sitting in a car, waiting and watching. But if they see someone sitting in the driver's seat for hours, it attracts suspicion.

The large windows facing the mall parking lot gave the man a view of the store's entire interior, illuminated as if on TV by fluorescent fixtures in the ceiling. He counted two employees, both wearing side arms. The customer count at any given time varied between one and three. Right now there were zero. Now was the time to make his move.

Before leaving his cabin and setting fire to it, Hanson had changed from his deputy's uniform to black sweats and a black hoodie. He pulled up the hood, put on some dark glasses, opened his car door and crossed the parking lot to the gun store. With one last look around the parking lot for witnesses, he pulled his Glock from his pocket, stepped inside the store, flipped the lock closed behind him and yelled: "Freeze! Both of you! Get on the floor now, hands above your heads. Do not reach for your guns if you want to live."

He stepped to the back of the first employee, planted his knee on the employee's lower back, removed the gun from his belt, and slipped a plastic zip tie around his hands. He frisked his pant legs for a hidden Derringer, and found none. Then he repeated the process with the second. He knew that gun store employees often carry a second weapon in case a robber disarms them of their primary gun.

"Do not move," he ordered. "I have nothing to lose, but you have the rest of your lives to look forward to. You can just bill this to insurance and everyone will be happy."

"Now, where's the key to this cabinet?" he asked, pointing to a display case of automatic weapons.

"In the till," employee number one replied.

Hanson rang open the till and found the key in the cash drawer. He unlocked the cabinet and selected an Uzi submachine gun and a dozen clips of ammunition. Then he went down the line and chose two other rapid-fire weapons, and the ammunition to go with them.

"I'm going to walk out that door now," Hanson said, "but I'm not going far. I'll have my eye on this store for a while, so don't either of you stand up and make me ruin your day. Just lie there and be grateful you have your whole lives ahead of you."

With the search heating up for Hanson, the last thing anyone needed was the distraction of another major crime, Shane thought.

A lone robber had entered a gun store on the outskirts of town, subdued the employees and gotten away with several automatic weapons. It was a serious and urgent matter requiring the full response of the department.

Given the type of weapons taken, it seemed likely the gunman had plans for them, and the department did not want to find out the hard way what those plans were.

For Robert and Shane, the big question was whether the gunman might have been Hanson. The employees described a shorter individual with a slight build, who concealed his identity in dark clothing, a hoodie and sunglasses. They said he seemed nervous, but that's true of most people when robbing a store where the employees are armed. He seemed to know what he wanted and what he was doing. He carried zip ties and knew how to use them quickly and efficiently. This could be Hanson but it could be a lot of other people, too.

It was yet another illustration of the alienation so many American men and boys feel, Shane thought. In a culture where males felt powerless and ineffectual, it didn't surprise him that many were angry and frustrated. As society demanded more justice for women and minorities, and made advances in pay, Shane had seen that some men felt the system was stacked against them. The loss of privilege can feel like persecution. Shane knew Hanson had been bullied mercilessly in school, called Shrimp, and the effects of that ridicule can last a lifetime. With the rise of social media, bullying had never been easier.

So it's not surprising, he thought, that guns seem like the last recourse for some men to get respect and leave their mark on the world. Easy availability of firearms, especially high-powered automatic weapons, made it worse. One individual with a weapon like that can kill a lot of people before he's stopped, Shane knew. Even a schoolboy can do it – a fleeting chance at immortality in the newspapers and history books.

Then there were the paramilitary and nationalist militias, a growing threat to police and civil society everywhere.

The problem was exacerbated by the large numbers of young veterans returning from the Middle East, where they had learned to fight and kill, to turn off their feelings or numb them to unspeakable horrors, but who were expected to assimilate back into mainstream society as if everything in their lives were wholesome and normal.

Every generation has its war, and every war exacts a price back home in ways that aren't always recognized at first. He wondered where this robber fit on that spectrum. He wagered this guy was a veteran, but it was possible his problem was drugs. Police dealt with these scenarios all the time.

Desperation

Shane dialed the phone and listened to it ring several times. "Haraldsen Ranch," Irene answered.

"Hi Irene," he began. "I thought I should check-in and ask how everything's going with you, and Brad, and Bolivar, and Kat."

"Unbelievably well," Irene said.

"You don't want to hedge that answer a little more?"

"Kat is doing famously. She impressed the heck out of Brad on the drive home yesterday from a long day in Boise."

"What happened?"

"By sheer good judgment, she avoided what could have been a serious accident on Banner Pass. The truck ahead of her lost a load of firewood but Kat was holding well back and was able to avoid the mess in the road and stop the car smoothly. Brad can't say enough good things about her."

"Wonderful."

"They are suddenly the best of buddies. I think she is his new fulltime driver. It's nice because these trips give her a few hours to look around Boise, maybe soak up some of the ambience of Boise State University."

"And how's Brad feeling physically?"

"About the same. The treatments are tamping down symptoms but he knows it's just temporary. He's fatigued all the time, and he's preparing himself psychologically for what we all know is ahead."

"I hope you're thinking ahead as well."

"I am," Irene said, "though I know you can never truly prepare. Of course I'm lucky to have Kat and Bolivar here to prop me up when I need it."

"And Bolivar? How is he?"

"Well, you can imagine he loves his new student. He has already taught Kat to ride as if she'd been performing in competitions for years. You should see her – tall and confident in the saddle. Bolivar calls her Annie Oakley, and I have to admit, the name fits. She's not afraid of hard work, either, pitching hay in the stalls."

"Is Kat anywhere nearby right now?" Shane asked. "I should give her a little update on what Robert and I are doing here. We're in Crossington, New York."

"She's with Bolivar. Let me call her on the intercom."

A moment later Kat's voice came on the line. "Annie Oakley," she said, and broke out laughing.

"I've heard the stories," Shane remarked. "You seem to have shown Bolivar you can ride a horse."

"Yes, and right now I'm showing him I can clean stalls. I'm down in the barn. I couldn't disappoint him; he's such a patient teacher. I can't believe they pay me to do this."

"I wanted to give you some good news," Shane said. "Robert and I are here in Crossington and Hanson is on the run. He's quit the campaign and bolted from the sheriff's department. We're going to get him. I'm certain of it – today, tomorrow or next week. I don't know which day, but we're very, very close."

"Can you get him for both murders?"

"I'm pretty sure."

"Well then this is an even better day than I thought."

At the sheriff's office, Stoltzfus reviewed video footage taken by two closed circuit cameras at the gun store. He ran it frame-by-frame on his computer. Most of the images were taken from a camera mounted from the ceiling, so it angled down on the head of the robber. Given the hood on the man's sweatshirt, and his dark glasses, his face was in shadow throughout the robbery, and the video didn't tell Stoltzfus much except his build, and how he walked, which he thought was cocky. He'd seen that swagger before.

When he turned up the audio on the tape, it told him everything. It was Hanson – no doubt about it. A few belt-level images taken from a separate camera mounted in the front counter of the store gave a better look at the face and confirmed the I.D. So now in addition to everything else, Hanson had committed armed robbery. He was digging himself a deep hole and clearly no longer cared.

Confirming Hanson's I.D. was both good and bad. It meant the department's effort was no longer split between two separate criminals, but that, in fact, they were looking for one suspect. On the other hand it meant Hanson did not seem suicidal by any stretch – he was accumulating guns for what was likely a last stand. But where? And when? Stoltzfus wished Hanson had gone through with his first inclination to end it all at the cabin. At least that was what he assumed from all the bottles.

Stoltzfus reached for the phone and called the superintendent of schools, explaining the urgency of tightened security till this was over. He reviewed the calendar of upcoming public events and gatherings, and itemized in his mind all the tall buildings and places of symbolic significance a shooter might go to attract maximum media attention.

Even in a small community like Crossington, the list of potential shooting locations was overwhelming. All he could do was warn building owners and government authorities at all levels to tighten their security until the suspect was captured.

The sheriff's department, city police and state patrol canceled all officer leave and put as many feet on the ground as they could. Within twenty-four hours they distributed Hanson's departmental portrait to upstate newspapers, along with pictures of the man in the black hoodie, and appealed to the public for help.

Hanson wasn't terribly worried about the pictures being circulated. His official portrait depicted a well-groomed officer, clean-shaven, with thinning brown hair. He knew tips from the public would come flooding into the department, based on that photo, overwhelming the resources of his fellow officers trying to return calls and follow-up.

Hanson already had stolen a car from a shopping center and driven to Watertown, where he stopped at a costume-and-party shop. He wasn't known in Watertown, so he chose it as the nearest good-sized city in which to purchase a dense black wig, fake mustache and stick-on sideburns. Then he hot-wired a different car, transferred his weapons to it, and headed back.

He looked a little like the mad professor now, but the important thing was he did not look like Lee Hanson. The car he was driving was stolen, to complete the picture. Of the hundreds of tips for officers to check, there might be one from some clerk at a party shop in Watertown, who thought he might have waited on Hanson. He doubted anyone would even return the call for several days.

With his disguise in place, Hanson checked into the Price Is Right Motel. The clerk was bored, pulled away from the Jeopardy show he was watching in the back room by the customer at the front counter. Hanson registered with a fake name, paid in cash, and then got into his car and drove to McDonalds, where he treated himself to take-out from the drive-through window.

The sixteen-year-old kid who took his money would neither know, nor care, that police were asking for help finding a nerdy, middle-aged guy with thinning, brown hair. After dark, Hanson would wrap his weapons in a blanket from the room and carry them into the motel. Till then he could nap and watch the news.

"Governor, this is Robert Yuka checking in." Robert had called the governor on his private line, knowing that his schedule today was light. "I appreciate you giving me the time to follow up on this New York case."

"It's all over the news out here," the governor said. "This deputy you're chasing sounds more and more desperate."

"No question about that. Shane and I came within an hour of catching him at his getaway cabin outside Foreston. We're pretty concerned about what he may do, now that he has armed himself with automatic weapons from the gun store robbery. The whole upstate region is worried he could show up almost anywhere, intending to kill as many people as he can."

"Frankly," the governor said, "I'm relieved Idaho is on the other side of the continent. No governor, county commissioner or mayor wants something like this hanging over him."

"I doubt he is thinking very far ahead," Robert said. "He's making it up as he goes. All the schools are on alert – along with public buildings, monuments, performance halls, shopping centers, movie theaters and other large venues. But there's only so much they can do. Whatever he's thinking, we expect to know soon. We just hope to be on top of it fast so he doesn't hurt anyone. I hope to be back at my post with you in just a few days."

"We're all rooting for you. Stay safe and I'll be looking forward to seeing you soon, with a good story to tell," the governor said.

At the Snooze Inn, Robert and Shane were taking a break in their room. It puzzled Shane that Hanson had dropped out of sight so totally since the gun store robbery. A stolen car would help explain it, but had he left the area entirely? If so, why did he want the automatic weapons? Did he have another remote cabin somewhere, or a friend who was sheltering him?

It was also possible he was hiding in plain sight, but had changed his appearance so much that no one could recognize him. The department still had dozens of leads to follow up, but they were days old and poor quality.

"What do you think, Robert?" he asked. "I'm out of ideas."

"We could shake the tree – call some motels. All it takes is for a clerk or a maid to see something that strikes them as odd. If he's wearing a disguise, they might pick up on it."

"Why not?" Shane replied. "It's better than waiting and doing nothing."

He suggested they divide the alphabet. He'd take the first half, Robert the second. They could use their cell phones so they wouldn't both be competing for the room phone.

"I think we should focus first on the mom-and-pop, budget motels," Robert suggested.

"Why's that?"

"He's a cop. Besides, it's where I'd go to get below the radar. Like this one, The Snooze Inn." They both laughed.

"Too many cops," Shane said.

"Well here's a fun one, The Price Is Right Motel. What kind of place can that be?"

"A place for people on a budget who love game shows. I'll bet it does a lot of business."

They started calling. The clerks were decidedly unhelpful. "No, nothing unusual . . . just tourists and regulars . . . the normal flow of customers . . . routine business . . ."

After a few calls Robert was tiring of the routine answers and becoming giddier. He dialed The Price Is Right.

"This is Robert Yuka. I'm a state trooper from Idaho looking for a suspect we believe may be staying in a local motel, and most likely is wearing a disguise and behaving oddly. I wondered if you have any suspicious characters renting a room from you now."

The clerk laughed. "All our patrons are suspicious."

"Does anyone strike you as wearing a toupee or disguise? Anyone acting especially secretive?"

The clerk laughed again. "Is this on the level?"

"I'm sorry to say it is," Robert assured him. "It's not a prank. If anyone comes to mind after you think about it, please give me a call. This guy is dangerous and we believe he is planning to hurt a lot of people." He gave the clerk his cell phone number.

"Nice to see you hitting your stride with the direct approach," Shane said. "That clerk will remember you."

"That's what I want. We've got to break through this wall of apathy with the motel clerks."

"It's almost dinnertime," Shane said. "Should we run over to the Bucky Beaver or order in?"

"Let's eat here and keep calling. I'll get us a pizza. We need to come up with something to show for this day."

In room one-twenty-two, at The Price Is Right, Leland Hanson checked his disguise in the mirror. He looked like a caricature from the comics, but if anyone asked he would tell them the wig was for cancer. Then they'd be sorry they asked.

He slipped on an overcoat he'd picked up at a thrift store. The day was too warm for it but it was the only way to hide his weapons. When he was satisfied, he opened the door, stepped outside and walked a bit stiffly to his car.

Robert's cell phone rang. It was the clerk from The Price Is Right. Robert raised his hand as a signal to Brad that something was up.

"Okay," the clerk said, "I've got a suspicious character for you. Is there a reward if he turns out to be the guy you're after?"

"You'll be a hero and your motel will be famous."

"This guy is a little shrimp, like you said, but his appearance is completely different from the description you gave me. He has a big mop of black hair and long sideburns, and a mustache. He's been paying cash, day by day, for the room at the far end of the motel, one-twenty-two."

"Is that all?"

"The hair is fake. Probably the mustache, too. He looks like he stepped out of a costume shop. He's not very friendly. Won't let the maid into the room. The one time he slipped up and opened the door, she noticed his wig and sideburns sitting on the dresser. The more I think about it, he's fishy as hell."

"Okay, thanks," Robert said. "I'll talk to my partner and we'll swing over that way. In fact you can count on it. Thank you for getting back to me."

Robert hung up and turned to Shane. "Do I look like a shrimp to you? I know I'm not very tall."

"There's nothing shrimpy about you. Trust me. You look like you could break someone in half with your bare hands. That's why the governor chose you as his bodyguard and driver – that and your sterling personality and pretty wife."

Robert filled in Shane on the call and they debated whether it was worth following up. Shane thought it seemed pretty thin. He had just paid for the pizza and they both reached for a slice. It was half-and-half – Hawaiian for Robert and pepperoni for Shane. It was hot and mouth-watering.

"We should probably get over to the motel," Robert said. "If it turns out this clerk was right and we don't do anything, we'll regret it for the rest of our careers."

"You're right," Shane conceded. He grabbed his Glock and they rushed out the door.

When they reached the motel, the clerk was standing outside room one-twenty-two. "You just missed him," the clerk said. "He came out of the room a few minutes ago and got into his car and drove away. He was wearing a tan overcoat, which is totally weird for a nice day like this, and was walking stiffly.

Without even asking the two officers, the clerk tapped lightly on the door. "Motel staff," he said, using his master key to open the room.

"Vodka bottles," Robert declared as he checked the wastebasket. "Same as we found at the cabin." He fished in the basket for some crumpled pieces of paper underneath the bottles.

Shane emerged from the bedroom with one of the automatic weapons taken in the gun store robbery. "No sign of the Uzi," he said. "I think he left this one behind because it was too much to carry."

"An Uzi is all you need to do a lot of damage," Robert said. He unfolded one of the pieces of paper from the wastebasket and handed it to the clerk. "Do you know this address?"

"That sounds like the Bucky Beaver Café, right next door to our competition, The Snooze Inn."

"I hope to hell he's just gone out for dinner," Shane said. "We've got to run," he said to the clerk. "Thank you for your help."

The two men got into the car and slammed the doors behind them. Shane started the engine, backed up, punched the accelerator and they sped away in a spray of gravel. He pounded the steering wheel. "I can't believe it. We're always one step behind."

"Closer this time," Robert said. "Only minutes behind."

At the café, Hanson entered and noted the "Please seat yourself" sign. The place was busy with diners grabbing an early dinner, but he was pleased that the booth by the window at the far end was unoccupied. He walked all the way to it and sat down, lowering the Uzi to the floor underneath his overcoat. He surveyed the people in the room – sheriff's deputies and city police, one or two firemen and several state patrol officers. He was delighted to see Stoltzfus but disappointed that Lindstrom and Yuka weren't there. You can't have everything.

It was obvious that nobody recognized him. Neither did they seem the least bit interested in the solo diner with the bushy mop of black hair.

The waitress dropped off a menu and filled his coffee cup, and then turned to walk away. Hanson grunted. Everything was so normal. He took a sip, and then reached down for the Uzi. He raised it above the table. Still, no one looked up from their conversations to notice. He pulled the trigger.

The waitress was the first to fall, hit by a spray of bullets in the back. Hanson stood and continued firing as he raked the gun back-and-forth across the room. People were ducking behind booths and tables. One or two officers found their sidearms and returned fire, but missed. Stoltzfus, twenty feet away, took careful aim with both hands, but collapsed on his table in a pool of blood before he could squeeze off a shot.

Hanson's Uzi went silent and the room was eerily quiet as he reached into his pocket for a fresh clip. In the kitchen, the cook and dishwasher seized the moment to bolt out the back door to the garbage rack. Hanson knew people were alive behind some of those tables and booths, but he couldn't see them. He looked for anyone on the tables or floor who was still moving.

Outside, Robert and Shane pulled up in front of the cafe and realized right away that a carnage was in progress. Hanson was so focused on what he was doing that he didn't even see them drive up. Shane walked to the window, drew his Glock semi-auto, and unloaded a series of shots through the glass. The window shattered and fell. Hanson's head and torso turned red as he folded, face first, on the table, dropping his Uzi to the floor. Robert was dialing 911, asking for every available ambulance at the scene of a mass shooting with many casualties.

Inside, they announced the incident was over. Several customers stood up, uninjured, and began aiding others who were wounded. Shane went from body to body, counting and identifying the dead. When he came to Stoltzfus he couldn't hold back his tears. He stood over the fallen officer and sobbed. Robert hugged him and cried, too.

"This is a terrible business," Robert said. "Terrible. I can't do anything to ease the pain. Nobody can."

Aid cars and paramedics arrived and took control of the room.

"Who's the acting sheriff?" Shane asked. "We need to call somebody."

"I don't know. For all I know, he's lying here dead."

"Then I guess we call the state patrol." Robert dialed 911. Shane walked up to several of the surviving officers. "Did he say anything – the suspect – before he started shooting?"

"Not a word," one of the officers replied. "Did anyone else hear anything?" They all shook their heads.

"Are you the guy who got him?" one of the officers asked.

"Yes. We came driving up and saw what was happening. I fired through the window."

"Thank god. I think he intended to keep at it till all of us were down. Who the hell was he?"

Shane grimaced. "Chief deputy Leland Hanson III, candidate for sheriff, and chief suspect in the murder of Sheriff Andy Dixon. How many did we lose here tonight? I lost count when I got to Stoltzfus."

"My god, one of our own," the officer said, shaking his head.

"We've got twelve dead, including the waitress and two tourists," one of the paramedics replied. "So that's nine law officers, and nine others wounded."

"It's a massacre. This town will never get over it."

Pain

"We got him," Shane told Brad and Irene when he reached them later that evening by phone. "But at a horrifying cost. Twelve innocent people are dead and nine others injured. Hanson is dead. He did not leave a note."

"Dear god," Brad exclaimed.

"He went insane," Shane said, "and took as many people with him as he could, especially police officers. My friend Peter Stoltzfus is dead. I wonder if we mishandled the whole thing – if it could have ended differently. The guy had a lifelong persecution complex and we turned up the psychological screws pretty hard."

"Where did the shooting happen?" Brad asked.

"At the Bucky Beaver Café, the preeminent police hangout in Crossington. Hanson chose it well – a soft target where he could find a lot of police officers with their guard down. We were focused on schools and shopping malls."

"Don't beat yourself up," Brad said. "You can't be responsible for the actions of a deranged person, especially someone who had murdered once and engineered the death of someone else to frame him. This was entirely Hanson's doing – not yours."

"I appreciate that. But the pain I'm feeling is beyond words. Robert and I were just minutes too late to save the lives of those people."

Shane said he felt he needed to tell Kat that Hanson was dead and had paid his debt for murdering the sheriff and Tim Wade. But he was so sick and upset about what happened, the staggering cost of it, that he wasn't sure he could talk to her right now. Brad said he would explain to her how things unfolded, and how difficult it was for Shane to talk about it till a little more time had passed.

He needed to hang around for another day or two to give statements to the various police agencies, since he was the one who shot Hanson. Robert was already on his way back to Boise, Shane said, feeling both elated and devastated they had solved the case, but wondering how he'd tell the governor about the terrible toll it had taken.

Brad suggested the whole group get together at the ranch in a month to talk about their feelings and find some closure. "I think all of you have some healing to do."

Shane called Elizabeth to let her know he and Robert were safe, and the case was closed. But he knew she could hear the sadness in his voice.

"Sometimes, winning doesn't feel like winning," he said. "When I get home I want to focus on good things for a while – Billy and our B&B, and the beauty of nature. I need to get all this out of my system and it's going to take time. In the meanwhile I'll have to come back here for a funeral."

D.B. Cooper

"I think we are gathered here for two reasons," Brad said two months later as he stood at the head of the big oak table, looking at the faces around him – Irene, Robert and Marie, Shane and Elizabeth, Billy, Martin, Bolivar and Kat. The whole group had flown to Stanley for this gathering at Brad and Irene's invitation, at the Haraldsen ranch.

"One is to give voice to our grief – to share our sadness about what we lost in the massacre at Crossington. That loss is much sharper and more personal for some of you than for others," he said, looking at Shane, and then Robert, "but it touches us all because when any of you are hurting, we all hurt with you."

Shane could see what Brad was doing, but wasn't sure it would make any difference. The sadness he felt at losing his friend, Peter Stoltzfus, and so many other good men was too deep, too sharp. Worse than the sadness was the sense of guilt – the sense that he could have done something differently, or better, to head off what happened.

"The other reason," Brad continued, "is to remind ourselves of all the goodness that surrounds us – our gratitude for one another, the camaraderie, friendship and love we share. We are deeply fortunate to live in a beautiful place, surrounded by so many reminders that life is good. It lightens my heart to be with you. I wasn't sure there would be another reunion here at the ranch. Difficult as the circumstances are, it means a lot to me."

Shane knew it had been a very tough year for Brad, with the cancer. He hoped he could remember these words, knowing the day was not far off when the tables would be turned and he'd be the speaker in front of this group, saying goodbye to his friend, who always had just the right words, and trying to comfort the people around this table. He suspected many of them were thinking the same.

"Now, I have a surprise because we have a special guest of honor who made the long trip to be with us," Brad said. Shane couldn't imagine who it would be. Brad opened the door to the next room and there stood Aunt Bonnie, with a big grin. It took a moment to register. Shane rose to his feet and went over and hugged her tightly. Elizabeth was right behind him.

"This is the best surprise of my life," Shane said. "Bonnie was our secret weapon, always our eyes and ears, and the keeper of knowledge about everything. I leaned on her hard."

"That's what I heard," Brad said. "We couldn't imagine a Pursuit Lake reunion without her. Bonnie just flew in from Ketchum a few minutes ago on a charter flight."

"Permission to approach the table?" Bonnie asked.

"Granted," Shane replied.

Bonnie sat down demurely with her hands in her lap.

"Whose aunt are you, anyway?" Brad asked, "because I can't get a straight answer from anyone."

"We'll get to that later if we have time," she said. "I'll keep my mouth shut while you finish your beautiful speech, Brad. And then I'll have something to say about all this police convention here, especially the ringleader, Shane. But while I'm thinking about it, you've got some nice digs here, Brad. I'm having a nice vacation. Loved that white-knuckle flight from Ketchum to Stanley."

"Wait a minute. Vacation from what?" Shane asked. "You're always on vacation."

"Yeah, and you're always at work, even on vacation."

Brad smiled and went back to his speech. Shane shook his head. For Brad to invite her was a masterful touch, a surprise he never saw coming.

"Life is ever changing. We lose someone we love, but find love in our hearts for somebody new, like our friends, Kat, here, and Aunt Bonnie. That's how we carry on and invest in the future. By the way, Elizabeth, I really must compliment you on your good judgment in recruiting Kat for us to come and help at the ranch."

"Actually, what I did was kidnap her for you," Elizabeth interrupted.

Laughter.

"If she washes out, let me know, because I might want the job," Bonnie said.

Brad ignored the remark. "I should also compliment Marie on her speed and agility in capturing Kat. If she hadn't been just fast enough to tackle her, Kat might not be with us right now."

Laughter spread around the table and Kat blushed. "That was a low blow. I still don't know how Marie did that, but I'm not complaining. Really."

Brad continued. "Our friend, Bolivar, here, has been in charge of Kat's extreme makeover."

Bolivar smiled and nodded. "It's a burden I cheerfully accept."

"He's the reason we call her Annie Oakley now. By the way, we saw you parade her across the ridge the other day to show off your work, Bolivar, and were terribly impressed.

"I can honestly say everyone at this table is above average – or at least the women. I'm not sure what the men contributed to the effort, except that you sure know how to complicate a vacation. And somebody here will never live down that stunt he pulled in the electrical storm."

More laughter.

"I tried to warn him," Bonnie protested. "When do I get to talk?"

The heck with Brad's polished speech, Shane thought. He'd trust Aunt Bonnie with his therapy. Brad was going down in flames and wrapped it up fast.

"Now," he concluded, "let's raise a toast to friends old and new, and get on with this irreverent free-for-all."

Everything was going to be okay.

But Shane couldn't stop thinking about D.B. Cooper. Maybe his father-in-law hadn't been the famous hijacker, but he had a lot of money and it came from *somewhere*. Every family has its mysteries, large and small. There are secrets in every marriage. He believed Elizabeth when she said she didn't have a clue where the money in the cookie tin came from.

Well, maybe he should rephrase that and say she didn't *know*. But he had a feeling she had a *clue*.

He realized now that there was more to his mysterious wife than met the eye. Oh, how he loved a mystery.

From *Final Deception: A Whidbey Island Mystery*
Book 1 in This Series
Available from Amazon.com and Whidbey Island bookstores

In the blackness, Bella Morelli pitched face forward in an ungainly dive, wind roaring in her ears. The four seconds took forever and she had two last thoughts – surprise and dread. She hit the water all wrong like a breaching whale, lungs first, a horrible impact, and that was the last she felt.

*

Deception Pass Bridge connects Washington's Fidalgo and Whidbey islands across a deep chasm. It is 180 feet from the bridge deck to the water, depending on tide. From there it's 130 more in icy darkness to the bottom.

A young person in peak condition, hitting the water feet first in perfect form, can survive if they miss the rocks and regain the surface before drowning or hypothermia. A 67-year-old cannot. Whirlpools and eddies reach out to clutch and pull them down.

*

Decades ago Brad had almost cracked the mystery of Bella. She had taken a road trip with him, taken a risk. Brad registered them in a Tennessee motel as Mr. and Mrs. Brad Haraldsen.

They hadn't discussed the sleeping arrangement – it just happened. They were two unmarried 25-year-olds traveling in the South in 1972. Gatlinburg was a honeymoon destination and the couple's eyes glistened with new love. Even in civilian attire, Brad carried himself with military bearing. That and his clean-cut, neatly trimmed hair were assets in the South where patriotism ran high.

As it was, the clerk didn't question their marital status – gave them a room by the pool in the nearly vacant auto court.

A heavy sky threatened afternoon lightning. Brad and Bella swam anyway and washed the miles from the road. Then, five years into their friendship, they made love for the first time as comfortably as if it were every day.

The lovemaking was slow and satisfying, their private secret as the storm rumbled through the lush hills beyond the thick curtains. Afterwards, they lay in each other's arms. Bella smiled and Brad felt her caution about him wash away.

A lifetime later, sitting on his mountain in Stanley, Idaho, Brad still teared up at the memory, as vivid now as it had ever been. That time, that place to which they had never returned, was the happiest of his life. Brad's eyes stung and he closed them to see it all again. He remembered every detail of that motel, that room, the long journey that led there.

From *Final Passage:*
An Alaska Ferry Mystery
Book 2 in this Series
Available from Amazon.com and Whidbey Island bookstores

The Matanuska inches ahead between flashing navigation buoys in Wrangell Narrows, changing course at each marker to stay within this twisting channel. Evening is falling and a campfire burns brightly on shore a hundred yards away. Sweet smoke from the fire drifts over the ship and takes Brad back to times he and Irene spent in the mountains of Idaho with their friends of a lifetime, Stu and Amy, both now gone. It's a bittersweet memory.

Brad imagines a family around that campfire, roasting weenies and marshmallows, or maybe good friends talking about their day. Smoke drifts toward the ferry from woodstoves in cozy cabins so close they could shout to the owners. A dog barks. A couple standing on their deck wave to the ship and Brad waves back.

*

Petersburg is a storybook scene on this quiet night. Irene is glad she made the effort to stay up. The lights of the town and its many boats must hold a thousand secrets of ordinary people and their Alaska-size dreams on the edge of the civilized world.

Moonlight bathes the snowfields of nearby peaks. This is the prettiest place she has seen on this trip, a pocket of humanity in the heart of wilderness, surrounded by water, mountains, glaciers and forest. She has this moment to herself, the other passengers having retired to their cabins for the evening. She lingers a while, then starts a leisurely circuit around the deck, taking in the view and the aromas of creosoted pilings, fish canneries, fir trees . . .

The impact from behind knocks the wind from Irene's lungs and sends her reeling forward, fighting for balance. She grabs wildly for the rail with her right arm and barely catches it, staying half on her feet, unable to breathe. Her heart pounds and her legs fold. She wraps her body over the rail and gasps in shock, staring down at the white bubbles where the bow slices through the blackness. Half a minute passes with no air. She's in full panic.

Then, ever so slowly, her diaphragm responds and her lungs draw air. She straightens up and wonders what happened. She is alone on the deck – no passengers, no crew. The ship already is in open water, accelerating toward Juneau.

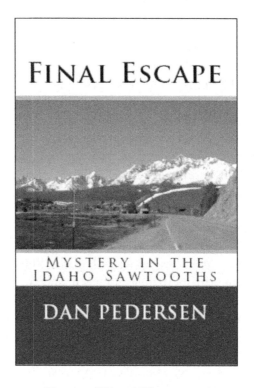

From *Final Escape:*
Mystery in the Idaho Sawtooths
Book 3 in this Series
Available from Amazon.com and Whidbey Island bookstores

On the porch after dinner, Brad breaks out two Mt. Borah Brown Ales for Shane and himself while Elizabeth and Irene clink glasses of wine. Brad notices Elizabeth looks especially beautiful in the soft light of the early evening, her long red hair catching the sun. Did she fix herself up a little extra? He catches Shane's eyes lingering on her.

In the distance, the soulful melody of a harmonica floats their way on the breeze.

"That's Bolivar," Brad says, "introducing Billy to the

harmonica. He's not bad, don't you think?"

Brad explains to Shane that the ale comes from a small craft brewery in Salmon, several hours north. "I think it's a delicious beer and it brings back memories of the time I climbed Mt. Borah in the Air Force."

"You were 20-something?" Shane asks.

"Yeah. About that."

"Reliving past glories," Shane laughs.

"Exactly."

Irene interjects. "He has a rich fantasy life."

Brad stares at her with a knowing smile. "I happen to like my fantasies," and then back at Shane. "Seriously, Shane, while Billy is with Bolivar and we have a few minutes, I wanted to ask your advice about a problem Elizabeth is having."

Shane leans forward and listens while Brad outlines the situation. When he finishes, Shane leans back and turns to Elizabeth, "Is it the same guy?"

"I don't think so."

"Because of the black hair? The pony tail?"

"Mainly that."

"I think it might be him," he says. "Otherwise it's an awfully big coincidence. It wouldn't be a hard disguise."

Brad adds, "There's something else. I didn't mention this to Elizabeth earlier, but we've started getting some harassing phone messages and hang-ups here at the ranch."

"What are the messages?"

"To keep our noses out of other people's business."

"Interesting! Well that takes it to another level."

"You think it's connected to me?" Elizabeth asks.

"I think there's a good chance. It all fits the pattern of a stalker who's obsessed with you and trying to make sure you can't have a life without him."

"Oh god," she moans. "This is bad."

"Not at all," Shane says. "We can handle this. I hate these creeps. They're predators and parasites, and push people around, but at heart they're pathetic and weak."

"But how would he even know about Brad and Irene?"

"He was in your house, wasn't he?" Shane asks. "Did he see your mail? Did he get into your computer?"

"Well he saw everything else."

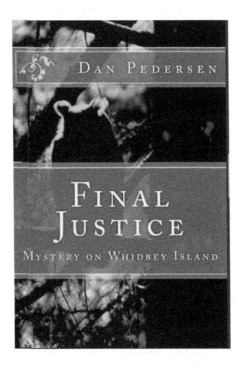

DAN PEDERSEN

FINAL JUSTICE

MYSTERY ON WHIDBEY ISLAND

From *Final Justice:*
Mystery on Whidbey Island
Book 4 in this Series

The body is on its side, in rigor, in the fetal position. The wound on the forehead is gruesome, deep and ugly. It bled profusely and leaked some gray ooze onto the ground. The man removes identification and personal effects, spreads a blue tarp and lifts the stiff corpse awkwardly onto it, dripping ooze, then grabs two corners of the tarp and starts to pull. It slides easily, confined to the tarp, leaving no blood trail, across the clearing to the forest edge.

At the hole he drags the body and tarp right up to it. The body lands in the bottom face up, legs up, staring at him with open eyes, in that classic expression of surprise. The last thing those eyes saw when they awoke was him holding a cinder block high overhead.

In a longer hole the body would lie flat but he dug this one deep enough that it doesn't matter.

He wads the rest of the tarp into the hole and refills it, starting with the head, throwing dirt into the corpse's face. Rocks and sand, little by little, erase those eyes.

He fills the hole all the way, smoothes and lightly packs the mound with his boots, and then digs three shallow depressions and replants the sword ferns he dug earlier. He spreads a layer of leaves, dry fir needles, rotten branches and forest debris around them on the disturbed earth. When he's done, there is little to catch the eye, just a slight anomaly in the undergrowth. It feels like rain, which will freshen the ferns. Weather and time soon will remove any traces.

He gathers up his tools, hoists them over his shoulder and heads back, whistling a few bars of "Whistle a Happy Tune," the happiest he's felt in some time.

*

. . . Two assistants roll a gurney into the room and position it alongside Brad's bed. One of them folds a warm blanket over Brad's legs and then, with his help, they slide him from the bed onto the gurney.

Irene blows him a kiss from her chair in the corner. "See you in a few minutes," she says as they wheel him out. It's a quick ride past several other bored patients, through double swinging doors into a cold hallway and then through another set of double doors into what looks like an industrial, stainless-steel kitchen or possibly a slaughterhouse where several women in blue scrubs are dancing.

Rock music blares from speakers in the ceiling.

"Turn that down a little, will you?" asks the woman who appears to be in charge. The volume drops. She leans over Brad's face so he can see her clearly and says, "It lightens the mood around here. Any requests? Led Zeppelin?"

Brad shakes his head.

"Jesus Loves Me?"

Brad winces. Is this a joke? Did she read the paperwork he just signed?

. . . "Ready?" she asks. "Any last words?"

From *Outdoorsy Male:*
Short Stories and Essays
Available from Amazon.com and Whidbey Island bookstores

Don't Photograph My Wattles

"I have only one vice," my old kindergarten classmate announces as she fishes a pack of American Spirit cigarettes from her bag and lights one.

A blue cloud engulfs us as we huddle under an awning in a chilly October-morning rain. Tammi has just finished a sesame bagel with cream cheese at the Bakery by the Sea in the quaint village of Langley, Whidbey Island.

"Well that sure was disappointing," she declares, screwing up her face.

"The bagel?"

"Yeah. Not that good."

"I sneak a glance at my watch because we are already late to the workshop she is presenting this morning."

"You say this is the only bakery in this backwater?" She asks.

"Only one."

"Crap."

Nodding at the cigarette pack in her yellow fingers, the points out, "At least they're all natural." She smiles for the first time this morning. "No artificial additives. No genetically modified tobacco."

Then she adds, "You can stop looking at your watch because I'm not going to rush this."

The smoke, which clings to us like burning tires, saturates my blue jacket and gray beard.

We are getting reacquainted after Tammi's first night in my garage guest apartment. I haven't seen her for about 60 years. She asks for a wakeup call, which I place to her iPhone at the stroke of 7:45.

"Yeah, I'm up," she answers with a voice like gravel, then apparently goes down again.

It turns out Tammi doesn't like the fruit and one-minute oatmeal I've stocked for her in the Guest Apartment by the Sea, nor the coffee. "I'm not an oatmeal fan, she says. "And to be honest I just didn't feel like cooking breakfast this morning." So at the last second she asks if I will drive her someplace for a bagel.

"I don't do dairy, sugar or wheat," she declares. "Or GMO."

As an afterthought she adds, "You only get one body."

I am struggling with every part of this.

Standing in the weather, she fills in a piece of her story. "My life is the shits. I know the reason I'm not wearing a ring on this finger is because I'm a nag. Well, that and some other things. That alcoholic turd I married wasted my best years. I've got nothing to show for it now but a bad back, a mountain of debt and a pack of dogs. I have this fantasy I'm going to meet a nice man on Whidbey Island, marry him and live happily ever after."

She sucks another lungful of smoke and blows it all over me.

"God, I hate being poor," she says. "I have no backup. Why does everyone else lead a charmed life but me?"

"It's all luck and timing," I say.

"I hate my gut," she remarks. "I swear I'm going to lose this spare tire. I know you plan to take pictures at the workshop. Keep in mind, I don't photograph well. I wave my arms and that makes my wattles hop around. Do not photograph my wattles."

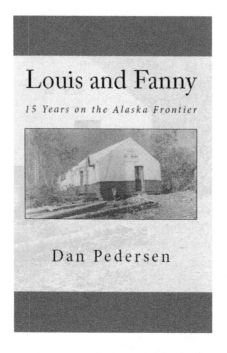

From *Louis and Fanny:*
15 Years on the Alaska Frontier
Available from Amazon.com and Whidbey Island bookstores

Trees sagged under a blanket of white. Boots kicked up powder in the streets of Seward, Alaska, as the mail steamer *Dora* pulled away from the dock. The ship trailed a plume of black smoke. Captain C.B. McMullen stood at the stern, taking a last look at civilization and pondering what he'd find on his return to Kodiak.

He'd just reached Seward with a firsthand account of conditions in the remote outpost of Kodiak. Mt. Katmai had exploded 100 miles from Kodiak in a volcanic eruption that was still spewing ash into the atmosphere. The *Dora* had called on Kodiak after tense hours sailing blind in conditions that could have cost McMullen the ship and all aboard.

Now he was going back with the minister's wife.

*

On Kodiak Island, ash filled the sky and blacked out the town for 60 hours. Landslides of ash swept away houses. People went hungry and expected to die. Lightning struck the Naval radio station, setting a fire and knocking out communication with the outside world. Ships' radios were useless with the electrical disturbance. Townspeople waited in darkness, their eyes and throats burning with dust, wondering if they could survive this, whatever it was.

Downwind, ash rained for a day at Juneau, across the Gulf of Alaska. In Vancouver, B.C., more than 1,000 miles from the volcano, people wondered if the sulfuric atmosphere was safe to breathe. It all happened just as the *Dora* was completing its westward run, bound for Kodiak a few hours ahead. It waited offshore till conditions cleared enough to approach Kodiak . . .

*

"The day was an exceptionally beautiful one and we were all on deck enjoying our cigar and the scenery when someone shouted: 'Look at the smoke.' Gazing off to the westward we beheld across Shelikof Straits, on the mainland, an immense column of smoke ascending skyward, its diameter seeming to be at least half a mile or a mile."

The volcano was 55 miles from their position, and Thwaites went on, "Of course we all thought of our cameras, but the distance was so great that the idea of securing a photograph was abandoned as impractical. We continued to watch the phenomenon when it began to dawn upon our minds that it was rapidly becoming dimmer, and that a dark mass of cloud was showing above the column, mingling with it and coming our way."

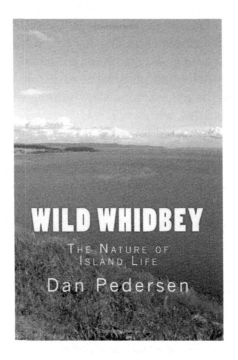

From Wild Whidbey:
The Nature of Island Life

In Full Color
Available from Amazon.com

People argue in circles about whether islands attract a certain kind of person or create them. I think it's both, but skewed toward the latter 30 years into my one-man study.

We make our big turns in life for complicated reasons, including luck and self-delusion. I had some romantic ideas about island life and they played a role in my irrational move to Whidbey Island when I still had a fulltime job in the city. I saw something wholesome here, wasn't sure how to explain it or get it, but hoped I'd figure it out . . .

The move was impulsive but soon became transformative . . . Waking up in a blissfully quiet place, I wasn't prepared for the birdsong. The woods act as a megaphone an hour before sunrise, when all the birds awaken with something to say. The songs change with the seasons and I started correlating the changes with seeing the first Rufous Hummingbirds of March, the first Violet-green Swallows, the first Black-headed Grosbeaks and Western Tanagers, even Great-horned Owls on foggy winter nights.

The spring migration is nature's timeless cycle. It's a barometer of how we are doing on this planet and takes place alongside but separate from our human concerns. To me it is comforting and reassuring amid the constant chaos of our world – war, crime and breaking news, politics, terrorism, jobs, divorce, drones, sickness, smart bombs and talk radio, and all the other noise that spews stress at us.

As time passed I started caring more about the cycles of nature than the cycles of news. In this I am well aware I am not normal or typical of most people and how they live . . .

I started counting the growth rings on the century-old tree rounds I was splitting, imagining the seasons those trees had seen. I found friends who cared about such details as much as I did. And I discovered the luxury of silence – the simple joys of a book and a camera, and some time outside.

Whidbey Island's abundant wildlife and forests, gentle people and creative community all claimed parts of my soul. All shaped my values and philosophy, and my temperament. I grew accustomed to kind smiles and cheery "good mornings" from both friends and strangers on the sidewalks of Langley and the trails in our woods. I stopped worrying about the person coming toward me in the dark.

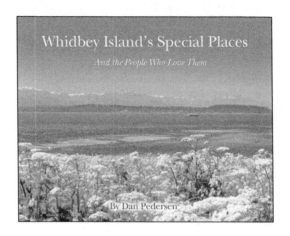

From Whidbey Island's Special Places
And the People Who Live There
Available from Whidbey Island bookstores

Standing in the shadows of giant old-growth firs and cedars at South Whidbey State Park, Elliott Menashe remembers a story. It's about a woman who attended one of his classes on forest management.

"She was imperious – a real tough cookie," he says, shaking his head. He'd been telling the class about forest snags and all the reasons to leave them intact as wildlife habitat, but the woman was not buying it. "I've got a 60-foot snag that's about six feet thick. "It's annoying me and I want it gone."

Menashe asked if it was a safety hazard. "No." And was it full of woodpecker holes?

"Yeah, it's got those. But I want it gone."

"You just moved here, right?" he asked, then offered her a deal. "Leave it alone, and in a year if you don't change your mind, I will pay for its removal."

About a year later a package showed up in Menashe's mail. "It's a bottle of really good wine. Chocolates. And pictures of, you know, baby owls, eagles, osprey, herons, kingfishers – all these pictures. She said, 'If you hadn't stopped me I would never have known what I was doing. Thank you so much. I look around me now with different eyes."

The story illustrates an error Menashe sees often as principal of

Greenbelt Consulting, a natural resources consulting firm. Newcomers often don't seek advice about living in harmony with nature. Arriving on the island from an urban or suburban setting of traditional lawns and landscaping, and with little previous contact with wildlife and woodland processes, their first impulse is to clear a big view, eradicate native vegetation and replace it with neat, manicured suburbia.

In the process they destroy all the best, most wondrous and magical reasons to live on the island.

A good place to become immersed in those wonders is the mile-long Wilbert Trail, across Smuggler's Cove Road from the entrance to South Whidbey State Park. Parallel parking for several cars is available at the trailhead on a widened section of road shoulder about 0.4-mile north of the park entrance. It is marked with a crosswalk and a small sign identifying the Wilbert Trail.

"This is not a true old-growth forest," Menashe clarifies. "It's a mature forest with old-growth remnants." The distinction is important but takes nothing away from the impact. A few steps from the highway, hikers enter a sea of sword ferns. Several hundred feet later they come to a mammoth Western Red Cedar, next to a bench on which to sit and contemplate.

"The Ancient Cedar" is estimated at 500 years old, but Menashe says it's probably not the oldest tree on this trail. Altogether, only about 1 to 5 percent of old growth forest remains in the Puget Sound Basin, and Menashe says every bit of it is priceless and deserves to be saved.

ABOUT THE AUTHOR

Dan Pedersen grew up in Western Washington. He holds two journalism degrees from the University of Washington and was a reporter and editor for several newspapers in Idaho and Washington, including a large outdoor weekly and a corporate marketing magazine.

In the 1970s he lived in Idaho while serving in the U.S. Air Force, hiking and camping in the Salmon River country, and growing to love the little village of Stanley. In the 1980s, his then-wife Suzanne introduced him to the Adirondacks of upper New York State.

This is his seventh book available from Amazon, and the fifth mystery in his series of "Final" books. In addition he is the author of *Trails Through Time*, available from Blurb.com, and a self-published book, *Whidbey Island's Special Places*, available directly from him and from Whidbey Island bookstores.

He writes a weekly blog, Dan's Blog, which may be found at https://pedersenwrites.blogspot.com.

Made in the USA
Las Vegas, NV
18 December 2022

63281776R00118